MAX WISECRACKS HOLLYWOOD (FOXTROTTING FOR JUSTICE)

A Max Royster Mystery

by Frank Hickey

Max Wisecracks Hollywood: (Foxtrotting for Justice)
A Max Royster Mystery
Copyright © 2016 by Frank Hickey

This novel is a work of fiction. All characters and events described herein are fictitious and wholly the product of the author's imagination. Any resemblance to events or actual persons, living or dead, is unintentional and coincidental.

Library of Congress
Catalogue-in-Publication Data

Max Cracks Hollywood (Foxtrotting for Justice) /
Frank Hickey
1. Fiction – Crime 2. Fiction – Mystery 3. Fiction – Hard-boiled

Published by Pigtown Books, an imprint of
Hidden Pearl Books L.L.C.

ISBN: 3:978-0-9970719-2-4

For further information, please contact:

info@pigtownbooks.com

10 9 8 7 6 5 4 3 2

Second Edition / First Issue

Dedicated to the Many Fine
Women and Men of
the Los Angeles Police Department.

CHAPTER 1.

Breezing
or
What's that?

That afternoon, I crossed Hollywood Boulevard, on foot, dodging traffic. Hearing shouts, I saw a Black woman in a dark blue LAPD uniform wrassling with someone underneath her.

"Stupid, you so stupid!" a woman shouted from under the cop.

The cop was trying to grab the woman's wrists. Both of them rolled on the concrete.

"Stop her, Jesus!" the suspect shouted. "Stupid po-lice! The Blood of Jesus is on Stupid!"

"That makes no sense," I thought. "Silly talk, messy arrest."

"Stop resisting!" the woman cop shouted.

The suspect punched the cop's face.

A soft, big man in an orange tank top stepped in front of me, blocking my view. He paid no attention to the fight.

By reflex, I sprang towards the cop.

The two women banged against a parked car.

The cop swung a black metal baton at the suspect. I heard the baton hit something.

Hollywooders stopped on the sidewalk. Cellphones blossomed in their hands.

"Damn, man!" someone else shouted. "Po-Po be tripping, yo!"

"Don't let them cars hit them!" another woman caterwauled in a Slavic accent.

My feet smacked the asphalt. It hurt my left knee.

The bad feeling kicked me. Memories flowed.

The cop lay on top of the suspect. The cop's mouth gaped, trying to suck air into her lungs. Her ribs heaved. She still held the baton. Sweat scored the cop's face.

A blonde wig tumbled from the suspect onto the gutter. Blood stained the wig.

Faded beauty flowered on the suspect's face. Something clicked in my memory. A suspicion grew in me.

I hoped that I was wrong.

The sidewalk crowd grew around us.

"Officer," I said to the woman cop, "you okay?"

Her hand snapped to her duty holster. Fingers gripped the gun butt.

"Hey," I said. "I'm an ex-cop, out of New York. Take it easy."

"Back off!" she shouted

"I had this same problem deal," I said. "Nobody wants to get collared any more. Where's the spirit of cooperation? Where's the love?"

Her other hand waved the baton. Blood stained the tip.

Someone slammed into me.

The Someone pinned me.

I went down to the sidewalk. My cheek scraped. Knee pain shot through me.

My arm flung out. It hit the woman lying underneath the cop.

"Stupid, Jesus," she moaned. "Blood of Jesus, on stupid."

"What are you saying?" I asked. "You're babbling."

"Stop resisting!" my Someone, a man, bellowed in my ear. "You under arrest! Right hand behind you! Don't move!"

"Police," I grunted. "ID in my wallet."

My head twisted, trying to see everything.

"Get on her after you hook this hardhead," the woman cop shouted to the cop on top of me. "Why didn't you jump in? She bit me!"

"Your arrest, she ain't moving," I said. "Get some ambulance jokers here."

"Tell me what to do!" the cop on top of me shouted.

Blond, wide and sweaty, he cuffed me too tight.

Metal pinched my wrists.

Seeing everything was important right now. I forced my head up from the hot sidewalk and tried to take everything in. This mess might lead to court, but I could not stay in Los Angeles.

"Let the police do they job!" a woman wearing shorts and a violet bikini top and shorts shouted.

"Why should we?" another woman, wearing an orange sari and black-rimmed glasses yelped back. She spoke in a lilting British accent. "All they ever do is harass us to make their ticket quotas. We're tired of it!"

"All of you, get back!" the man cop bellowed, as if he were slipping his anchor. He waved his arms at the crowd. Unlike his partner, he wore short sleeves. His arms burst out against the dark blue fabric, like two living bodies packed with muscle. They spoke of years of serious weightlifting. He moved his forearms around as if he was proud of them.

The crowd skittered back a few feet and then surged back in like the ocean. They surrounded the three of us and the Black woman stretched out on the sidewalk. The crowd kept growing. This cop needed reinforcements.

"Why, man?" a skinny skateboarder in broken-toed sneakers and hairy legs asked. A cigarette dangled from his mouth.

"Because I say so!" the cop hollered.

"Always a winning line," I muttered.

Skateboarder stepped closer,

"We ain't doing nothing wrong!" Skateboarder shouted. "You don't want us watching you? Everyone film this! Get your cameras going!"

Right now, my own arms felt like boiled celery stalks and about as useful. They strained against the metal handcuffs as I tried to stand myself up.

Sweat stung my wrists as I worked them raw, trying to rock sideways.

I kept searching for any witnesses in the windows above us, somebody who would still be on this street tomorrow. But nobody appeared. All the witnesses were down here, surrounding us.

Hollywood traffic slowed behind the cop. Drivers leaned out of their windows, palming their phones in their free hands and trying to work their steering wheels and phone-cameras at the same time.

"Request additional units, this location!" the man cop shouted into his radio.

"Unit broadcasting, stand by," a woman's voice said from his radio. "Hollywood units, stand by. South Traffic Unit, read off the Triple-A number for this driver one in your incident."

The radio kept buzzing.

"South Traffic Unit, go ahead," the radio dispatcher said. "Read off the number."

"That dispatcher brings back old memories," I said. "Happy halcyon days in Patrol."

Two cars barked each other's fenders and slammed to a stop.

The first driver leaped out of his Chevy as if legions of insurance fiends were chasing him with their pitchforks. Sweat matted his white hair against his piggy head, and he danced a light two-step in front of the other car.

"What's the matter, you?" he shouted. "You too, stupid, watch where the hell you going?"

"Rhetorical question," I said.

The driver in the other car, a pinkish-and-gray-primer-coat Honda, looking about twenty hard years old, gunned the engine and spun forward. It just missed the first driver, skidded and kept going down the side street.

"Hey, where you going?" the Piggy-Pig hollered.

"He got no in-surance!" the woman in the sari said. "Probably he is here illegally. No papers. Like my ex-husband."

"Git a rope!" someone in the crowd shouted in a country drawl.

"He looked Mex to me!" Skateboarder said. "That's why he ran. They never got insurance. Restrict immigration, that's the answer."

"I'm gonna get his insurance!" the driver said. "Not paying this gol-danged deductible."

He vaulted his bulk back into his car seat and his Chevy shot forward, down the same side street.

Some of the crowd stepped after him. Maybe they were hoping to see a clash of the gladiators in a fight.

More onlookers swelled the mob in front of us.

"Crazies," the man cop said. "Both of them."

"All units, continue to stand by," the dispatcher on his radio said.

Rocking from side to side, I managed to roll my bulky self up onto my right knee.

"Stay down!" the woman cop said to me. "If you try running, we're gonna Taser you."

That was worth ignoring. She had her hands full.

The concrete bit my knee and hurt, but I was not going to stay down like a trussed turkey awaiting the chef.

Straining not to fall, I made it up to my feet and leaned against a trashcan, breathing hard. Something steely seemed to cut into my lungs. Years of marbled fat steaks, bourbon and cigars were taking their toll. My whole body ached to go somewhere and flop down.

Again, I searched for someone at the windows.

Nobody.

"Hey!" the woman cop shouted at her partner. "You get us any additional units here?"

"He's trying," I said.

"Clear the air!" a new voice said over the radio. "This Triple-A stuff is taking too long."

"Amen," I said.

Strain made my voice wheeze.

Some drivers in the traffic jam in front of us gave up and left their cars to see what was causing the mess. They added to the crowd that was overflowing onto the street.

"This gonna be on the news?" the woman in the violet bikini asked.

My heart pounded like a runaway horse, slamming against my chest wall.

"Your arrest woman looks familiar," I panted.

"Shut your fat face!" the man cop shouted.

"Looks like Callie McKissick, the actress," I said. "Used to be famous."

"Doesn't matter now," the woman cop said. Her voice pitched high from nerves, "'cause she and her vitals ain't responding. She's going down. Circling the drain."

Chapter 2.

Deciding, Then Sliding
or
Mob Rule

"Officers, CPR might keep her going," I said. "Please try it on her."

"Try shutting up," the man cop said.

Drivers saw us. Horns screamed. Other horns joined in.

"Patty," the man cop said to the woman cop, "these looky-loos are getting bad! Need some additional units here!"

"You're repeating yourself," I said.

The scene seemed unreal in the perfect LA day under a hot blue sky.

"Po-po brutality!" a youngster shouted.

"They all the time do us like this!" a large Latina woman in a red T-shirt bellowed. It read "Kiss The Cook."

Rap music got louder behind me. Nerves made me want to hurl.

"CPR her!" I said. "Right now!"

"Re-tard, you telling me what to do?" my cop, the wide White guy, said.

Sweat wet his pug nose under narrow muddy eyes. His black leather gun belt and shoes gleamed against the dark blue uniform. Sunlight caught the etched gold-and-silver oval badge on his chest.

"You're under arrest, ace," he said.

"You want her dead?" I asked. My voice climbed. "Get moving."

"We can't give her CPR," the woman cop said.

She breathed heavy, a wiry woman in her forties, in a long-sleeved uniform shirt. She stood about five-foot-three inches, crouching under one-thirty pounds. A thin gold watch bobbled on her wrist.

Without the uniform, nobody would see her as a cop. She looked too small and tidy for this kind of street combat.

Bunched curls waved on her head. The tin nameplate on her chest read "Alwer." Flecks of rust pitted the plate.

"If we CPR her," Alwer said, "and she goes DOA, PSB can throw us into prison."

"You talk lots of initials," I said. "But not doing nothing. Uncuff me. I'll CPR her."

"Man, you ever hear of custody?" the man cop asked. "We uncuff you, we lose a prisoner."

His badge read "Grack."

"Better than a life," I said. "Get an ambulance here. Now. Or else, I start remembering things for the record."

"She brought it on herself," Alwer said. "If she really is hurt."

"Officer, just look at her," I said.

"Try looking at my arm, champ," Alwer said. "Ripped right through the sleeve, there. Broke the skin. Blood and stuff. Like they said in the academy, bet she's a carrier of airborne pathogens."

"You know those wild showbiz folks," I said. "Loose morals. Know a few of them myself."

The radio buzzed again.

"Any unit with a message, go ahead," the dispatcher said.

"It's about time," Grack said.

"6A11, request an RA on Hollywood Boulevard and Gower," Alwer said into her hip radio. "Female Black, about seventy, not conscious or breathing. Possible PCP suspect on drugs."

"Why PCP?" I asked.

Nobody gave me no ear.

"I've got a towel here. It'll stop the bleeding," a man's voice said behind me.

"Keep back," Alwer said, like a reflex.

"Gimme," I said.

My body ached as I edged my handcuffs around my gut and took the towel from the man. The last thing that we needed was a towel contaminating the forensics here.

The man was slim and supple, ageless. He sported a white silk shirt with flared sleeves, like something in an old pirate movie, black toreador pants and gleaming black shoes.

"Why're you in handcuffs?" he asked me.

"Distraction tactic," I said. "Calm the crowd. Get them focused elsewhere."

"Don't pay him no mind," Alwer said. "He tripping."

For lots of reasons, I needed the name of Toreador Pants right now.

"I'm glad that you got the guts to come out here," I told him.

It was salesman time again at a crime scene.

"I'm Max Royster."

"Florida," he said. "Van Florida."

His brown hair spiked over eyes the same color, forehead lined with worry. Now this scene was changing his looks, aging him.

"You parked right here?" I asked, wanting to see his license plate. By now, I was way witness-hungry. He could get me free of this mess.

"No. I just saw this outside my window there," he said. "Opened up my dance studio this week."

"Good luck to you."

"Thanks."

"What window where?"

"Right over there, on Gower. See? Still open. I was sweeping up when I saw this."

"What did you see?" I asked.

"How come you took the towel from me?" he asked.

"Because she's dead."

"Dead?" Florida said. "You mean, really?"

"Graveyard dead," I said. "Is there any other kind?"

"I can't stay here for that. Oh, my God!"

His black shoes moved fast, and he was gone back into the crowd.

"Good dancer," I thought. "Very light on his tootsies."

The window on Gower was at street level and still open, like he said. Later on, I would use that.

Car traffic spliced past. More bystanders bunched and swelled on the sidewalk.

"They killed that woman!" one weepy-looking blonde with caked makeup around pinkish eye sockets said. "For nothing! Film this on your phones, everybody!"

"Get me a supervisor here!" Grack said into his radio. "And some black-and-whites."

"Look out!" Alwer shouted.

A bottle smashed near us. Shards hit my leg.

The smell of beer and something rubber burning hit us.

"Chunk at them!" a rail-thin whiskered man with milky pale skin shouted, waving a gray rock in his knobby fist. "They the ones towed my ride last Easter!"

"McKissick was famous before," I recalled. Hollywood published books about her and her letters to friends. But she was gonna be more famous now.

"Their rap is weak!" Latina Cook said. "Talk down to everyone!"

"What's this PSB that scares you so much?" I asked.

"Professional Standards Bureau," Alwer said. "Internal Affairs. They headhunt us coppers, jail us and ruin our lives."

"Cheery stuff," I said. "I know the trouble. But you better get some witness statements now to cover yourselves."

"We can't," Alwer said. "Everyone hates us, this division."

"Got the detectives for that stuff, statements and things," Grack said.

"And where are they now?" I asked. "Officers, get thinking sharp here. McKissick dying is going to hurt you. It'll be big stuff with the media."

"Told you. I never heard of her!" Alwer shouted.

"Maybe not," I said. "But you're going to."

Chapter 3.

Real Life
or
The Rule Book Dies

"Watch out for the units!" Grack shouted.

He reached inside his patrol car and yanked a pump shotgun from the console.

"Here they come!" Alwer gave out. "Took 'em long enough! Lazy slugs!"

Three black-and-white LAPD cars roared down Hollywood Boulevard. Red roof lights bled. Sirens keened. My ears ached.

"Check out them headbreakers!" Latina Cook shouted. "Like that lady said, they stupid! Jesus! The Blood of Jesus is on Stupid!"

"Whatever that means," I said.

A shave-headed cop vaulted out of the first car. Something flew and hit his car.

"GET BACK!" he roared. He racked his own pump-action shotgun. It looked like a toy in his huge hands.

"Airship over Hollywood!" a voice shouted from Alwer's radio. "Block off all south entrances to Gower."

"Airship, go to Simplex!" a woman said.

"Wilshire units responding," a Latino man's accent rasped from the radio. "Show 7A33 en route."

More bottles flew.

"The Blood of Jesus!" a man shouted from the crowd.

Others chanted with him.

"Yo, this ain't the way," I whispered to myself.

"Why do we take all their guff?" a beery-looking type asked, his blond haircut in a mullet.

"Aw, shut up," I said. "Mullet-Head. You got to be real de-evolved to cut your hair like that."

He was about fifteen feet from me and could not hear me. But I felt better anyway.

"Officer Alwer," I said. "You got to talk to these folks. This Blue Meanie military machine stuff just makes it worse."

"You nuts, spacey-cadet," she said. "It won't work."

"Thinking that way grows the problem," I said.

I stepped closer to the crowd from behind Alwer's car. A couple gaped at me.

"Get those jacked-up po-po out of here!" snapped a Latino man. He wore a formal black mariachi suit stitched with cream-colored designs. A guitar was slung across his back. Small metal chains ran down both his pants legs, making a tingling noise. His belt showed hand-carved cuts and silver *conchos*, small em-bossed medallions. "All they do is run us down!"

"Afternoon, everybody," I said. "Got a favor to ask. Can we clear this street so that the ambulance can get through?"

Mullet Cut nodded. Maybe I had reached him.

Then he winged something at me.

With handcuffs on, I could not move fast.

The something broke on my belt buckle. It hurt.

A mayonnaise bottle.

Mayo spattered all over me.

It smelled acidic. Probably a cheap brand.

Others things flew at me.

They made me duck.

Alwer glared at me as she squatted down next to McKissick, a black Glock in her hand.

"Told you, hardhead!" she shouted at me.

"Officer Alwer, you are right," I panted. "LA folks act dif-ferent from New Yorkers."

A helicopter buzz sawed overhead, drowning out the crowd sounds.

"Get back, or I'll teargas you!" a crew-cut Asian cop shouted at two kids waving skateboards.

The mob grew.

Debris winged at us.

Cars stopped and spun around, fleeing.

"Grack!" I shouted over the noise.

His head whipped around.

"Don't use my name, re-tard!" Grack shouted.

"Yeah, yeah. Can't you get a bus here for McKissick?"

"A bus?"

"Sorry. New York cop talk. Can't you get an ambulance here for McKissick?"

"Dude, you my sergeant now or something? An ambulance can't get here until the scene is stabilized!"

"But they might keep her alive!"

"Alwer!" a chunky senior cop with a white moustache against his black skin shouted. "Stuff this turkey in your unit! Right now!"

"I got him!" Grack shouted.

He yanked me by the handcuff chain and wedged me into his car. My wrists stung.

"You're under arrest for Inciting to Riot," Grack said. "And other stuff, too."

"Officer, I've got to be in Miami by Friday," I said. "Or else, I lose a job."

"Forget Miami," he said. "You ain't going nowhere."

CHAPTER 4.

Balance
or
Nothing Simple

"Can you crack a window, please, Officer Grack?" I said. "This seat here smells like a baboon's sock."

Grack slid the plastic partition open between the front and back seats. Alwer jangled into the seat next to him.

"Better not spit," Grack said. "That's Assault on a Police Officer."

"Wouldn't dream of spitting," I said. "I graduated from a private prep school."

"You talk too much, hardhead," Alwer said.

The smell in the backseat shifted. Before, it had smelled of wet blue jeans. Now it changed to a bouquet of beer and-tobacco.

Grack's phone on his side of the car played some Muzak. Maybe real music scared him.

"I don't know Los Angeles real well yet," I said. "But I figure that if even the happy-go-lucky singing mariachis woof at you, it means you just lost Los Angeles."

"You don't live here, right, dude?" Grack said.

"No," I said. "But right now, I'm learning fast. Most realistic New Yorkers see their cops as roly-poly loud kids with guns, none too bright. Being a White fool like I am, I think that most of New York doesn't fear our cops. Politicians try to milk that talk for their own ends."

"You making a speech?"

"Maybe. I don't care about race or looks. I start out liking everyone. Here, in your Los Angeles, the cop is seen by some as a ramrod-straight warrior athlete, just itching to use his muscles, ticket book or piece against you."

"That's why your New York City is out of control, dude."

"Is it?" I asked. "How many murders New York got last year?"

"That's your problem," he said.

"Means that you don't know," I said. "Like most cops, you live by TV news and your own impressions. We had 328 murders last year in New York. That's a success."

"Why?" Alwer asked.

"Because, twenty-five years ago, we had six murders a day. Came to 2245. Now, we have less than one a day. And Los Angeles had how many?"

"Told us once at roll call," Grack said. "Somewhere around 260, I think."

"And you got half the population of New York," I said. "Just four million. Proves my point. Scaring citizens makes cities more dangerous. Nobody who is afraid of a cop will tell him anything. So nobody talks. Nobody prevents."

"Let's stop all this BS," Alwer said. "Got work to do."

"Yeah, man," Grack said. "Beats me how he got me all distracted like."

"It's a gift," I said.

"You need tough cops," Grack said.

"Not angry ones," I said.

"Gotta deal with PSB," Alwer said. "The District Attorney's Roll-Out Team for all Death-In-Custody cases. Chief of Police office review. Then, the media. And those church groups, screaming for my butt. Shoot to sugar, why I gotta put up with all this?"

"Because if you don't," I said, "who polices and saves lives?"

Alwer turned to squint at me.

"Man," she said. "You be one corny dude, you know that?"

"You ain't moving that car!" Latina Cook said.

She planted herself five feet in front of the LAPD black-and-white.

"Try running me down, gringos!" shouted Latina Cook.

"Put those baby-pumping hips somewhere else!" Grack hollered at her. "Can't stop us like that!"

"They're doing it," I muttered.

"Hit us!" Skateboarder cawed. "I'll have my lawyer get all your badges for it!"

"We ain't letting you take our backseat brother there to jail!" Latina Cook shouted.

Dark sweat smears decorated her T-shirt armpits.

"Our brother?" I hissed "When did I become her brother?"

LAPD helicopters crisscrossed low above us. Their engine noise sounded monstrous, throbbing against my own ears.

"Those helicopters up there making a mad racket," I said. "Like they're trying to punish us."

"Shut up, man," Grack said.

"Maybe they are," I said. "Los Angeles Punishment Department. LAPD."

Alwer leaned back from the dashboard.

"Can't run these fools down, partner," Alwer said.

"We better!" Grack said. "They gonna swarm us!"

"I'm cooling it," Alwer muttered.

"Good idea," I said from the back seat.

The glass partition between the front and back seats slid open and shut. Then it stayed open. They could hear me.

"Why don't you try it, Grack?" I asked. "Cooling it, I mean."

"She dead," Alwer said. Her head tilted towards the gold-and-silver oval badge pinned to her left breast pocket.

Her voice dipped down as well, like someone grieving at a gravesite. This was the part of policing that the public never saw. She shook her head side-to-side. "What a mess this gonna be."

Something winged towards us. I ducked. A wet plastic bag split open against my window. Light blue soiled baby diapers spilled out. Some stuck to the car.

"For the cop who has everything," I said.

"Gun this 'hooptee' at these Adam Henrys!" Grack hollered. "Lights and siren!"

"They're already on," I muttered. "Guess that hooptee is LAPD cop slang for 'car'."

Another plastic bag splattered against our hood.

Whiskers drank from a flat small bottle, put it in a plastic shopping bag and whirled the bag around his head. At the right time, he released it.

The bag smashed on the front passenger door.

"Old Whiskers thinks he's David with the slingshot, fighting Goliath," I said. "And we're Goliath. Can't have civilization without plastic bags."

A green Mercury came up on our left and blew through the stop sign. It headed for us.

"Damn!" Grack hollered.

The car braked. It bucked and skidded. The front fender tapped ours.

"Re-tard!" Grack bellowed. "He's getting a cite!"

"Don't do it!" Alwer shouted.

But Grack was already bounding out of his seat. His keys jangled. Our car rocked.

Grack bulled up to the Mercury's driver, panting, his mouth open.

Some of the crowd pelted trash at us.

"We can't take this stuff!" a young Asian cop shouted. "Grab those suckers and take them down!"

The other black-and-whites whipped around the crowd and shot away.

"Why they abandoning you?" I asked. "Seems nutty."

My question hung in the air.

"Is that the LA way? No camaraderie? Not like New York."

The driver, a youngster about twenty-two, teal-colored framed glasses, blond hair thinning fast, wore a necklace outside his orange polyester shirt. His yap yawned and shut.

"You won't like the ticket I'm gonna give you!" Grack shouted.

"Officer, I didn't –"

"You talk when I'm through talking, re-tard!" Grack sputtered. "Not before! Why you driving like that, man? Trying to kill somebody?"

"Officer —"

"Didn't I tell you to be quiet? Name?"

"Woodrow S. Cullen."

From my seat in the cop car, I could hear everything Grack and the driver were saying.

In the rear view mirror, I could see Alwer's frowning face.

McKissick dying would change her life. Guilt monsters would crack her peace. Sleep would flee from her.

From my Patrol years, I remembered those nights where shadows had stalked me until sunrise. Alwer needed distractions right now, anything to stop her worries. Or else, the devils would eat her up and then burn down what was left of her.

"Officer Alwer," I said. "When I was an NYPD cop, safety came first. You can back up your partner there. I'm not going anywhere."

"I KNOW that's right," she stressed. Shock changed her tone. She was dropping the official voice and talking Black, like she was off-duty with close friends. "You really a cop back in New York?"

"Got suspended a lot."

"In the 'hood'?"

"Flatbush. Ninety-eight percent Black. But I'm an idealist-type. Not color-struck. Everyone gets a chance to play the fool. Or the saint. That's democracy. That's America. Treated everyone right and made my beat safer."

"Then I can tell you," she said. Her voice changed and loosened up. "But Grack wear me out sometimes. Why he giving out tickets now, front of a 415 crowd? Child's got a devil."

"Crowd's quieting down to listen," I said. "They enjoyed seeing someone else get condemned by the cops. Just so it's not them."

"What's that?"

"*Schadenfreude*," I said.

"Or some kinda BS," Alwer replied.

"*Schadenfreude* is a psychology term," I gassed, trying to distract Alwer. "Means giggling when others step in mud. And there's a lot of that going around."

Grack hopped to the cop car fender, squinted at where the Mercury had tapped it. He blew out a breath and ran his fingertips over the fender.

Whiskers and Latina Cook stepped closer to look at our car.

"Figure that every Angeleno is an expert in car damage," I said, to distract Alwer more. "And over-aggressive policemen."

"Our captain say that you try to hide a fender-bender bump, he gonna get you fired," she said. "Goodbye, pension and health plans and everything else. So, we gotta be real careful, behind all that."

"You way mad lucky that your heap didn't no real damage on my unit, Woodrow," Grack shouted at the youngster. "Callin' you Woody, right? Else, we can charge you with Vehicular Assault on Officers –"

"Sounds like a weak case to me," I muttered.

"Royster, stop with the annoying," Alwer said.

"I kid you not," I said. "You might want to tell Grack that he's standing too close to the door and that driver. The driver can reach for a piece before Old Grack can react. Please pull Grack's coat to that. When he's calmed down, that is."

"Grack do like he please," Alwer said.

"So I see."

"Nothing I can do," Alwer said.

"Try apologizing," I said. "Always worked for me. Cause I made mistakes every hour. And I always said so. Everyone gets it that way."

"Maybe that works in New York," Alwer said. "Being a crazy place, like I hear. But it won't fly out here."

"Try it," I said. "Just this once."

Outside our car, the little traffic scenario kept on rolling.

"I might just cite you anyway!" Grack shouted at Woody. "Gimme one good reason why not!"

"Officer, can I please tell you –" Woody began.

"I'll tell you something, re-tard!" Grack hollered.

Even at this distance, I could see the sweat shining on his face. The crowd growled and grew and grew around them.

"You say one more word and I'll have you getting about six tickets and a ride on the tow hook!" Grack bellowed. "You want that?"

Woody shook his blond head.

"Then MOVE!" Grack shouted.

Woody moved. He switched on the ignition, the engine caught, and the car lurched forward.

"OW!" Grack shouted. "You ran over my foot!"

"Officer, I tried to tell you!"

"Shut up!" Grack shouted. "You know what you did? I can charge you with Battery on a Police Officer! If I go to the hospital overnight, that's Felony Assault! You can go to Pelican Bay State Prison for that."

Grack turned his head and saw the crowd drinking this all in.

They had stopped a-chunking things at us. This was more fun.

"Officer, I tried to tell you!" Woody said. "My goodness gracious. But you told me to shut up. I knew that your foot was near my tire. You said you'd give me a ticket –"

"Aw, stop whining," Grack said. "Making my foot hurt."

"Y'all hear him shouting like that, the poor guy?" Whiskers hooted. "Just for driving too fast!"

"And hitting his car," I said. "Don't forget that."

"That's how they do us!" Latina Cook said.

"Damn," Alwer said.

She breathed heavy, like an overworked mama correcting a child. Then she stepped out of the car and addressed the crowd.

"Everyone, listen up! No ticket! No impound! We apologize. Grack, let's go."

Everything slowed down. Somebody guffawed.

Whiskers said an atrocious adverb. Alwer had taken away all their material.

"Hell with this," a Latino man walking a collie said. "Got other things to do. Get my dog outta here."

The crowd looked at each other, shrugged and seemed to melt away.

"Never heard any cop say sorry before!" Whiskers said.

He was fast losing his audience and looked like he was talking to himself.

"Good work, Alwer," I said. "THAT'S what I call policing."

Chapter 5.

Shake-Up
or
What's your Dee-Eye-Cee Gotta Do With Me?

The back seat kept smelling evil. Their radio kept shouting.

We drove away from the growing crowd. Traffic was snarling everywhere. TV vans had stopped, and their crews were filming everything. Sloppy tourists in Middle America funwear slouched on the corners.

"Look at that character scratching his privates while TV cameras film him," I muttered to the unlistening officers in the front seat. "This ain't the Hollywood tinsel-town of Bogart and Bacall anymore."

More helicopters buzzed overhead.

"Officers, can we speak before you book me?" I asked. "I can do you some good."

Grack spun the wheel. I slid on the seat.

"Just shut your hole," he said. "You're under arrest."

"You already said that," I said. "It's not news."

"Then SHUT UP!"

"Now, that's never easy for me," I said. "I'm a born wisecracker. Third generation. Grandma Royster was a Brooklyn wisecracker."

"Hardhead, you in trouble!" Alwer said.

"Again, not news. I can tell that from your body language. And where I'm sitting. But let me speak with your oldest sergeant, your most senior, once we get inside. Okay?"

"Why the oldest sergeant?"

"Because I'm an age-ist. Like a racist or a sexist. Maybe your oldest can comprehend me. We're about the same age."

"Alwer, you got me into this cluster," Grack said. "Man, a DIC caper will mess up my package forever."

"What's a DIC caper?" I asked. "Dee-Eye-Cee? Dick? Is President Tricky Dick Nixon involved?"

"Dee-Eye-Cee means a Death-in-Custody caper, you knucklehead," Alwer said.

""Caper?'" I asked. "'Knucklehead?' That's kid talk. From old TV shows. Like Bozo the Clown. Does anyone in Los Angeles ever grow up?"

ℂ

We pulled up in front of a boxy, gray stone building under a red stucco roof. A bronze sign read "Los Angeles Police Department – Hollywood Division." Gunport-style windows looked down on us.

Latinos with pushcarts waited for hungry, angry customers to come out of the holding pens. With their last bits of loose change, the customers bought roasted corn, *churros* and *tamales*.

We parked in the back.

Cops in riot helmets and shotguns trotted to their black-and-whites.

"That's not our assigned car!" a Latino cop shouted to his Asian woman partner. "You dodo bird! Are you a frickin' loser or what?"

"Same old police talk," I muttered.

Behind his back, the woman made an ugly face and flipped him her middle finger.

"Calling for additional units on Sunset and Vine," a red-haired woman sergeant said. "Looks like these fools are spreading out."

Alwer grabbed me by the bicep and hauled me out of the car. It hurt.

"Easy, Officer Alwer," I said. "You can see that I'm still full of mayonnaise."

"Full of something. Never heard such bull-crap in my life."

"Mayo all over my pants," I said. "Right around the Controversial Area. Look like a reject from an unsuccessful orgy."

Alwer rolled her eyes and made an ugly face.

We unhappy three came out of the car and to a coded door. Grack covered the hand punching in the numbers with his other so that I couldn't see the code. Maybe he thought that I was planning to break into the station tomorrow.

A scar scored his neck above the dark blue collar. It could have been from a car crash. Or maybe someone had tried to cut his throat.

℃

The hallway was long and gray and depressing, rank with the smell of someone cooking macaroni-and-cheese. A TV played a game show with a cheering audience.

"Look at you," a chunky Latina cop said. Her dark face twisted in a grimace. Her hair piled like rope on top of her head gave her a solid look. Big eyes ruled her face, and she rolled them at me. "Smiling. Looking all around. Disrespectful. You think that you're funny?"

"I'm a riot," I said. "Sorry, wrong word right now."

Her nickel nameplate read "Quizal."

"You just think that you're funny. But you're not."

She stepped back to let more cops race down the hall.

"Los Angeles is a tough audience," I said. "Now, take my own arresting officer. Please."

"Very un-funny," Quizal said.

Alwer and Grack led me into a gray stone cell smelling of unwashed bodies. The cell ran about eight feet by ten, with smooth yellow walls, decorated with graffiti and gouges.

We went through the pockets and shoes and wallet routine. Grack took everything from me, scrutinized it and bagged it.

Then, I waited alone.

Part of me drifted back to high school days at Saint Blaise's School for Young Men. They always predicted that my wisecracking might land me in a place like this.

A gray-haired, uniformed cop appeared in the door.

"Sir, I'm the Watch Commander," he said in a dry Midwestern accent. "Sergeant Poole. Officers said that you wanted to speak with me."

He looked fit, like someone who walked to a steakhouse and then jogged home after eating. His red outdoor face held blue eyes. A scar marred his right upper lip. Maybe someone had cut him. Cops like him and Grack carried their mistakes on their faces.

He smelled of aftershave and fresh leather polish. His black shoes shone like mica. Five hash marks scored his left shirt cuff. That meant at least twenty-five years of service. He carried two sets of handcuffs on his Sam Browne belt. That meant that he was always ready to leave the station and help his cops in the street when the cow-flop hit the fan.

"Sarge, can you check my wallet for my police ID?" I asked.

"Already did. But there's no police ID. Just a slip saying that Police Officer Maxwell A. Royster lost three vacation days for working overtime without asking permission first."

"Can you think of a better police ID?" I asked. "Sarge, I can help you and your cops by telling the truth."

"Hold up, there. You're in custody. Detained, not arrested. Your rights –"

"I'm waiving them. Any lawyer will tell me to shut up before the Preliminary Hearing. By then, you'll have a riot on your hands."

"You're risking years in prison."

"Got to. I saw McKissick being irrational and shouting about the Blood of Jesus. I don't know how it started, but I saw her and your Officer Alwer wrestling. The whole mess came from somewhere. Alwer didn't start it."

"You'll testify to that?"

"If needed to."

"Oh, it's needed to," he said. "Don't worry about that. Now, what do you want?"

"I got no pension, Sarge. No cash. I just landed myself a dream job as security on a cruise ship line. Central and South America, two month voyage.

"Good salary and free trip. Union membership. But I gotta be in Miami by Friday. Or else, I lose the job. And my cash deposit. And get blacklisted in the cruise industry. So, can you get me out by Friday?"

"I'll do what I can," he said.

CHAPTER 6.

Double-Talk
or
Think That One Over

"Where is this hammerhead Royster?" a nasal voice bounced at me from outside in the hall. "Let me see him. Is he for real?"

"As real as it gets," I said.

"You Royster?" a slim customer in a tan poplin suit asked. Designer eyeglasses swung on a neck-chain. Gray shot through his hair, over a reddish face and startling cobalt eyes. He looked like a noisy fifty.

"I'm Detective-Sergeant Tyke, PSB," he said.

He came inside the interview room.

His partner, a solid Asian woman with long hair bleached tan, followed him. Her eyes flicked over me. She bobbed her head as if her partner had abashed her into silence.

"You're going to talk turkey right now or go into prison for a while, yeah," Tyke continued. "Inciting to Riot is a heavy charge, if anyone gets hurt. So you better –"

"Hold on, sports fans," I said. "I was never busted. And I'm not arrested now. I'm here, trying to Be a Darn Good Fellow. But I can slide on out."

"WHAT?" Tyke shouted.

"That's right," Poole said, coming in behind them. "Mr. Royster is free to go, as soon as we complete our warrant check on him."

"No way!" Tyke said. "He stays until I finish with him."

"You just did," I said.

My legs worked inside the khaki shorts, and I rocked to the door.

"Tyke, you're one of these jokers, no matter what I say, it's going to be wrong. So, it's been real."

The cops let me pass.

"Wait here for the warrant check," Poole said. "Should just be a few minutes more."

℃

In the lobby, pandemonium reigned.

"Go ahead!" a Black man holding two kids by the hands said. "I saw wrong out there! Lock me up! Bring me to the ass-whipping room!"

"Saw that po-lice throw her stick and hit that gal from across Gower Street!" a wattled blonde woman with mirror sunglasses said. "And if I'm lyin', I'm flyin'!"

"Then you're flying," I said to her. "Because you're lying. Now hit the road!"

"Can't do that, Royster," Poole said, coming up. "I keep pulling you out of a mess. This lady is a witness. Have to take her statement."

"Tell him, Officer!" the woman said. "Make him shut up! Gimme his name and badge number, and I'll report him to the chief, my assemblywoman, my reverend and those TV folks!"

"Don't forget the U.S. Senate Sub-Committee on Premature Aging," I said.

"Them, too!"

She stepped to the desk cop and started unwinding her fairy tale.

"You write her jazz down?" I asked. "Even if she's lying?"

"Doesn't matter. We've had about eleven witnesses come in already. They're all lying."

"So toss them out," I said.

"We can't. They'll say that we were covering up. Scream to the media. You're the only normal witness, trying to tell the truth, that we dug up so far."

"Nobody ever called me a 'normal witness' before. Or a 'normal' anything. What happens if I just drift on?"

"Then we're stuck with liars, kooks and boobs hustling to pry cash out of the city. They'll testify. And Patty Alwer gets ruined." He pronounced the word "roont" in his Middle America drawl. "Hear that you were a New York cop. So you know how it goes."

"Yeah. Unhappily."

"What?"

"Unhappily," I said. "Because the City of the Angels now has a famous dead Black actress. No weapon. What crime was she doing?"

"5400(A) 1 California Vehicle Code," Poole said.

"Which is what? Insider Trading? Defrauding-an-Innkeeper? Kissing-on-the-First Date?"

"It's against the Vehicle Code to post a sign on your car that you want to sell it," he said. "It makes other drivers slow down and causes accidents."

"Really? In Los Angeles?"

"Stop cutting the fool, Royster. So, when we see a sign, we sometimes ticket the owner. Reduces accidents. The owners will hire a homeless guy to take the sign off the windshield when we roll by."

"Is that why your cop Patty Alwer stopped McKissick?"

"Seems like. Alwer saw her take the sign and try hiding it. We keep calling the R.O., Registered Owner, of the car. No answer. Probably wants to duck the citation. But we got three of ours injured, eight fat-heads in custody for Disorderly Conduct and Misdemeanor-Assault-on-a-PO and the media rolling out."

"Poole, the rest of America won't believe that LAPD goes after the homeless for Vehicle Code Bolshoi like that," I said. "The public will burn Alwer at the stake as a modern-type badge-wearing witch."

"They're doing it now," he said.

Again, it was decision time and it felt hard. It usually did. For the last time, I wondered why I could not be like everyone else.

"I can't let that happen," I said. "Royster has got to be Royster. So, goodbye Miami new job and hello PSB goons like Detective-Sergeant Tyke. Let me slink back into that room."

CHAPTER 7

Messing Up the Mess
or
The Hair Ball Rolls

Poole ferried me back into the interview room, then left me alone with Sgt. Tyke and his Asian woman partner.

They sat at angles with me facing them. I felt like a Christmas turkey with two butchers coming to carve me up. Behind us was a table with a fat tape recorder. Maybe it was there to scare the cops into good behavior. Or me into telling the truth.

"You gonna activate that tape recorder?" I asked.

"I'll decide that," Tyke said.

"Kind of defeats the purpose," I said.

Years of police secrets echoed from framed pictures on the wall – grave, mustached LAPD uniformed cops in cavalry cloaks and Stetson hats.

Tyke looked like somebody was goosing him. He leaned closer to me, smelling of peanut butter and shoe polish. His new shoes creaked.

"What's this, you Adam Henry?" he snapped.

I blew out a raspberry.

"I got it, Tyke," I said. "'Adam-Henry', yup. Means the word 'Ass-Hole', without really saying it. In case the adults are listening."

"They say you used to be an officer?"

"Let's not swap resumes. It would be too depressing."

"Come on, play ball and tell us, Mr. Royster," said his partner.

A lilt to her words marked her as Filipina-American. Her full body pushed out against her dark red pantsuit. She looked about thirty, half my age, and wore no wedding ring. Her eyes looked like she could laugh long and loud if the adults allowed her. But something held her back. Maybe she had been reared in some Catholic missionary school where the nuns would spank her for hooting or skylarking.

To her today, the LAPD was just another stern institution where you could not enjoy life without permission.

"I'm Officer Rhea Shadap of PSB. See whatta mean? Tell us, okay, no problem. Wha' happen? That way, we understand you."

"Good luck with that," I said. "Ask my ex-wife."

"Spill it, Royster," Tyke said.

"How elegant," I said. "NYPD cops are so different from you LAPD robots. Like I said before, most New Yorkers don't fear or hate their cops. On the other hand, a lot of Angelenos do."

"You got the answer why?" she asked. "Wha' happen?"

Emotion pinked her face and chipped at her English. The lilt grew strident.

If she were under stress, shouting into a radio, I could never be able to understand her. I wondered how the LAPD oral panel had passed her on speech.

"I read up on it," I said. "I used to love policing in New York. You LA cops go right out of your Academy and into a radio car with a veteran. You speed past all your information sources with your windows up and the AC turned to full blast."

"We need to hear this?" Tyke asked.

"Your partner thinks so," I said.

Officer Shadap glanced at me. Maybe I was reaching her.

"A New York cop walks for his first two years," I rattled on. Like a salesman, I was hustling to make them see me as a person and not an object. "At least, two. Some, ten years. That teaches you how to deal with everyone. Crazy, safe, rich or poor.

Our radios don't work everywhere. Too many big buildings block the signal. So, most times, you can't call for help."

"Wha' happen?" Officer Shadap said.

"Never mind," I said.

"No coppers walk here, man," Officer Shadap said. "Unless they wanna. And nobody wanna. Maybe, couple of minutes, okay, no problems. No harm, no foul. But we spread too thin. Not enough coppers, like it is. Liberals tell people, don't join us. We an occupy army, yeah."

"And it's too damn dangerous," Tyke said. "They would kill any foot cop. This is the most dangerous city in America."

"'Do You Know What It Means to Miss New Orleans'?"

"Huh?" Tyke said.

"Title of a catchy tune by Satchmo."

"Huh?" he repeated.

"New Orleans is a slaughterhouse for murder. Ever heard of Detroit? Los Angeles is no way near the most dangerous city in America. Try Camden, New Jersey or North Little Rock, Arkansas. You believe that LA is so dangerous, that justifies you treating everyone like a killer."

"You quite a speech guy, Royster. Never shut up, huh?"

"Maybe you should read something once in a while, Tyke. No matter how much it hurts."

"I know enough already."

"And you LA cops act angry at everyone," I said. "That's your style. Don't try it on me, Tyke. Now, what do you want to know?"

"Git that camera out my face, you media vulture!" someone shouted outside in a Southern drawl.

Officer Shadap took me through the routine ID stuff. Tyke sat back and let her do the boring stuff. He was probably priming himself for matters more grand.

Sure enough, he swooped down on me.

"Tell us what you saw, Royster," Tyke said.

"I didn't see the incident start," I said. Nerves pitched my voice higher. "But as I was crossing, I saw both Alwer and McKissick wrestling. McKissick kept saying 'You so stupid! Stop her, Jesus. The Blood of Jesus is on you, stupid.'"

"And just what did McKissick mean by that?" Tyke snapped.

"It's your city," I said. "You tell me."

"What did Officer Alwer say?" Shadap asked me.

"She kept saying 'Stop resisting'," I said. "Must have said it six times or more."

"Officer Alwer, man, she say anything else?" Shadap asked. "Like racial stuff? You know? Black stuff?"

"They're both Black," I said. "Remember?"

"No, they ain't," Tyke said. "One's blue. And the Department prohibits ANYONE using racially derogatory terms. Even if they're Eskimo."

Tyke stepped back to his chair. Maybe I was tiring him out.

"You mean 'Inuit', don't you, Detective-Sergeant Tyke?" I said. "Because the word 'Eskimo' is racially derogatory. You want to watch that term. Just ask any Canuck."

"Including THAT word. Stop all this BS, Royster," Shadap said. "You some kinda nut?"

"My own kind," I said.

"Royster, did Officer Alwer say any kind – racial stuff, slang, you know? "

"Not that I remember now."

"What kinda answer that?" Shadap asked.

"The kind that a cop needs, fighting for her life," I said. "Should my answer vex you, you may enquire of those prime witnesses outside, a-clamoring in the lobby. They'll tell you everything but the truth."

"Did Officer Alwer's partner touch the suspect?"

"Not that I saw."

"Royster, ya see the suspect's hands anywhere, you know, near Officer Alwer's firearm?" she asked. "Get me?"

"They were wrestling. Both their hands were going everywhere."

Tyke leaned forward in his chair.

In the lobby, shouts grew. Los Angeles was coming apart because of McKissick. They would stream her old movies on their TVs and computers, when she looked like a teenage beauty queen.

"So it's possible that the suspect was NOT reaching for the officer's gun?" he asked.

"You just interrupted your partner," I said. "That chagrins me anew. So do you, Tyke."

"That's all right," Shadap said.

"Maybe to you," I said. "Not to me. I think we'll have a little law here. Let's get an Assistant District Attorney talking to me for the record."

"Why?" Tyke asked.

"Because you're a twister," I said. "No matter what I say, you will twist it. The DA won't."

"Ohhh, don't know about all that mess, gas-bag," Shadap said. "But take my card. You call any time."

"Any time?"

"We can discuss the case."

"Very pretty card," I said. "LAPD badge in all its pageantry on the back. And your badge number. It's almost the same as Alwer's."

"Wha' happen?" Shadap said.

That phrase "Wha' happen?" seemed to be how she handled the mysterious world outside her. Her speech was slipping again. My wisecracks were getting to her.

"Maybe thinking, like you a cop again," she said. "But you ain't. Remember that, man. You just a jacked-up janky kinda witness."

"Did you come through the Academy together?" I asked.

"Wha' happen?" Shadap asked. "That your business?"

"Ten minutes on a computer and I'll find out for myself," I said.

"She got through, class after me," Tyke said.

"You're not in the same age group," I said, trying to loosen them both up.

Shadap smirked.

"Because LAPD got no upper age limit," she said.

"Then, maybe I'll join," I said.

"You wouldn't fit in," Tyke said.

"Pro'ly not. I didn't fit in back in New York."

"Are you trying to guess my age?" Shadap asked.

"Wouldn't dare," I said. "Your name on the card reads 'Police Officer Rhea L.J. Shadap, PSB'. What does 'L.J.' stand for, please?"

"L.J. means 'Lady Jane'," Shadap said. "My mother like that name. Way independent-type woman back in the Philippines. Ran her own business. Selling banana leaves."

"Cases like this, dealing with cops, probably make you wish that you were back there now," I said. "Pricing the banana leaves."

CHAPTER 8.

Talking It Up
or
Lady Jane Speaks

"I gotta call the skipper," Tyke said. He sounded like an important man-of-affairs, dealing with weighty matters. But his light eyes showed fear of something, I noticed a bald patch now near the crown of his head. I had a vision of how he would look twenty years from now, retired and still angry, shouting at people from his suburban front porch.

"Here's your phone and personal stuff back," Shadap said. She handed me back the plastic bag with my wallet and phone. Breathing relief, I pocketed everything. "That's just our procedure, you know? Do it with everyone."

"Thank you, Officer Shadap," I said. "I'm trying to make your job easier. No matter how it looks."

"Officer Shadap, keep Royster chilled out, okay?" Tyke said. "Don't let him jump in front of those CNN cameras."

"I never watch TV news," I said. "It makes you too uncomplicated."

Tyke left us two alone, closing the door behind him.

"Shadap, this is a silly time for a history mini-lesson," I said. "But, once, while I was a seaman stuck on a long voyage, I had only one book to read. A Dutch paperback, looking at American race riots. Practically memorized it."

"Wha' happen?"

"You ever get stuck with just one book like that?" I asked.

"Don't read much. Guess I oughta. Too busy working, driving around. Having dinner with friends."

"Some like reading. Sailors kinda got to on long voyages. In 1967, this country suffered race riots. Do you know how many, in one year?"

"How could I?"

"153. Can you imagine that? 153 cities tore up by this Black-White ring-around dance. Black folks have it very tough in America."

"Is that why they always break the laws and disrespect us, man?"

"What do you mean 'always break the laws'?" I asked.

"You know what I mean."

"Why? Because I'm a White ex-cop? I'm not White. This is just a pigmentation disorder."

"Wha' happen? You like hacking around, right?"

"Blacks have it tough," I repeated. "They can't live where they want, work where they want or get the same breaks that everyone else lives by. Stuck in high-crime areas that they can never escape."

"Not anymore, man."

"Yes, right now, man," I said.

"Then they should fix it themselves."

"Try it, when you're twenty, no job skills, no high-school diploma and no family or cash to help you. Sure, you can join the Army, get through Basic and combat and claw your way to a small pension of twenty grand and medical benefits. But it's not easy."

"My folks did okay."

"Asians ain't Blacks. What I'm trying to say, almost all those riots started with some cop stuff. Usually Brutality against a Black Person."

"That's not our fault."

"Why do you say 'our fault,' Shadap? You weren't a cop then. You sure don't know what happened to start those riots."

"Don't believe that many riots, gas-bag. Just can't be."

I leaned closer.

"Why not?" I asked.

"Because those talking heads on the History Channel would be talking all about it. Man, 153? Didn't know that there are 153 cities in the whole United States."

"What you said is the nugget of 'why?' that draws me," I said.

"You sure talk funny for a cop. For real."

"Maybe I was never much of a cop. But what fascinates me, Officer Shadap, is the fact that those talking heads DON'T talk about it. Nobody remembers. Or wants to remember."

The room seemed to grow around us.

"It's on the Internet?" she asked.

"The big riots, Detroit and Newark, are, yeah. A lot of books were written about them. But nothing about the smaller riots. There's no list of where they were. Just the number 153."

"So what? This is all, just talking BS, you know. Doesn't matter now."

"I think that it does," I said. "Somebody would have to be old as me or older, to remember that Long, Hot Summer of '67. Hippies called it 'The Summer of Love.' But, it wasn't. We sweep it out of our memories. Then it doesn't exist. We tell ourselves that it never happened. Or that conditions for Blacks have gotten so much better."

"So what?"

"So, it did happen. And conditions ain't that much better. Riots make it worse. Nobody wins in a riot."

"This is just trash talking, man. Doesn't get us anywhere."

"Are you sure, Officer Shadap? Let's not start another race riot here, today."

Chapter 9.

Promise?
or
Legally Speaking

Quizal, the chunky Latin officer, brought the Deputy District Attorney and Sgt. Pierce inside the interview room.

"That's Royster there," Quizal said. "He's not funny."

The DDA boasted blond hair in a razor cut and baby blue eyes. His smooth face rode above a pricey black suit that looked hot in this LA climate. His shoes gleamed like he was ready for a courtroom appearance and not riding a death case in Hollywood.

He looked like one of those lawyers who worked hard on his appearance to impress the jury. He would intimidate a hostile witness with his looks and his loud abusive questions.

"Good luck with this fool," Quizal said as she left.

"Mr. Royster, I understand that you're helping us get to a clearer understanding of what took place today?" the DDA said. He had a flat hard delivery, with no doubt slowing him down.

"Trying," I said.

"Super," he said. "Let's get you down on paper as to what happened."

"You are?" I asked.

"Wendell Brookings, of the District Attorney's office."

"Mr. Brookings, you're going to run a background on me, sooner or later. So, I'm an ex-cop out of New York,"

"Honorably retired, I take it?"

"You'd have to take it. Nobody else would."

"Give him a straight answer," Shadap said.

"If you can," Tyke said.

"The straight answer is that I have a job opening for me," I said," but I've gotta be in Miami for it. Not here."

"Good job?" Brookings asked.

"Haven't worked in seventeen months. Any job is a glorious wonderful job."

Something tugged at Brookings' lip. It might have been a smirk. Or it could be a twitch, maybe from nerve damage.

"This job is a shot at a new career," I said. "And the man don't want to hear no excuses."

"What kind of job?" Brookings asked.

"Cruise ship security," I said.

His mouth twitched again.

Maybe Brookings did not approve of cruise ship security.

That did not ruffle me much. Because I approved. They would feed me, bed me and pay me to travel.

"Let's see what we have here, first," Brookings said. "I think that I can promise you that we won't keep you from your new job. We want to keep you happy."

"Then let me get to Miami."

"Absolutely," Brookings said. "Now, let's solidify a bit here."

Brookings dandled his briefcase on his knees and drew papers out from it. I felt like a sixth-grader back in Saint Blaise's School for Young Men with the principal reading my "naughty-boy" letters.

Tyke slid a video camera from his briefcase and voiced a heading.

"This is Sergeant Willis Tyke, serial number 32877, assigned to Professional Standards Bureau," he said. "I will be operating a Department approved Cuska video camera in the matter of the McKissick inquiry against Officer Patricia Z. Alwer, Hollywood, Patrol Division."

That heading meant that it was evidence for court.

Alwer was getting hit with charges.

I was not.

But a cop's fear still iced my lungs. The NYPD had put me through this same slow torture, and I had been innocent of everything except joining the Department. After these years, the fear still rode me.

The lobby noise grew. More shouts swung through the air.

Outside, sirens and helicopters kept ripping their noise.

The cellphone buzzed in my pocket. Tyke and Brookings fixed me with stern professional looks.

The phone felt hot against my ear.

"Max, this is Koy," a soft woman's voice, Chinese-accented, said on the phone.

"*Gna oy nay,*" I said, butchering the Cantonese as usual.

"No time for love talk," she said. "You know that my parents trying to get back China, right?"

As always, under stress, her English suffered, and she spoke with Cantonese syntax.

"They take their *lay see chin,* the Chinese New Year's money in the red envelopes, from their families and save it and buy airline tickets to Guangzhou."

"That's a lot of red envelope cash," I said.

"So, they already there, in the old flat," she said. "They ask me to come, help them. So I gotta go. With Snowball, but he must go thirty days in quarantine."

Koy trained animals for a living. Snowball-the-Wonder-Dog was her favorite, a cream-colored Great Pyrenees hound who loved to eat, snooze and put his wet nose on my thigh.

"I don't know when I come back," Koy said. "Or if I ever come back."

The others in the room glared at me.

Shutting my eyes, I could see Koy's black hair framing her exquisite face.

This was not a call that I wanted to hear.

"So, you can do what you want," Koy said. "With all the ladies. You too old for me, anyway."

"You keep telling me that," I said. "It ages me."

"Do what you want," she said.

"To do that, I'd have to be in China," I said. "With you and Snowball."

"Royster," Brookings said. "We've got work here."

It was time for another decision.

"Call me when your plane lands," I said. "Please."

The cellphone felt very heavy when I put it away in my pocket.

Brookings talked me along as the others listened.

"Patty says that she was trying to cite the suspect for the CVC violation," Poole said. "The suspect hit her in the neck –"

"Sergeant!" Tyke snapped.

Shadap gasped and leaned forward. Her face hardened.

"With something hard, like a screwdriver and tried to grab Patty's gun," Poole went on.

"You can't tell him that!" Brookings said. "That'll bias him."

"Sgt. Poole, leave the room," Tyke said. "You just put your career in jeopardy."

"Got thirty-two years in, anyway," Poole said. "My wife wants me to retire while I can. Then we can travel."

"Sergeant, you need to get yourself a defense rep," Tyke said. "You may be facing criminal charges here for witness tampering in a capital case. Don't say another word in here. You just disgraced yourself and all of us."

"Don't know about that last part," I said.

Sgt. Poole left, walking tall and military past the PSB Team of Tyke and Shadap. Nobody made eye contact with anyone else. Allegiances were falling apart everywhere.

"Brookings, if Patty Alwer felt something hard hit her throat," I said, "and McKissick was grabbing for her gun, that justifies Alwer using lethal force against her. It's a survival move."

"That's not your call," Tyke said.

"Maybe not," I said. "But I just called it."

"We just want what you saw and heard," Shadap said.

"What killed her?" I asked.

Nobody answered.

"I saw Alwer use her baton," I said. "Then I saw that the tip of the baton had blood on it."

Brookings scribbled that down.

"We'll cover all of you with the Blood of Jesus!" a man bellowed in the lobby.

"It's getting noisier outside," Shadap said.

"I think that it's going to get worse," I said. "And we know why."

"Us coppers need to show who's boss in the street," Tyke said. "Get in a little stick time and fill up our jail."

"That is why," I said.

"That's not germane right now," Brookings said. "You remain our most important witness to this incident."

"I have to say again that I did not see this incident begin," I said. "I heard shouts. When I looked over, both Officer Alwer and McKissick were wrestling with each other."

Brookings scrutinized me.

"That may change," he said. "Now, as a former law enforcement officer, I can understand some reluctance to rush to judgment."

"Or as a human being," I said. "Rushing to judgment is for youngsters younger than I."

"Alwer had just gotten promoted to P-3," Tyke said. "Even though she's a relatively new officer. Everyone at the station says that she was really proud of the promotion.

"Which might be why she insisted on wearing the Class-A formal uniform with the long sleeves. Even on a hot day. Maybe that promotion went to her head today. Maybe she came down a bit too heavy on the victim. D'you see what I mean?"

"Sure," I said. "You're guessing."

"Not really."

"Yes, really," I said. "Seen Internal Affairs types in action in the past. When you clear away all the hard evidence, if there is any, you try your pop-psychology guesswork on what you think that the cop did.

"With no real training in psychology, you try to get inside the cop's head, please your bosses and move ahead smoothly in your career."

Tyke opened his mouth and closed it and shook his head like a boxer taking punches.

"Royster, does New York have a psych test for people like you who want to be cops?" Brookings asked. "Can't imagine how you passed it."

"I done it with mirrors," I recited.

"Enough of this," Brookings said. "You know, that Ms. McKissick had eight ballpoint pens in her pockets when she died. Who carries around eight pens?"

"Kleptomaniacs," I said.

"Stop it, Royster."

"Homeless people use them to stab each other," I said. "And nobody will arrest them for it."

"And three notebooks," Brookings went on. "All covered with handwriting. What does that tell us?"

"Hypergraphia," I said. "Compulsive writing. Like Lewis Carroll."

"Did you see the officer do anything criminal?" Tyke asked me.

My breath corkscrewed. Brookings shot Tyke a look that would scrape ice off a windshield.

"You favor the subtle tack, do you, Sergeant?" I asked.

"Just tell us what you saw," he said.

"Interviewing is more delicate and fine than that," I said. "But that's all that I saw."

"Maybe you can give us more, later on," Brookings said.

Something icy frosted me again. My head swiveled to his.

"What 'later on'?" I asked. "I'm getting my act together and taking it on the road."

Tyke tapped me on the elbow with a folded paper sheet. His touch was gentle mocking.

Then he dropped the paper onto the floor.

"I'm not picking that up," I said. My voice cracked.

"Doesn't matter," Tyke said. "You're served. That's a subpoena. You gotta stay in LA until we let you go."

Chapter 10.

Me Being Me
or
Acting Out

"How about I just kill myself, the first chance I get?" I asked. "Seems the only way out of this mess."

"Then I'll see about getting this subpoena voided," Brookings said.

"You could just take it back now," I said,

"Well, no, not actually, I couldn't do that. It would upset the judge who signed it, no end."

"Not to mention your boss," I said.

"But we're going to get you on that flight for Miami," he said. "Here's my card. My phone is always on. Reach me, day or night."

"Yeah," I said.

Some lawyers had told me that before

"You're our best bet at closing out this case quickly," Brookings said.

He closed his black leather briefcase with brass fittings on it. "Except that you are a former officer. The tabloids will scream that you're helping your fellow cops and they will scream 'cover-up. So, it's going to be a delicate tightrope walk using you."

"Gotcha," I said.

I tried to think of a wittier reply but nothing came to mind.

"Call you tomorrow, counselor," I said, rising to my feet.

"Wait a sec, Royster," Shadap said. "Can't just walk out of here, player. The looky-loos, the nosy guys, they all saw you come in. Might battery you, yeah."

For a second, I wondered if getting me into a car alone was one of Officer Shadap's interview tricks.

She shifted in the dark red pantsuit again. Her thighs melded together.

"There's a riotous assembly outside," Tyke said.

"Aggravated by whom?" I asked.

"They'll grab you up out there," Shadap said. "Let us give you a ride, at least."

"I'm a New Yorker," I said. "We walk."

"Make sure that you got all your property back," Tyke said. "Wallet and phone and cash. Count your money in front of us. So you can't accuse us of stealing from you later on."

"Don't worry, Sergeant," I said.

"Just making sure," he said.

"That kind of Puritanical fear hangs all over this station house," I said. "And your whole Department. Stop worrying about things that don't matter."

We went past the front desk, where Officer Quizal was talking with a clump of taxpayers. They were shouting about their rights as phones rang and radios burped out calls from a PA system on the wall.

"Why all this electronic noise?" I asked Shadap. "One radio speaker without that PA system would be enough."

"Need to know everything that's going on," she said. "Radio calls and announcements inside the station. This is a dangerous town, Royster."

"Gets more dangerous when cops can't speak to locals," I said. "Or each other. Especially with all this hullabaloo."

"We gotta use all the communication stuff that we got," Shadap said. "Or else they'll take it away from us some kinda way."

Nobody in the crowd paid me any attention. They were enjoying themselves too much. This was like reality TV and they were the stars of today.

The noise set my teeth on edge. There was too much of it spewing out of the high-tech electronics all around us.

"Hollywood Units, Hollywood units," the PA system barked. "Any unit in the vicinity. 415 crowd destroying property, Hollywood and Sycamore. Unit responding?"

Two young jogger-type uniformed cops shambled towards the parking lot.

"No Hollywood units available," squawked a fat radio box on the wall. The speaker's voice sounded like Donald Trump suffering from dog distemper.

"Air Three responding from Harbor Division, ten minute ETA," rasped out another voice from the same radio box

"Any Hollenbeck Unit, shots fired near the station." the first radio box voice said.

"If the system wants precise and smart police work," I said, "why don't they give cops better systems to hear these calls? This noise will make anyone angry. Even me."

"Huh?" Quizal said.

"Cops need clarity. And clarity begins at home."

"You, Royster!" Quizal called. "You're not funny."

"Are you talking to me?" an aged Black man asked Quizal.

Shaking my head to clear it, I stepped outside the front door.

℣

Outside Hollywood Police Station, three rows of screamers were hitting their own high notes. By my guess, more than eighty shouters and ranters were grouped around the station.

"We gonna get that officer and have him fired for what he did!" a man with the classic profile of a white-haired Roman senator voiced.

I bet that he was an actor between jobs. This was Hollywood, after all.

"Wasn't a 'he' who did it," a red-haired woman, in a floppy orange sundress with mustard stains on it, said. "Was a 'she'."

"Whomever," Actor said.

He stepped closer to the cops and clenched a fist above his profile.

"Nobody in this Department truly protects and serves!" he announced.

"You tell it, senior!" Red Hair shouted. "Right between their eyes!"

"Ms. McKissick was an actress much better than her movies!" Actor shouted. He was working himself up. "I know because I acted with her in Funny Bunny Hunts the Horn Bug!"

"Missed that one," I muttered. "And glad of it."

A burly Latino sergeant with short, spurred sideburns took off his riot helmet.

"You're all scum!" Actor shouted. "Fascist murderers!"

"Yon actor's starting to get sucked in by his own material," I thought.

He leaned forward until he was almost touching the Sergeant.

"Scum!" Actor shouted. "Filthy scum!"

He was an unknown to me. Maybe getting busted would help his career.

The Sergeant's neck muscles swelled. But he just grimaced at the Actor. His expression might have been a smile.

"Whatever, dude," the Sergeant said.

The Sergeant wedged his riot helmet back on his head and walked on.

"Hey, John Barrymore!" I shouted at the Actor.

Staying in character, he surveyed me.

"Sir?" he intoned.

"You're an actor," I said. "Do the Method here, the Stanislavski ragtime. Get into that cop's head."

"Mmmm," he said.

"You're a Black woman cop, and you just killed another Black lady, homeless at that," I said. "Do you think that you care about losing your job? Does it matter that much? When you lie down at night, do you fret about lost income and getting another job?"

He thought about this.

A helicopter swooped down closer.

The noise stung my ears.

Actor turned back to the crowd.

"Scum!" he roared. "Fascist bullies!"

He was back to being a showboat again. He had forgotten all about my penetrating question. Somehow, that hurt my feelings.

Blue uniforms in riot gear faced them off. More black-and-whites rocked into view.

Farther away, other police cars blocked off streets.

"I want no part of this," I muttered. "Daddy must eat. I want a Nathan's jumbo hot dog, mustard and sauerkraut and a large coffee to keep me going."

Red Hair was getting louder, if that was possible.

"Excuse me extremely," I asked her.

She halted her mewling enough to look at me, sniff and keep hollering.

"I'm probably dense," I said. "But I don't see where screaming at a building will assist with this very complex social problem of police brutality."

"They didn't have to kill her over selling a car!" Actor shouted. "That's crazy! California IS a car culture!"

"Po-po brutality!" a Middle Eastern-looking teenager with a goatee shouted.

Then he looked at me, four feet away.

"You're not shouting, mister," he said. "Why not? Got no guts? What do you say, huh?"

"I say that police brutality is like pornography," I said. "Nobody can define it. But they know it when they see it."

Striding away from the poor man's mini-riot, I needed food. I must translate the cuisine from New Yorkese to modern California dialect.

☙

A white wooden eatery with chipped blue doorway stood halfway down the block. Broken glass lay on the sidewalk below a duct-taped square of cardboard. Maybe a disgruntled diner had tossed a bowl through the window to protest the Soup of the Day.

Cigarette butts dotted the dusty linoleum floor.

A stumpy Asian waiter with a twitchy left cheek and a beaten look met me at the door. He was scratching himself without beauty.

"We closed," he muttered.

"Now?"

"Sure, slick. Listen to them helicopters and stuff. There gonna be a riot."

"No, there won't," I said. "And, anyway, I'm hungry. Riot or no."

"We closing," he repeated. "So are all the other restaurants around here now. They don't wanna get jacked up and stuff."

"But I'm hungry," I said. "Now, this is getting serious."

CHAPTER 11.

LAPD's Story
or
Tell Me Why

"Coffee?" I asked.

"It's pretty old" he said.

"I'm not too young myself," I said.

"Okay," he said, stepping aside. It looked difficult for him to allow me entry. "But I closing up pretty damn soon, you know."

"Bless you, my son."

My body thanked me for folding it into a splintered wooden chair.

"We got no cream, milk, bro'," he mumbled.

"Just atmosphere and love," I said.

Police Officer Shadap bustled into the restaurant. Like most Angelenos, she looked rushed. Traffic jams always did that to normals.

"Gotta talk to you, Royster," Shadap said. "So you can kinda get a handle on what's the real deal here."

"Then get me an interpreter."

"Wha' happen?"

"Because LA ain't New York. We don't speak the same language."

"Wha' happen?"

"Officer Shadap, are you going to keep asking that question, 'Wha' happened?'"

"Aww?"

"Trouble with us cops is that we repeat our same words, the same 'cleesh', all the time. Radio jargon that we figure everyone understands."

"Royster, you a real New York City know-it-all, huh?"

"Possibly."

"So, I need to get you straight on this stuff, whatever you call it, LAPD talk, or else you gonna screw up, hard head. Order food yet, you?"

"Not yet. The service personnel here seems to be mulling things over before they move. That means that I still stay hungry. And grouchy. And talkative."

"Motor-mouth gas-bag, yeah," she said.

My coffee arrived and I tried drinking it. It took a strong imagination to get half of it down.

Two dollars bills crisped out of my pocket and onto the table.

There had to be a better cup somewhere nearby. Needing coffee reminded me that I was fast hardening into a bleak old age.

Hunger was still wiring through my temples and gut. If this kept up, I might act irresponsibly. Getting older did that to me.

"I'd rather walk outside," I said. "If you're going to talk. These joints got video cameras for robberies. Tends to inhibit me."

"We can drive. Where's your car?"

"In your LA imagination, officer."

"You got no car? Jeez Louise, how can you get anywhere?"

"You're saying that, that's Los Angeles versus New York all over again."

"Okey-dokey, we'll walk. OMG."

All her slang sounded odd, coming from her traditional Asian face.

ʚ3

We stepped away from the restaurant. The waiter looked glad to see the last of us.

The sky buzzed with police and media helicopters. Something smelled like a rubber fire nearby. Groups in Dollar General Budget Wear eddied and swirled away on corners. Loud voices fought pounding rap music.

"My captain's a history nut," Shadap said. "And I had to drive him all last year. Chewed my ear off about the Department. What you know about us LAPD guys , anyway, Royster?"

"That you don't like to laugh."

"Smart ass," she said. "Think that you know everything."

"Working on it," I said.

"We used to be big-time corrupt, in the Depression." Her speech and words got more formal now. Maybe she was quoting her captain. "Us coppers used to stop migrants at the California state line, 200 miles away. Bighead Chief said the LA city limits began there. Nobody poor getting into here."

"Took a broad view of his territory," I wisecracked.

"Chief just said, 'Do it. I'm chief,'" she said.

"That's the problem with policing right there," I said. "In that one sentence."

"Whatever, motor-mouth. Coppers collect cash off gambling capers, white slavers and dopers. Everything had a price."

"That made everyone happy in the City of the Angels," I said.

Maybe that other officer, Quizal, was right. Maybe I was not funny.

"Well, some boat-rockers called it 'corruption' but most called it 'doing business.' That's what they did. Chief Davis put together his gun squad, and the Mayor backed him to the hilt. Whatever the chief wanted. Remember, this whole country was freaked out by the Depression and what the Japs were doing, chewing up Asia and what Hitler was pulling in Germany."

"So your LAPD decided to save America by beating and handcuffing it?"

"Never got enough coppers for our big city, motor-mouth. So we hadda find the right ones and teach them to hit fast and hard. Still got to paste the perps like that."

"That's propaganda, Shadap. You're not the only joker bored by a history nut. New Orleans, Chicago and New York had worse crime troubles. Only Los Angeles had decided to hire cops who saw themselves as warriors, not officers. Cops should solve problems and not just nightstick anyone they see as wrong."

"Got it all figured, huh, Royster?" she asked. "Including what happened today?"

"I've walked one city and policed another," I said. "Not being modest, maybe I learned some things."

She looked bulkier in her Department-approved business attire. Talking made her seem more solid.

"And everyone in LA was too scared to buck the Department," I said. "Nobody tried to, right?"

"Couple troublemakers, pot-stirrers, can't-leave-well-enough-alone types did," she said. "Hired a private eye to get the real deal on us coppers. The PI was a smarty-pants like you, Royster, making all kinds of trouble, talking big and going to testify."

"So, what did you cops do to him?" I asked.

CHAPTER 12

**Dispute
or
He Said / She Said History**

"We blowed him up," Shadap said.

"Truly?" I asked. "That will give you a black eye among police reformers."

"Well, he was talking all kinds of smack about the Department."

"Can't have that," I said.

"Mean, dude, whatever, blowing him up was weak stuff."

"Glad you disapprove," I said. "If I'm interpreting your Angelese rightly."

"Royster, you gonna keep making fun of how I talk? Or are you going to figure out the Department?"

Part of me enjoyed bear-baiting Officer Shadap. The other part toyed with the idea of her inviting me home for shelter and talk. Maybe she lived alone. Maybe she would not have to explain me to traditional Filipino parents.

"They might be one and the same thing. Your Department should teach some real communication skills."

"Bull-crap."

"Shadap, I was a cop who never caught on. Always running to keep up with the real cops. Got through less than two years, with suspensions and punishment details."

"How'd you get a pension like that?"

"Got no pension. Some bosses back there are still trying to lock me down into Bellevue Hospital for life. Tossed me out for depression. Which I don't have, by the way."

"No, you don't. Seems more like you never shut up."

"But I figured out that when cops don't communicate well enough, they may have to hit, to kick, to spray, to choke and to shoot. When it ain't needed."

"Man, that touchy-feely stuff'll get you wasted out here with these knuckleheads."

"'Knuckleheads,'" I said. "Again, you're using kid words in an adult predicament. I've noticed that a lot of you LA cops talk alike. Use the same expressions. Like you're a club and the rest of the world is outside of it."

Her eyes softened a bit. Maybe she was gauging me, thinking about a forbidden tryst.

She moved closer to me. I tried to look harmless and wise. I probably failed.

"That's touchy-feely stuff, man. You gotta keep moving and not go around H-U-A."

"What does that mean, 'H-U-A?'" I asked.

"Too many questions, man."

"I'm a stranger in a strange land."

"H-U-A- means your Head-Up-Your-Ass. Not paying attention. Now, I need my energy drink. And some sunflower seeds. Let's stop talking so much."

"No, Shadap. I want to talk."

"Player, you're nuts. You're getting me all hacked-off mad, you know."

"Then, maybe, you should control yourself, Officer Shadap. You can't shout and bully your way out of every problem, you know."

"Don't know any such thing. Trying to teach you something about LA that you should know and you just keep wisecracking."

"You cops waste a lot of LAPD energy insulting people and calling it 'police work'," I said. "That's not history. That's current events."

"I don't get what you're trying to sell me, player. When this reformer-type, Harry Raymond, got blown up back in the thirties, he didn't die.

"LA turned all mad at us cops and the mayor. They could handle gambling and vice and girls but not dynamiting this fool. They screamed against corruption. So they threw out our police chief and mayor. First mayor of a big-ass city ever recalled from office. Now, they wanted honest policing. No more corruption."

"So, they elect a 'Goo-Goo' mayor," I said.

"Wha' happen? What's a 'Goo-Goo?'"

"Good Government," I said.

"The police captain who blew up the reformer's car got ten years for that."

"Ten years? For attempted murder like that? After serving as a captain? That's a bit light, yes?"

"Nobody likes a troublemaker," she said.

"How well I know," I said.

She moved away a bit. Maybe I had missed my chance.

Going for broke, I took her hand. She hesitated and then pulled it away. I touched her knuckles again and held her hand. She shook her head and let our hands stay together.

"These reformer fools scrapped our badges and handed us new ones. The old badges were kinda sharp, teardrop design. Cheap and tinny. Smaller."

"But the new badges, ones you wear today, are oval," I said. "Pretty, too. Mixed silver and gold.

"Looks almost like heraldry. Something from the Middle Ages. Jewelry. Those things on the badges top border. They are lines etched into the metal. D'you know what they are?"

"No. What?"

Shadap, the young girl buried inside police procedure came out from under it. Her brown eyes searched mine.

"Tell you later, Officer Shadap. Right now, you're too fragile to hear about those things on top of the badge. Fasces, they call them. A symbol of the early Fascist party in Italy.

"Whatever," she said. But her head cocked like she was interested.

"Fascists began in Italy," I said. "This may seem like dry history to you now. But you should know that Fascists could execute troublemakers, like you call them, without trial," I said. "No judge, no warrant, no jury."

"Now you're calling us murderers!" she said. "Just like those idiot radicals out there on Hollywood Boulevard. Why am I listening to you?"

"Because nobody else will dare tell you this stuff," I said. "They won't dare. Not your lover, your family, your partners or your civilians. Everyone's too scared of your anger."

She smiled a bit.

"You did me angry, with that 'Fascism' stuff," she said. "Gets my goat, all right. Maybe you just better stick to the history lesson, tell me more about our badge."

"It's the most famous police badge in the world now," I said, playing for time. Every word, every human connection, might get me closer to Miami. "And some groups who don't know real life claim that all cops are Fascists. I don't agree with them."

"Those groups, like you say, they all janky," Shadap said. "Shady Gradys.'"

"And, what, pray tell, is a 'Shady Grady'?" I asked.

My words quickened because I wanted to sell myself to her. She might cut me a break. If she invited me home and I accepted, that might show me as owing something to the LAPD. And Brookings could not show me as an impartial witness. Escaping to Miami was still possible.

"You know. Someone who don't look right."

"Fascinating, Officer Shadap. Drive on, please."

"After we blowed up that reform character. they picked a rulebook guy, from South Dakota, be our chief. Religious-type, reformed drinker. This Chief, Parker, swore he'd nail any cop who embarrassed the Department by taking money."

"Okay," I said. "That covers corruption. How about brutality?"

Traffic hooted behind us. Cars rattled their engines past, turned a corner and were gone. More crowds showed, far up the block. Even from far away, they looked organized and angry at everything. Bottles and sticks showed in their hands.

"Under Chief Parker, we got real famous," she said. "Best uniforms, pay and training. Civilians forgetting about our past stuff."

"That's because nobody reads in Los Angeles," I said. "They drive, instead. From books, I tumbled that a small-time actor named Jack Webb got the idea to hero-worship you new and clean cops with his radio show, Dragnet."

"They clean coppers. Didn't have to jack around with no Bloods and Crips three-striker parolees," she said.

In California, three felony strikes on your rap sheet, even for some types of drug possession, meant you would go to prison for life.

"Makes 'em fight harder, when we stop them."

"Jack Webb's hustle pushed your department to fame. And respectability. Webb was a performer and every performer needs a gimmick. Or else, his act falls flat. Then, he's nobody special, no dream, no fire. So, who would want to buy a ticket to see someone ordinary? Webb's gimmick was the LAPD."

"Some coppers got in some stick time on Rodney King," she said. "Video made us seem like we were brutal. Dunno about that."

"I do," I said. "That WAS brutality. And I hate it. I've had to warn or slug cop partners not to play too rough with the clients."

"So, now, we're all reformed," she said.

"After today, I'm not sure," I said.

"The old-timers say, before Rodney King, within the manual, somebody talked back or fought you, you could do ANYTHING to them. Anything, player."

"Like shoot the mayor for jaywalking?" I asked.

"Anything."

CHAPTER 13.

Po-Po Logic
or
I Know What I Mean.

"I worked West LA and Pacific Palisades," Shadap said. "Rich White places. Don't matter. Everyone gets in our face. They just don't like cops. Nobody does."

"Might depend on your approach," I said.

"Bull-crap, man. Like, they just wanna speed with their tinted windows and oversized tires and break traffic laws, like. Check it out."

We were far from Hollywood Station now. The blocks looked more ragged, graffiti sprawled on the walls of the dead buildings. Loud-talking Angelenos in football jerseys hung outside. Rap music blasted from a cherry-red Honda.

"Lemme show you, man," Shadap said. "Like a experiment, whatever."

She stepped closer to the group of scraggly White kids on the corner. They were hanging out, smoking and joking and doing nothing else.

"Hey, hey," the oldest one said. He wore a moustache, too young to be full, under heavy brows and pearly teeth.

He pointed at Shadap, chunky and respectable in her red business pantsuit.

"Fat sistah here look like Po-Po. Po-po in the house, yo! What's up, po-po?"

He was straining to sound ethnic and cool, anything but ordinary Hollywood White.

"Where you from?" Shadap asked Moustache. "Got any tats?"

Shadap meant the "tattoos." The LA slang was getting through to me.

"I'm not from nowhere, yo," he said.

"Alienated modern youth," I muttered.

"I don't bang," he went on. "No gangs. That's the real deal, Neil."

"Yeah, he do!" one of his pals shouted. "He a stone killer."

"You wearing a lot of green," Shadap said to the oldest one, the one who started talking. "That the colors here? Armenian Power Gang, maybe? Huh? Who got ID here?"

"Man, we done nothing!" the oldest one bleated.

To me, it felt like I was watching a dance. They had all rehearsed their parts before.

"Who on probation, parole?" Shadap said. She lifted a small radio from her belt and spoke into it. "6K12, request additional unit Yucca and Cahuenga, possible George activity."

That radio code "George" had to stand for "Gang." A tough code to crack.

"Roger, 6K12," the radio came back.

"Shadap, what are you doing?"

"Shove it, Royster, Just stay out of the way."

"Man, what we do?" asked another one with a Mohawk haircut. Silver studs dotted his left cheek near a green monster throat tattoo.

"Good question," I said.

"All of you turn around," Shadap said.

"We don't gotta," one said.

"They don't gotta," I said. "Constitution might agree."

Shadap shifted her jacket and gripped the black Glock in her hip holster. I flinched. The boys froze. Her blunt trigger finger stayed on the gun's frame, the right way for safety.

"Put your hands on your heads," Shadap said. "Interlace your fingers. Face the wall. Get down on your knees. Do it now."

"'Interlace?'" I said.

It sounded like an official term taught in the academy. Just so as not to offend anyone.

Moustache spat on the ground and put his hands in his pockets.

My breath sucked in.

"Hands!" Shadap shouted.

She yanked out the Glock and pointed it at the ground.

"Yo, po-po," Moustache said. "I can't kneel. Had knee surgery, like. Hurts too much."

"Got a doctor's note?" Shadap asked.

"Huh?"

"Kneel!"

Moustache knelt.

The others knelt.

Shadap's gun shook slightly. I knew the feeling. On the NYPD gun range, my hands had always waved everywhere. My palms sweated. My own civilian doctor never knew why. Maybe I never belonged there. I had kept it as one of my secrets from the NYPD.

"Shadap," I said. "You're outnumbered here. Cool it and let them walk."

"Your package, real weak, player," she told me.

"My knee hurts," Moustache said.

"Suck it up," Shadap said.

Her radio gurgled on her belt.

Locals stopped and frowned. I could feel their eyes scraping across me. The anger felt like a blast of hot summer air on the subway.

A black-and-white slewed around the corner, lights and sirens working. It slammed to a stop, and a small Latina woman cop jumped out, shotgun aimed upward at high port.

"Freeze!" she shouted in a strong Spanish accent. "Don't nobody move nothing!"

"Think that one over," I muttered.

Being scared always turned me to wisecracking.

Her shotgun stayed pointed skywards.

Other LAPD cars rocketed to us.

Cops in dark blue uniforms that looked black in the strong sunlight smacked their boots on the sidewalk and clustered near the kids.

"Keep your hands on your head!" a spindly blond cop with wire-rim glasses bellowed. "Move and we jack you, man!"

"You always do us this way!" Moustache whined. "Get your name and sue you! Get you fired, yo!"

"Take your hands off your head and see what happens!" the blond cop answered. "Or I'll lock you down for Obstruction!"

"Two youngsters woofing at each other in bad temper," I muttered. "Except one of them sports a badge."

Big hands from the other cops ran over the sagging blue jeans, worn low in gangsta style by the kids, America's future.

"Detective, we got some weed off the loudmouth there," said a Black cop with a gold shooting medal on his shirt. His thumb jabbed at Moustache. "Maybe enough for a sales charge."

"Righteous," Shadap said. "Yeah, I smelled it on him."

"You did?" I asked. "I didn't."

"Gave me probable cause to stop them," she said.

Moustache's right hand scratched his own kneecap below the surfer short pants. The dirty fingernails rasped against the skin.

"I didn't smell it," I repeated. "And I was closer to them than you were."

"You some kind of fruity liberal, Royster?" Shadap asked.

Moustache's fingers kept working. The skin on the knee-cap got red.

"This isn't the bust of the century here, Shadap," I said. "How are you going to process this significant arrest and work the McKissick death at the same time?"

From sad experience, I realized what Moustache was doing with his un-cuffed hand. His fingers kept scratching the skin.

"I'll take the arrest," the Black cop said.

"How?" I asked. "You smelled the marijuana, too? Try humming that past a jury."

"Not your problem," Shadap said. "Maybe you belong back in New York."

"If only you knew," I said.

More cop cars zoomed up. Doors slammed.

Some cops squinted into their mobile computer terminals and checked the other kids for warrants. The older cops held the list of names and repeated them over their portable radios.

"Hey!" Moustache shouted. "I'm a juvie!"

"You a loudmouth!" the Black cop hollered. "Can it!"

"You pulled your gun on a juvie!" Moustache wailed.

He was lying. But it sounded good.

"And I told you, my knee surgery! You kept me on my knees anyway! Now, look at it! All red and stuff and it hurts bad! I'm gonna have my moms sue you. Get your badge and all, bacon!"

Trying not to stare, I walked away from this scene.

"Hey, Royster!" Shadap shouted. "Where you going, fool? Get back here!"

Chapter 14.

Changes
or
A Woman Named Yan

Trudging, hunger hollowing my gut, I went past three more restaurants closing up.

More groups roiled through the streets. Some knocked over trashcans. Glass broke and speckled the sidewalk.

"The Blood of Jesus is on stupid!" one teenager with a swinging baseball bat and a drill sergeant's bellow kept shouting.

Others chanted it.

Hollywood lived on catchphrases. Old expressions like "You oughta be in pictures" to "Boulevard of Broken Dreams," had dominated movies from their start. Hollywooders thought like movie audiences. Many lived as if they were in the movies for their whole lives. Give them an audience, and they would keep on acting until they performed for the undertaker.

Slogans like "Slap the Jap" and "No Taxation Without Representation!" could unify any loose group. This new slogan "The Blood of Jesus is on stupid!" might rally these street people. They could rip the City of the Angels apart.

One bar-back character with a shaved head and a Russian cavalry moustache was mopping up the patio of the fourth restaurant.

"What's the deal here, cousin?" I asked him. "Hollywood shuts down at six? I got that cash. I'm hungry. And nothing is open."

"My boss says to close up in case they have another riot," he said.

"ANOTHER riot?"

"Daddy-o, America's worst race riots always hit LA. Watts started it. In the Rodney King riots, they burned down the police booth right outside the downtown cop headquarters. That's fricking close, daddy-o."

"Why are the race riots so bad here?" I asked. "Why not in the South, for argument's sake?"

"LA is a pretty damn tense town, daddy-o," he said. "Maybe it's the traffic."

"Got any non-tense beanery where a low-rent kind of guy like me can eat to keep body and soul together?"

"There's one spot on Wilcox," he said.

"Why you making that pouty kind of face?" I asked. "Are you so very dainty where you dine?"

"Well," he said. "It isn't that CLEAN."

"I promise to snub the cockroaches," I said. "Where on Wilcox?"

"Right near the police station."

"Seems like I'm walking around Hollywood in circles," I said.

"Whatever," he said.

"In case you didn't hear, there's a bit of a minor insurrection going on there," I said. "I don't think any normal restaurant will be open."

"You'll be surprised," he said.

And wouldn't say any more.

My feet pointed me back the way that I had come.

℃

Along Wilcox, near the Hollywood Station, another crowd had mushroomed. The Actor was holding court with a cadre of funny-looking types, probably scruffy cinema geniuses.

More LAPD cars kept vaulting through the streets. The cops emerged to string out yellow tape that said "Police line. Do not cross," and glare at the crowd.

Screwing up my courage, I walked back towards the crime scene on Sunset and Gower.

Black-and-whites still parked on the corners. A group of detectives, silver-and-gold badges pinned to the lapels of good suits, conferred next to a yellow chalk outline. McKissick's body had lain on that spot.

Outside a closed restaurant, I scored a copy of the LA Free Press and scribbled down everything at the scene on the free space. All the civilian license plate numbers, descriptions of each cop and their patrol car numbers went into this raggy journal.

Nobody paid me any mind, penning words onto a newspaper. If anything, they probably thought that I was playing the Lotto. If Los Angeles had a Lotto.

The folded newspaper wad went into my hip pocket.

Something kept hammering into my head, about McKissick and all her pens and notebooks. She must have been writing something to someone.

❦

I picked my way along Gower Street to the window that Van Florida, the dance teacher, had fingered earlier at the death scene.

For once, my luck held.

The street door held a sign reading "Free First Dance Lesson / with Van Florida / Hollywood's Best Dance Teacher. No Appointment Needed. Come On In."

The door creaked as I opened it.

"Besame Mucho" played from a shiny new speaker.

The large room had three windows that looked out at street level on Gower. The death scene lay about seventy feet away. Depending on the traffic, Florida might have seen the whole mess start.

Florida was holding a class with three solid-looking women, staring at him as he went through steps. All three looked like the long-suffering wives of petulant grocery store assistant managers. They microscoped me. Their eyes showed me that they found me wanting in many ways.

"The rumba is a slow, sexy kind of dance," Florida said to the class. "With an easy four-step movement. Slow, quick, quick, slow."

His eyes hopscotched over me.

"Now that we have another man here, we can practice this," he said. "Ladies, this is Mr. Max Royster who has danced just about everywhere. Let us start right now."

"I don't know," the oldest woman said in some kind of European accent. Frosted white hair framed her baby-blue eyes.

"That's okay," I said. "Because I know. Come, my dear. They are playing our song."

Making a face, she let me step up and take her into rumba position.

She stepped on my foot. It hurt. She was no tiger lily.

"Good move," I said. "Just shorten it up a bit. You're doing good."

"But I stepped on your foot," she said.

Now her accent sounded German. Maybe she wanted truth and precision. I never did.

"You should never say that when you're dancing with a man," I said. "You should only say one thing."

"*Ja*? What?"

"Tell you when we finish this dance," I said.

Her face said that she would hold me to that promise.

"I'll dance with Gayle," Florida said.

His partner was a green-eyed blonde woman, stylish in her white pants suit.

"And then, Barbara," Florida said. "Let's enjoy this."

"You know that my name is Max," I said to my Bigfoot partner. "What's yours?"

She pressed her lips together and did not answer.

Trying to cheer myself, I thought that maybe my grace had made her speechless.

Somehow, we labored through the dance.

"All right," she said. "What should the woman say to the man? You said that you would tell me."

"Whenever two are dancing and the man makes a mistake, a gaffe, a faux pas, steps on the woman's foot or something dumb like that," I gobbled. "The woman should only say one thing to him."

"And what is that?"

"She should say, 'Sir, you are wonderful,'" I said. "That's all that the man wants to hear anyway. He'll never pay attention to anything else. He will just think that the woman is brilliant to have discovered the truth about him so rapidly."

The song faded out.

"Everyone did very well," Florida said. "Now, please take a water break. Sit, stretch or relax. We'll resume in five minutes."

Florida stepped over closer to me. Nobody could hear us.

"Working on my rumba break-step," I said. "What hours are you open? D'you have a card?"

"What for?"

"Well, my goodness gracious," I said, trying to buy time. "I just came from a death myself. Don't you think that I need some sweetness and light after that? Told you that I was a dancer. You saw me move just now. I can help your new studio get off the ground."

"Why?"

"Because I like to dance, that's why. Don't you?"

"Why did the police arrest you before?"

"They didn't," I said. "That was just to calm things down, like I said. Trick move. We were laughing about it at the station."

"I didn't see anything worth remembering, nothing physical or medical, about that woman dying," he said. "Here's my card, anyway."

"Sure. Let me help you with the rest of the lesson. What do you charge?"

"The first lesson is free, like the sign says. Let's get back to dancing."

About an hour later, I left Florida's classroom. Like always, everything felt better after dancing.

✍

My Manhattan feet betrayed me and I got lost again on the Hollywood streets. My sense of direction needed the Lex Ave Number 6 line to stay on course.

Feeling my way, I blundered onto Wilcox Street and back in front of Hollywood Station. A crowd of street people still hung out in front. They held signs reading "Justice for McKissick!!!!" "Wake Up, AmeriKKKa!"

LAPD cops in riot gear, with gray helmets and visors down, stood in a skirmish line outside the station.

TV vans and their crews, along with green plastic temporary toilets, like you see at picnics and jamborees, choked the street.

"Excuse me, sir," a blonde woman in an orange windbreaker said to me. Her bright emerald eyes dominated a tanned model's face. "I'd like to speak with you."

"Speak away," I said without thinking.

"You were here before. The police brought you outside. You're a witness, right?"

"Not right now. I'm almost homeless."

"We can put you up in a motel."

"Who is 'we,' pray tell?" I asked.

"Oh, I thought that you knew. Gretchen Ekstrom, *Channel 63 News.*"

She pivoted on showgirl's legs and showed me the back of her orange windbreaker. It read "LA Street News – Channel 63."

"He's a witness!" someone shouted.

Too late, I recognized the Latina woman wearing her "Kiss The Cook" outfit from before. She had a group around her.

"I saw him when she died!" she shouted. "He saw everything, the whole real deal, people!"

My guts corkscrewed again.

The crowd encircled me.

"What's your name, sir?" Gretchen the reporter asked.

"Just call me Johnny Faust," I said. "Selling my soul for a motel room from Gretchen."

"You gotta tell what you saw!" the Latina Cook woman shouted. "We all demand it."

"Be right back," I said. Nerves made my voice crack.

Running would get the crowd chasing me like a wolf-pack. So I had to con them somehow.

"Take a shot of him!" Gretchen shouted to a camera crew standing near a van. "Get a close-up!"

Her group sprang into action.

Other crews heard her and pointed their hand-held camera units at me.

"Man up, player!" a chunky Black man with sideburns and a beard said. "We gotta right to know."

"Where you going?" the Latina Cook said.

"Toilet," I said. "Porta-Potty over there. Real bad. Emergency stuff. Getting old."

My thumb pointed to the green plastic toilets,

Nobody would film me going into the toilet. It was not good TV.

The crowd followed me for a few feet towards the toilets.

"Can't talk now," I said.

They stopped following me. I kept walking.

Gretchen followed me. She took a microphone from a shoulder bag and held it in front of her.

"Get me in your van, away from here," I said. "And we'll talk. Lots."

"Sure thing?"

"Would this face lie?" I asked.

The Porta-Potty temporary toilet had been cleaned up recently.

"Thank God, LA is not New York," I said aloud, trying to calm my nerves. "Not in here, anyway. Most of these things back home would make a rat hurl up his flapjack breakfast."

Outside, I could hear people stepping away from my shelter. Human nature might win the day.

One by one, I weighed my choices. None of them looked that good.

Gretchen would need more time to get my plan in operation. But I knew that she would do it. Her assignment editor and her career would push her for it.

Heat warmed my green plastic walls.

Doors slammed outside. An engine caught and came closer to my hide-out.

"Time to gamble everything," I whispered. "Sure can't stay here much longer. Some Angeleno might need it in a bodily-function kind of hurry."

The engine noise stayed put.

This might be heavenly Gretchen in the rescue van. If I pitched it right, she probably would invite me to her own private place for some quality time. She would have a more upscale place than Officer Shadap and a lot fewer personal rules.

McKissick's death might turn me into Hollywood's oldest gigolo.

Breathing hard, I stepped outside my hide-out.

Gretchen's van driver did it just right.

The van lay between me and the crowd with the side panel door open.

It looked innocent.

Gretchen was in the front seat. Again, her beauty drew me.

Ducking my head, I went fast into the open side panel door.

"Hey!" someone shouted. "He's getting in that car!"

"They're stealing him!"

"Block the van!"

"Try it!" the driver said from the front seat. He was a lean, tense Latino about thirty, with hair in a pony tail and tattoos on his knuckles gripping the wheel. He moved the van out, dodged a thick man holding a sign reading "Stop Police Brutality!"

Nobody was standing on the sidewalk, so he lurched the van up onto it.

He floored it.

"Stop that van!" a voice shouted on a loud-speaker. It sounded like a cop. "Officers on the perimeter! Traffic violation!"

"Let's not start that all over again," I said. "Traffic rules started this whole hair-ball."

"Reminds me when I was riding for the White Fence gang against the Crenshaw Cruisers," the driver said. "I was their best wheel-man, sport."

"Now you're mine," I said.

"You'll get a bonus for this, Alonso," Gretchen said from the front seat. She gripped his bicep with fingernails that were long and elegant and painted to match her windbreaker. "And some other favors."

We were back on Hollywood Boulevard now. Nobody was chasing us on foot.

"Close that door all the way, Mr. Faust," Gretchen said from the front seat. "Wouldn't want you to fall out."

We stopped at a red light.

"Me, neither," I said. My legs got me out of the van and onto the street. It felt good.

Gretchen yelped something. Traffic noise covered her words.

"Hey!" the driver shouted. He cut the engine, came around and got in front of me. His face flushed under an outdoor tan and his fists clenched.

"You ain't leaving us like this!" he bellowed.

"Touch me and that's assault," I said. "Think it over. I'll charge you and sue your station. Could sure use the cash."

"Let him go, Alonso!" Gretchen shouted. "Please! And you, Mr. Faust, you lied to me! You lied to the press."

"Facing a mob," I said. "Sure, I did. What would you do?"

☙

One restaurant, Tiny's Sandwich Shop, lay still open. Four tables and a small kitchen in back and a wall TV blaring out the latest outraged crowd coverage.

Something twitched inside me. Maybe Gretchen and her TV van were still tailing me. I looked around.

My skin felt itchy, like someone was following me.

Back in New York, Internal Affairs used to follow me all the time. Being under surveillance gave me a feeling that never went away. Right now, I felt the same way.

A scarred stumpy character, with a huge muscled chest and both arms as big as logs, tattooed with crawly blue snakes, puffed on a broken cigar in the doorway. He looked about fifty, Latino and watchful, casting his eyes at the crowd maybe 300 feet away.

A throat tattoo read "Tiny."

" Wassup out there?" Tiny asked.

"Self-realizing," I said. "Sometimes, I get the feeling that everybody down the block is acting out their favorite part. The fools want and need to act foolish. And cracking down on their nonsense makes the blue suits feel fulfilled. They both have their exits and their entrances, to quote the Bard."

"You betcha," he said.

His grey moustache wagged as he spoke.

The feeling of being tailed hung with me. My eyes checked the street outside. Nobody looked suspicious to me. Maybe I was getting cuckoo from the stress.

"Why're you still open?" I asked.

"'cause, yo, man, give respect to the po-po, man. See my tats? Down for my hood, my homeboys, done my share, dumb crap, beat down and locked down for it. Police, they got a hard job to do, homes."

"And you used to be the hard job that they had to do," I said.

"Yeah, you right, homes. And I know they gonna have another riot. So the po-po, la jura, they need to eat. Me, I stay open to feed them. Anyone don't like it, gotta deal with me."

"Thank God for you," I said. I dropped into a chair just inside the door, after scanning the street again. The feeling of being followed stayed with me. "Cup of coffee and a menu, please."

Both came. So did a hot turkey sandwich with gravy. A second one seemed necessary, so as not to hurt the cook's feelings.

Three blocks from Hollywood Station, I felt jittery and nerved up eating my sandwich here. Some more cops might come in and roust me.

"Is it safe to eat here?" a woman's voice asked behind me.

My head turned.

"Very safe," I said. "The safest that you can imagine."

The woman giggled. Her face was finely carved and not young but ageless.

Delicate black eyelashes rimmed brown eyes. They looked liquid in this light. No artist could do such fine work in black pen-and-ink work against pale parchment paper. Her eyes screwed themselves up at the sight of me putting away coffee cup number three.

She stood about ten inches or so under my six feet and in perfect proportions at that height. Her body inside the cream-colored peasant blouse and blood-red skirt looked like an Olympic swimmer in top condition. She wore her longish black hair loose and off one shoulder.

"Do you mind if I sit here?" she asked. "You look like a good protector. That commotion down the street scares me."

CHAPTER 15.

Woman Talk
or
More of Yan

"Maybe we should discuss all that," I said. "That's my catchy opening line."

She smiled. It was like watching a sunrise over the water.

"I'm sure," she said.

"Fear not, fair damsel," I said. "This stout Sir Knight here will save you from all dragons."

She smiled again.

"Whatever," she said.

That word, so very Los Angeles, made me smile along with her.

Taped mariachi horn music from passing cars mixed with the helicopters buzz-sawing overhead.

"Do you know what happened down the street?" she asked.

"Whatever it is, it will depress me. I'd rather learn about you. Are you from Los Angeles? Because, nobody is."

"Hawaii," she said. "And you?"

"I'm of New York City."

"And you're here on business?"

"Not hardly. Have you ever suffered through a New York winter?"

"Never ask a Hawaiian that question."

"I'll try to remember."

"So you came for the weather?" she asked.

"Got some old shipmates in San Pedro and I wanted to see Hollywood."

"Were you in the Navy?"

"No. Foreign ships, Ordinary Seaman. Very Ordinary."

"What do you think of our Hollywood?"

"You don't want to hear me slam your city, do you?" I asked.

"That depends. I hope that you're not a nut."

"I'm as normal as the next guy," I said.

"Because I know enough nuts already."

"My name's Max. I'll bet that you have an enchanting name that I shall never forget."

"Maybe you are a nut. But my name's Yan."

Tiny handed Yan a menu. A scent of frying ham came from the kitchen behind him.

"Don't wanna interrupt or nothing," he said. "But the TV says that the po-po stopped that lady for some BS traffic violation. She resisted. So they shot her."

It was time to weigh in.

"Nobody shot," I said. "No shots were fired."

"Please, let's not talk about it," Yan said.

"That's what they saying on the TV, bro," the man said. "That she was an actress, a star, big time."

"Leave it to LA to get the actress part right but gack up the important details," I said.

"Never heard of her," he said.

"Before your time. She was a young Black actress decades ago," I said. "Beautiful to watch. Those Blaxploitation films were full of Afro hairstyles, dope dealers, flashy clothes, eight-inch heels and karate fights. Far as I know, she hasn't acted for years."

"I'll have a BLT sandwich on white bread, no mayo," Yan said. "With a large iced tea, no sugar, please."

"Gonna be one big chingadera," he said, moving away.

"I hope that everyone just lets it pass," Yan said. "It's so ugly. Hawaiians are more tolerant and laid-back. And I'm not even Polynesian. My grandma was Welsh. Do you have this much anger in New York?"

"A different kind of anger," I said. "We reserve it for slow waiters."

Yan was drawing my attention to her. Gretchen the TV reporter had gotten to me the same way.

My friends would say that I never learned.

"What d'you do in New York, man?"

"Lifeguard in a car wash," I said.

Something about Yan's innocent eyes made me hide that I was an ex-cop.

CHAPTER 16.

Like The Song Says, "Where Do We Go From Here?"
or
Love in LA

"I realize that I'm not dressed for it," I said. "But this is Hollywood, after all. Where do you Hollywoodians go to dance?"

"Why do you want to dance now?" Yan asked.

"Why not? I tried to stop the riot. But I couldn't. So I might as well dance."

Yan's dark brows knitted prettily.

"You got 'trouble' written all over you," she said. "Don't know why I let you talk to me and stuff."

"Because peace and love can stop a riot."

"Do you have to use that word 'riot'?" she asked.

"Ah, you're right. This is Los Angeles, after all. The home of soft euphemism. You don't have riots in Los Angeles. Not since Rodney King, at any rate. Let us then call it 'civil unrest'. Does that suit you?"

"There's no place to dance around here, Max."

Her saying my name warmed me.

"I've heard about the Roosevelt Hotel," I said. "Surely, they must have a lounge with a piano hacking out something in the background and a piece of free floor three-foot square."

"That's not much space," she said.

"Dancing close can be very liberating."

"Don't have the cash to dance anymore."

"Downsized?"

"Don't joke about it. My landlord's evicting me next month. Would you like to be a woman in some homeless shelter?"

"Excuse my wisecracks," I said. "Being broke is no fun."

"Argh, I may squeak by again. Hanging out, waiting on a check. But nix on the dancing for a while now. Never thought that I'd be in this kind of jammed-up deal."

"Nobody does."

"So I'm in survival mode right now."

"Of course you are," I said.

To my own ears, I sounded like a glad-handing salesman, trying to close a deal.

"Money worries like that does make you feel like you're buried in a box and can't breathe."

"Ding-bat economy is scary right now," she said. "Don't know what to do. Everybody wants something for nothing. I can get back on my meds, maybe Social Security or something. Tell the docs that I'm depressed again. Get a crummy li'l check that way. Lots, people, do that now. Brag about it."

An idea hit me. I leaned forward the way that I used to at Handgun Qualification at the NYPD Range. I fanned out my wallet to show her some bills.

"Here's some pictures of the dead Presidents," I said. My cracking voice hurt the moment. "Get some food to your home. I recommend Bush's Baked Beans and Hormel's Smoked Pork Picnic Shoulder for true consumer value."

"Breaks my rules, that one there. Can't take money from you, *brah*."

"You better," I said. "That way, I can deduct this meal as a business dinner."

"What business?"

"I'll think of something," I said. "Maybe monkey business."

"I won't forget this," she said.

"Sure thing," I said. "Because I won't let you."

"I have to go now," she said. "That money is just a loan, okay? Do you have a card?"

"Let me walk you home. These are perilous times. You called me '*brah*.' Pray tell, what is that?"

"Hawaiian slang," she said. "Meaning 'guy'. Friendly-type term, you know."

"In that case, I should walk you home."

"No, thank you. I got to see my girlfriend on the way home. Thanks for the loan, man."

Something in her face made me want to push things some more.

"May I see you again?" I asked.

"Why would I want that? I don't like people knowing much about me. Or where I live."

"Then, compromise," I said. "Can you meet me here to-morrow at eleven? I'll buy you an early lunch and we can talk more. I promise not to pry into your private life."

"Maybe," she said. She scribbled on a notebook page and handed it to me, just her name, Yan, and her phone number.

"I don't know why I'm giving you this. Maybe because I hate being stood up. Do a lot of things that I can't figure out. That's today. See how I feel tomorrow."

With that, she raised up and eased her way out of Tiny's Sandwich Shop and maybe my life.

Tiny ogled her as she walked through the door.

"Dude, she fine," Tiny observed.

"The supreme compliment," I said. "From a veteran con-noisseur."

"Hey, Tiny!" a huge, shaved-headed LAPD cop shouted from the sidewalk. "Been capering, my man?"

My head swung.

The pair were frowning. They looked like Armageddon about to erupt.

Then Tiny guffawed.

"Officer Kraus, you know I don't caper no more, *guëy!*" he hollered. "C'mere, and I show you! No new tats!"

The cop swaggered inside the shop, riot helmet held under his arm. His tall black boots gleamed. So did the long holster on his right hip.

The holster held an old-fashioned revolver with a long barrel. Once upon a time, California cops all carried long-barreled revolvers. Thirty years ago, most departments switched to semi-automatic pistols with sixteen-shot magazines.

"Two roast beef sandwiches on rye, onion and mayo, Tiny," the cop said. "Need those carbs today, bro. Our knuckleheads are breaking bad."

"Eat all that," Tiny said," and you won't be able to chase me, running me all over Pico-Union and stuff, like you used to."

"Officer Kraus, we should do a l'il old footrace," Tiny said. "Just for old time's sake, *guëy*. See who's still got it."

"These knuckleheads gonna take my strength tonight," the revolver cop said. Silver and gold medals winked under the badge on his left tunic pocket. "Maybe we'll try that race sometime later."

"You gotta tell your po-po homies that it's just for fun," Tiny said. "Not like before, when you locked me down in Eastlake."

Chapter 17.

Homie Cronies
or
Plain Talk

"Eastlake Juvie Hall was all messed up *chingadera, tipo,*" Tiny said. "Nobody didn't got it together there,"

"Sleeping just one night in there would kill me," Kraus said. "Scare me straight."

"Worked for me, man."

Kraus nodded at the restless crowd outside.

"That is some hairy mess out there."

"Them kids, them gang-banger wannabes," Tiny said. "They don't got it figured yet. Gonna go down screaming about this lady who got herself killed and mess they lives. Or get shot. Wisht I could tell them."

"They won't listen, Tiny. No more than you did, you fifteen and stuff."

"Called up my little *sobrinos* and told 'em, 'Stay put in the house. Be chillin' like a villain. Don't go outside till this situation is played out, dudes.'"

"Nobody's gonna listen," said Kraus. "This suspect tried messing up Hollywood officers three times last year. But TV's calling her a great actress who fought for civil rights years ago and is a victim of police brutality. So now the young cops wanna play war. Can't talk them out of it."

"They angry, boss," Tiny said. "And it eats them up. Just like the girls in my family. In their twenties. They all involved with having kids, getting *embarazada*."

I understood enough Spanish to know that the word "embarazada" meant "pregnant," not "embarrassed."

"Forget about school, 'cause they in love, and it gonna last forever. Then they find their man don't care that much, and he strayin' and playin' around, cheatin' and all that. They get angry and stay that way the next twenny years."

"Seems to me like everyone in LA is angry," I said. "Maybe it's the traffic."

My same phrase, that one, echoed from before.

Kraus surprised me by reacting mildly. He just looked at me over his sandwich.

"Yeah?" was all he said.

"If it's like the Army," I said.

I was probably making a fool of myself. Again.

"The new ones do dumb stuff cause they're angry," I said. "That's in their first hitch. Then they spend the next sixteen years trying to live it down on paper until they can retire."

"You're an old Army man, huh?" Kraus said. "It shows all over you. I can always tell an Army man."

Aside from the NYPD cops, I had never joined anything like the Army. At all. The Audubon Society had thrown me out for smoking a cigar in the men's room after a glorious champagne dinner.

Kraus ate as he watched the LAPD cars zoom past

"Gotta go, Tiny," he said. He smacked his gut with a slap that made my ears ring.

"Maybe I see you at Zona Rosa later," Tiny said. "Buy you a beer. If this mess don't blow up worse."

"It will," I said, under my breath.

CHAPTER 18.

Digging for Apples
or
Picture This

The cellphone came out in my hand, but it took me a minute to remember what I had planned to do. Each year, that kind of thing happened more often. Then I recalled my idea, and my fingers punched in the number for the American Hotel.

I asked for three more days stay.

"Nossir," the room clerk said. "Can't do that."

"Why not?"

"That movie convention here this week, sir," the clerk's voice sped up and got more singsong. "Your room is already booked for another guest tomorrow."

"Then move me to another room."

"Can't do that, sir." Now he sounded bored. "This convention took all our space. Don't think that you're gonna find another room anywhere. Nossir, no way. Uh-huh."

Feeling that old despair settling back in, I kept dialing information for hotel numbers as I hunted for a room.

"These answers are depressing to Our Hero," I muttered in between colorful cuss words. "Just like the Bible says, there is no room in the inn."

Pouncing on the number of that whiz-bang crackerjack DDA Brookings, I fingered in his number.

A cool voicemail assured me that DDA Brookings would return my call ASAP.

"Mayhap, he is doing whatever Learned Counsel does for self-realization," I said. "Perhaps refreshing the missus."

On Tiny's TV set, more Angelenos chanted, 'The Blood of Jesus is on Stupid!"

I pocketed my cellphone.

"What does that mean to you, Tiny?" I asked. "'The Blood of Jesus is on Stupid'?"

"Just *cháchara* from some *tonto*," he said.

"Back in Manhattan, a psycho jumped and hammered a TV anchor on classy Park Avenue," I said. "He kept asking the anchor, 'What's the frequency, Kenneth?'"

"What that mess mean?"

"Nobody knows, Tiny. But it became part of Manhattan culture."

"It don't make no sense!"

"'The Blood of Jesus is on Stupid!' is no example of crystal-clear communication, either," I said. "It may rank right up there with 'The business of America is business' and 'As New Hampshire goes, so goes the nation.'"

"Why you say that?"

"Because everyone is an instant expert on police brutality," I said. "Whether they're a crackhead in the alley without no shoes or a Supreme Court Justice. We civilians, we spectators, all think that we know it all. That we are geniuses, that we are the cat's ass."

"But you gotta stop it, homes."

"And keep the streets safe at the same time?" I said. "Just tell me how."

"Huh?"

"When you make cops too scared to move against clients, because of cries about 'brutality', get ready for some teenager funerals," I preached. As usual, I was talking too much. "More weeping. That cuts deeper than TV news spots."

"Beats me, *guëy*."

"Other cops will resign. Still more cops will work inside, at clerical jobs. And criminals will run rough over you, your family and your city."

"I dunno. Was she really a movie star, that lady?"

"Back in the Seventies, directors made movies aimed at Black audiences," I said. "Me and my buddies snuck into the double-feature bills on the Deuce –"

"The what?"

"42nd Street before it turned into Disneyland. Never knew that there was such a big audience for the films like that.

"The films dealt with drugs, racism and crime. For the first time, Black actors and actresses starred in popular movies that millions enjoyed.

"Critics called them Blaxploitation. Most of the actors were happy to work. Like all actors, they needed to eat. And we were glad to watch them. Flashy clothes, beautiful women and a slang we never heard before."

"And this lady was big-time?"

"Don't know how big she was. But she starred in a few. I remember her real well. Had the actress's knack of holding your attention. Spoke up against typecasting. Some civil rights groups used her as a popular spokeswoman. She talked at rallies and wrote pamphlets. As an actress, she knew how to have a rowdy crowd see things her way."

"Then my mama would know her name."

"Almost every older Angeleno would. Los Angeles is still a company town for movies."

The TV set burped out more noise.

The screen showed Officer Alwer coming down the steps of the Hollywood station. A white-haired Black man with gold eyeglasses and a wispy moustache held her arm.

A TV reporter, dark and Latino, pushing sixty, lunged at Alwer with his mike.

"Officer Alwer!" he shouted. "Did you target Ms. McKissick because she had made civilian complaints against you in the past?"

"Don't answer that," the white haired man said.

I hoped that he was Alwer's lawyer. She needed one.

"No way, Jose!" Alwer snapped.

"My client does not wish to speak now," the man said. So he was her lawyer.

"We have papers saying that she had 'beefed' you," the reporter said. "Why do you call me 'Jose,' Officer? That's not my name. Are all Latinos 'Jose' to you, Officer Alwer?"

Alwer tore her arm away from the lawyer.

"Listen up, man," Alwer said. "That crackhead was trying to grab my weapon! So I used whatever it took."

"Shut up, Patty!" I told the TV set.

"Weren't you just harassing the homeless, like you Hollywood Division officers always do?"

Alwer's face melted into a mask.

"The law is the law," she said.

"BLEEP!" the sound went. "BLEEP! BLEEP!"

"Officer is saying bad words," I said. "And she's pushing folks away with what she says. Including me."

My cellphone buzzed.

"This is Deputy District Attorney Brookings," the hurried voice said. "I understand your plight as regards housing. But, unless you want to go to a city-run homeless shelter, there's very little that I can do. Our Emergency Housing Program takes three days to activate."

"Then, maybe you should re-name the program," I said. "Call it the Semi-Emergency Housing Program,"

CHAPTER 19.

Night Sweats
or
Despair Is the Only Answer

My Hollywood motel lay off Sunset and right now did not look too sparkling.

Neither did I.

"Despair is the only answer," I muttered. "But Our Hero must cheer up and press on."

The Asian clerk's look told me the same thing as he had on the phone. His huge gut strained against his blue jeans under an orange dashiki and a bored look.

"Royster in 26," I said. "We spoke on the phone. Are there any rooms free tomorrow?"

He shook his head and his black pigtail slapped against his neck.

"Told you no, sir," he said. "Movie convention, got all the rooms. Nobody got nothing. And tomorrow, your checkout time is nine a.m."

"Nine a.m.?" I said. "That's not checkout time. That's boot camp reveille before the five-mile run."

"Nine a.m.," he said. "Or else, we call the cops to throw you out. That's policy."

"Go and whistle for it," I said.

With that cheery riposte, I dripped my way up to my room.

❦

Two small windows, shower only, no bathtub, and a TV chained to the wall greeted Our Hero. The bed sagged like a sway-backed pony on shaky legs. The walls showed sponge marks. Dust collected in the corners.

Seeing Hollywood's beauty would cost more cash than I had.

I flopped down on the hard bed. I had to make plans.

Breathing hard, thinking of Yan's smile, I stretched out my bones and sinews on the mattress. Her landlord was shoving her out soon. LA looked like a hard-edged place to be homeless.

The TV news showed more footage of the crowd around Hollywood Station and the usual loudmouths who push themselves in front of reporters to explain life to the media

"Officer Alwer was assigned to Day Watch at Hollywood Station," the reporter, a young Middle Eastern woman said. "Advocates for the homeless have complained about the LAPD harassing the Hollywood homeless to clean up the area for tourists. Officer Alwer was one of these."

"That tells me nothing, Glassface," I said aloud to the TV set. "'Officer Alwer was one of these.' One what? A Hollywood cop? We concede that. She ticketed the homeless? She killed one for fun? What? Typical airhead TV news."

They showed some film clips from McKissick's Blaxploitation movies as a beautiful, angry teenager, karate-chopping white villains who looked like Mafia thugs. Her eyes glowed. She kicked and punched and smiled her way through the B-films. She looked too young and beautiful to wind up homeless and a Death- in-Custody LAPD case decades later.

"These clips will get the viewing public more riled up than before," I said aloud. "Thank you, TV assignment editors of America."

Calling your lawyer at night usually only disappointed you, but my attorney Skip Cossee played and laughed and guzzled through the nightlife.

I punched the digits into my cellphone and got Skip's voicemail.

"Skip, this is your favorite pink client, Foxy Maxy calling," I said. "In trouble. Surrounded by straight-and-narrow jokers. Letter of the law-type cats."

Skip jumped into my voicemail message.

"That do be trouble," Skip's thunderous Black voice rolled across America on the phone. "Tell me. Tell Daddy Fix."

Going through the whole story sounded fake, even to me.

"Melodramatic vacation, huh?" I said. "Wish that this beautiful land and weather was matched by the Angeleno people."

"Many tourists to LA feel the same way. Don't see me living there, do ya, Maxwell?"

"Now you tell me. This room smells like unclean ox blood on a hot afternoon. A mattress hard enough to ram a baby whale."

"As a respected and honorable officer of the court, I by Jesus sure can't tell you to duck this subpoena," Skip said. "But they can't turn you loose. Too swinging important for their case. All Los Angeles wants to dig what you saw. You the Big-Man-of-the-Month."

"If I leave, I can stay away until this cools down," I said. "Disappearing is one of the few skills I have left."

"Right on. Seen you in action. Them law-cats , rule-book freaks, never find you."

Nerves made me snap my fingers.

"But I won't leave," I said. "Good citizens, media and PSB will eat Patty Alwer up if I do. I'm her only wit."

"After this mess, like the Rodney King case, the Feds could subpoena you for their own civil rights case. Might drag on for years."

My mind pictured Skip, wide and solid as a cigarette machine, ebony-colored, turned dapper with other people's money.

"I get the feeling that I'm trying to ride a thunderbolt," I said. "What would YOU do in this little trick bag that I'm in?"

"Call my lawyer."

"You're a lot of help," I said. "And what would HE tell me?"

"Dunno."

"You don't know," I said. "But you'd call him. That's certainly circular logic right there. As a cop, I used to feel sorry for wits who got caught up in the machine. Now, I know why."

"Research this a bit," he said. "California codes. Squeeze some fools for favors. Slant things your way."

"How much is this going to cost me?"

"Aw, Maxwell!"

His wail came through the phone, lingered over the cornfields of Kansas and corkscrewed into my ear.

"Every breath you suck in costs somebody somewhere some cash," I said. "Or some pearl beyond any price. I just want to know beforehand. This time for a change."

"Cynical, Maxwell. Downright bitter. Don't you know that you're my favorite honky?"

The phone call ending sounded very loud from where I was.

A shower wetted me but did not bring sleep. My ear kept pounding against the pillow. Noise grew in the hallway.

The Hollywood movie conventioneers were cutting up out there. Slamming down giggle water, panty raids and tossing bags of water out their windows. Keeping Our Hero awake.

Chapter 20

This Won't "Woik"
or
Ain't You Technically My Baby?

At eleven the next day, keeping our meet like I'd schemed, Yan swept onto the corner, hair loose and flying and eyes laughing like we were old friends.

That made me wonder about her again. Something about her seemed off-key.

"How you doing?" she asked.

"Concerned about your walk," I said. "There was a big truck crack-up on Romaine Street. Made me worry about you."

"Oh, you're learning the area here. Like, cool. No, I trucked down Fountain."

"Short walk?" I asked.

Her face tightened.

"You're still trying, figga out where I live?" she asked. "What do you think I am?"

My insides jumped.

"I think that you're someone who has to be careful," I said. My slow voice gave me time to think. "Lot of Hollywood sharpies bouncing around. But, nobody can live happy without trust. You don't have to be careful about me. Lower the gate and relax."

Traffic noise came between us.

"We'll see about that," she said.

Like, cool, all right, I thought.

"Tiny's restaurant here is still closed," I said. "So, let's go somewhere new. Please show me your city. I'm happy seeing you and getting an extra night in my motel. The new guest cancelled so I keep my room one day longer. That makes me landed Hollywood gentry. A man of property."

"But just one more night?" she said. "So you're looking for a place to crash."

My breath went in. She was figuring me out too well.

She looked and scented fresh from the shower. That meant that she had just left home. So she lived near Fountain Avenue, just north of us. Somehow, I had to know just where she lived.

"I been away from home since I was a kid," she went on. "Lot of guys hitting on me. Greyhound station, Taco Bell tables and park benches."

"Not me," I said.

"You're kinda different, all right," she said. "So far."

"Put on the old feedbag with me?" I asked in a dopey Brooklyn accent. "I mean, you look bee-you-tee-full."

"'Feedbag?'" she asked.

Her face stretched. I could not blame her. This act was turning me into a clown-type.

"Charming expression, what?" I said, trying to sound clipped but charming, like Cary Grant. "Lunch. Or supper. Anywhere that you wish."

"Oh, like, I don't know."

"Don't know what? Are you fasting? Some kind of political expression through self-denial?"

"Like, you know lots of stuff. Maybe too much. It kinda weirds me out."

Her tone scared me. I needed this hustle.

"Ms. Los Angeles," I said. "I promise not to know too much."

"I mean, it's like, you know."

"I just know that we both need food. Let's get some."

Behind us, Angelenos coursed by in a flowing chrome-and-fiberglass stream of traffic.

"I mean, I don't know you," she said.

"What's to know? I am cute and fun. The last of the boulevardiers, a raconteur and a student of the cocktail. Come, let us study together."

"Don't know."

"Maybe you think that I can't buy lunch," I said. "Don't worry. I can. And this friendship is gonna 'woik'."

"'Gonna work?'"

"That's what I said. It's gonna work."

"Even if LA, like, goes up in smoke?"

Her words chilled me. They reminded me of something. But right now, I could not place it.

"C'mon," I said. "All my life, I'm coaxing other beautiful women to do things that they don't want to do."

That tickled her. That was okay. Guys always tried to talk her around.

"Listen," she said.

I did.

"It's like, I'm way hungry right now, and my plastic isn't working," she said. "That money you gave me, hadda spend it right away on food to keep me going."

Maybe she gave it to her pimp, I thought.

"My credit card, I called, the toll-free number, yata-yata-yata. Like, due to high caller volume. Call back, same tape, later for that."

"I know," I said. "Like tech support for my smartphone. Fingernails on the blackboard. Just awful."

Yan considered me.

"Watch out for the traffic here," I said.

"Everywhere."

"Those cars all tear up these quiet Hollywood streets," I said. "Some of these places seem so peaceful, shady and green. Then, you turn a corner and it's six lanes of Hollywood Boulevard traffic, huge chrome eighteen-wheelers screaming at you from on high. Can't believe that it's the same neighborhood."

"Yeah," she said. "Way nutso."

"Sorry for boring you," I said. "I forgot that Los Angeles doesn't really enjoy neighborhoods or understand what they are."

"Sure, we do. Neighborhoods are where you live."

We reached a cafe-type restaurant across from a storage place and vacant lot for sale.

"You see?" I said. "But that's enough hot-air sociology. Here's a brunch spot that I scouted out before. Tables outside, some shade and a dance floor. Our little hideaway."

❧

The waiter, a lank leaning-against-anything type with a shock of inky black hair over a dark, scarred face, took our orders. His rubber sandals slapped the floor.

A speaker played "The Exodus Theme" somewhere above us.

There was something weighing on me that I had to tell Yan.

"Yan, I'm involved with another woman," I said. "Known her for years."

Yan's brows knitted.

"Is she here in Hollywood?" she asked.

"Hardly. China. Maybe permanently."

"What kind of a thing you two got?" she asked.

"She travels a lot. Trains animals."

"Did she let you off the leash, give you your freedom?"

"Oh, yes."

"Then, you got no worries from me. And you shouldn't sweat it yourself."

"Are you sure?" I asked.

"What's the matter with ya?" she asked. "You a Catholic or something? Got the guilt there?"

My breath came out and I sagged in my chair.

"But I really like it that you told me first," Yan said. "That kind of honest talk goes a long way with me. And it turns me on."

We both scanned each other.

"May I have the pleasure of this dance?" I asked.

"Man, there's no one else dancing."

"Ah, the high-school prom," I said. "Gee whiz, what'll the other guys say?"

"Mean, it's like daylight and all."

"The sun will go down, my Yan. Happens every day. Darndest thing that I ever did see. Absolutely everything goes dark and mysterious and romantic."

"Can't they put up a squawk if you dance without they got a cabaret license or something?" she asked. "Call the cops?"

"Cops are kinda too busy today," I said. "Are you serious about that?"

"Los Angeles, they're always watching you, brah. Tiniest little petty stuff. Back home in Hawaii, we used to smoke weed with them when they weren't working. Real laid-back guys there."

"Let's discuss different policing styles as we dance," I said.

It felt like I was trying to lift up a loaded dump-truck by myself.

Yan rose when I looked at her and tried out my boyish smile, beat up by the years. She did not smile back.

But she came into my arms in dance position and we started a slow foxtrot to 'Exodus.'

"Isn't this song about dead Jews fighting and war and stuff?" she asked. "And it's too slow and draggy for dancing."

"Well," I opined into her shoulder. "It's better than no music at all."

CHAPTER 21.

**The Craft, The Secret of Life
or
Blue Suit Chit-Chat**

Somehow, through grit and sound family values, I managed to pull myself through that night, into a shower and in front of the motel desk clerk at eighty-thirty the next morning.

"I'm packed and ready to slide on out," I said. "How about I leave my bag with you at the front desk?"

The clerk squinted. Small, blondish, with chalky skin under quick brown eyes, she looked me over. If people were animals, she would be a parakeet on a perch.

"Nossir, we can't do that," she said. "That's a liability on our part."

"And why is that?"

"That is our policy, sir."

"This isn't the Dred Scott Supreme Court decision," I said. "Just some extra duds from the Sharing Is Caring Thrift Shop."

"But, sir, we can't."

"No more snappy dialogue," I said.

My hand hoisted the bag up to the desk and left it on the counter. She stared at like it was the hoof print of the Fiend.

"I'll be back for it as soon as I can," I said.

"Sir! Sir!"

My legs kept me walking from her. Stopping now would invite disaster.

Then, civilization crumbled.

The petite blonde parakeet drew in a lung full of air.

"HEY, YOU!" she caterwauled.

Stepping outside the door made me technically homeless. So, I stepped and crossed the street.

Stares from passersby made her retreat back into the motel office.

Sunset Boulevard was waking now, with pools of sunlight in between the black etched shadows. I could still feel the cool of night air blending with the warm air of morning.

Drifters stretched and patted their pockets for the morning smoke. They eyed me for a handout, but I looked and moved too much like them.

"Where you going?" a man asked. "Get back on that curb!"

An LAPD cop stood too close to me, silver-gray hair combed back from a tanned Latino face. His black-rimmed glasses bobbled as he spoke, He was pushing fifty or so, with sun-lines etched into his neck. His dark blue uniform, bound in black leather, looked new. The gold-and-silver badge glinted on his chest.

"You trying to get yourself killed in this traffic?" he asked.

No traffic came along Sunset. That made it rare moment in Hollywood.

His tone made my body sting with shame and my ribs heave.

"Excuse me, officer," I said. "I'm an ex-cop –"

"Hold on, fruitcake. You talk when I'm finished talking."

If people were animals, he would be an owl. There was something owlish about the he way that he raised his voice and cawed at me, while the glasses bobbled.

"Break out some ID," he said. "No more flapping your mouth."

My body sponged sweat.

In the cop world, there was no need for him to confront me like this. Nothing felt dangerous or tough here. I looked like a paunchy, harmless tourist in clean clothes on a busy middle-class street.

My rookie days in the NYPD came back to me. Street life moved sweeter when the cop tried to get along with everyone, even the crooks. That was the Craft, the secret of life.

It had taken me months to learn that.

"Here's the ID," I said. "Plus, some paper from the NYPD."

"Okay. Let me see," he said.

My feet stepped away from him as I tried to loosen down the cords of my body.

Nothing seemed to work. So I tried watching the sluice-mill of fiberglass and chrome again starting to roll down the streets.

Something else tugged my attention.

Back in New York, whenever a cop stopped a pedestrian, rubberneckers would blossom from the concrete. They would stare and offer the loser-in-life advice.

That street chorus had three favorite shouts:

"Get his shield number!"

"Call Fox News!"

"Contact Internal Affairs!"

Here in LA, nobody on foot stopped. They looked away from me and this cop. It seemed like they did not want to get involved. Maybe they were scared.

Newsreel photos of the Afghanistan secret police kidnapping innocents went through my mind. Here in Los Angeles, nobody was going to interfere with this officer.

This did not feel like America any more.

"Sign here," he said. "Not an admission of guilt, just a promise to appear. If you do not appear a warrant will be issued for your arrest."

My shoes stepped back.

"Officer, did you see my paper from the NYPD?" I asked.

"Start walking," he said. "Nothing says that I have to read what you got. Now, get out of my face."

CHAPTER 22.

Rappin'
or
Community Standards

"Body's hot and humming-mad," I said aloud. "Dealing with bullies like that always does it to me. Is this is a police state? Is this Poland with palm trees?"

Mad-striding away from the cop, I angled into an alley and a parking lot.

"Los Angeles," I went on. "Six parking-lots in search of a city. Part-time adults racing around."

Los Angelenos loved their cars so much that they planned carports and driving alleys like this everywhere.

Something rubber was burning nearby.

Another cop-copter punished us normals with the buzz-saw noise.

"Look, Mommy!" some kid shouted off to my left. "Another ghetto-bird!"

"Stereotyping," I thought. "Hurts us all. And Hollywood's no ghetto. Just filled with the youngster arty ragamuffins who want to huddle clear of the ghetto."

"Yo, dude!" someone said behind me.

I turned to face a mixed knot of locals. Some looked like computer nerds. Others moved like thugs. It was the American dream, a melting-pot mob.

"You were talking with cops, man," one said. It was the Actor, the guy shouting in the crowd before, when they were acting up. These jokers looked like a splinter of the same group.

"Here come the arty ragamuffins right here," I whispered, voice choppy from nerves.

"We saw you talking with the head-breakers," the Actor said.

"Had to," I said. "They got guns."

"What do you mean?" he frowned.

Good-looking and poised, he was thrown off by what I said. Mother Royster always said that it was easy to fool an actor.

"They jacked me up, like they always do," I said, trying to make it a whine. "Wanna see the summons he shoved on me? Just ain't right, man."

"You're not a snitch?"

"What would a snitch be doing walking around free?" I asked.

It was time to angle for some logic again, even to this crowd.

"He'd be with another group, wearing a microphone, getting videos, more evidence and names and stuff."

"Right on, bro," a scrawny white skateboarder with a black ski cap on said. Tattoos pulsed around his neck.

"Look," I said. "No gun or nothing electronic, man."

My fingers yanked up my shirt and displayed my bare beer belly. My stomach showed nothing but neglect and too many dinners. Being Southern Californians, they expected everyone to have movie-star abs and a perma-tan.

This group made me trembly with being scared. They could turn on me right quick, just out of restlessness.

"You brothers and sisters sure scared me," I rattled on. "'cause I don't go showing my gut to just anyone, unless I got a real good reason."

"And I can see why," a young South Asian woman in the group said in a clear British accent. "That much fat is disgraceful."

Her nose, with a silver stud in it, wrinkled at my display. Her long black braid swung behind her, over her punk rock T-shirt. A metal hammer hung on a loop in her belt, but she did not look like a carpenter.

"Everything has gone to seed," I said.

"You need to join a gym," she continued. Maybe she was the fixer-upper type.

"Wounded am I," I muttered. "Listen up. I was in puppy-love with McKissick the first time I saw her in *Sawed-Off Shotgun-Shooting Susie* back in the Blaxploitation days. It's all wrong, her living homeless, and then cracked by some wild copper."

"Amen," said Scrawny. "And I knew some people who tried to get her straight, you know? Take her in for a night, clean her up. But it didn't work. She would just write them letters and stay on the street."

"Which people?" I asked. "They deserve recognition."

He shook his head.

"They gone from here now," he said. "Welfare threw them out of Cali, man. But they know that I'm a movie freak and they told me about her."

"Heard she wrote a lot of letters," I said.

"Man, she was nutty on letters," he said. "Went hungry to buy envelopes."

Keeping my cover, I could not ask any more about McKissick. They would sense something wrong.

"Some critics slammed Blaxploitation films but they shouldn't," I said, nodding to the Actor. "What do you think? Didn't you act with her?"

"Of course I did," he said, right on cue. He could not stand leaving center stage.

Mama Royster was right. Actors acted. They rarely thought.

"You worked with her?" Scrawny asked.

The others made admiring noises. They stepped closer to him, feeling fame by association.

"Everyone here all sick on knowing Someone In Showbiz," I muttered, too low for them to hear me. "I better blow town before this same disease takes me, too."

"Of course, I did," the Actor said. "That's why I'm here."

"Which mo-vie?" Hammer Lady asked in her sprightly accent.

"*Truck-Stop Loving*, for one," the Actor said. "And *Chocolate Sunday*, for another. But they were bit parts, uncredited. I looked so different then. You would hardly recognize me."

"I bet," I said under my breath.

"Longer hair, frizzed out for the pictures," he said. "What they called a 'Jewfro'. Like an Afro, you know. And we wore love-beads, headbands, bell-bottoms."

Their smiles heated as they looked at the Actor with new eyes. He had acted with the dead McKissick. Maybe they had enjoyed a one-night stand on the movie set. He might have known her that well. They hungered for flesh gossip.

"Was she really an activist or was she just playing another part?" I asked.

This question pushed him deeper into the forgotten star's orbit and cranked his ego up higher. His eyes skittered around the alley where we stood. He did not look like anyone respected or important. My questions gave him a chance to expound.

"She was committed and sincere," the Actor announced in a voice like someone giving a funeral oration. "McKissick rode with the Freedom Riders in Alabama and survived the Mississippi Burning summer when the Ku Klux Klan was dropping activists like flies. It was America at war, and she was in the middle of it. She pushed for a movement that we are still in, thanks to her.

"They should put up statues to her. Not have her homeless and murdered by some police who wants to kill innocent people."

This audience in the alley would never read enough to learn about McKissick's work. So the Actor held their attention.

"Damn, man," Scrawny said. "Didn't know. My parents weren't even born yet. Too long ago."

My breathing eased. Maybe they would let me slide. They were getting entertained for free here. That might distract them.

"McKissick pushed for hot lunches for all school kids in Lowndes County, Alabama," the Actor went on. "She showed her courage marching against the segregated lunch counters at the local Country Vittles restaurant and forcing it to open up. Met and ate with Dr. Martin Luther King, James Forman, Stokely Carmichael. James Baldwin. Big times for this country."

"Never knew about that," the Skateboarder said.

"She urged young Black women not to get pregnant or drop out of high school," the Actor went on. "She gave talks about that in the Chicago housing projects."

"She must have been doing something right," said Hammer Lady.

My feet started moving off to the side. Running away seemed like a good idea. But this crowd was like a wolf-pack. If I ruptured our trust by trying to run, they would chase, catch and maul me.

"Direct action," Scrawny said. "Why we do this."

He unrolled his ski cap down over his face. Two plastic eye holes showed in the cap. He looked like an evil spirit.

"Wear this, gloves and long sleeves," he said. "And the Man's tear gas can't getcha. No skin showing. Our brothers and sisters in Germany designed this. They call it 'die schwartze Block.' That means 'the black bloc.' It ID's us to each other. Makes it hard for the system to see who you are. Good luck trying that case in court. Can charge the cops and they tear gas and not feel nothing."

"Pretty risky?" I asked.

"Naw, dude," he said. "When was the last time that the Man killed a demonstrator in America? Kent State, maybe, during the Vietnam War. They can't hurt us too bad no more. Rubber bullets, overnight stay in the hospital.

"When the Black Bloc first started they dang sure hit the German cops by surprise, injured 400 of them in one day. Just think of that, man! 400 cops hurt!"

He sounded like a glutton talking about pork chops and biscuits in hot gravy.

"Some of them will be in pain or crippled the rest of their cruddy Fascist lives. The Black Bloc also racked up about 500 non-violent demonstrators. non-stop revolutionary action for you, bro. And we can do the same thing here in pig Los Angeles."

"Cops chase you forever," I said. I tried to keep my voice neutral, not taking sides.

"Oh, man, don't you know?" He seemed puzzled. "Dudes like me, we found entire towns in the Pacific Northwest, with populations going down. So we filled that town with us.

"Opened food cooperatives, farmed and lived off the land. Our own lawyers, businesses and doctors liked living there, in the country. Now we got everyone living there into the movement.

The others moved away, died off or got forced out. We all work together, without the State interfering. If we have to strike against anyone and hide out, we can stay in those towns. No government will ever find us there, man. It's like a hidden kingdom."

His words made me forget everything around me.

"What about the cops up there?" I asked.

"Ain't many, to start with, man," he said. "Counties up there got no cash for a big sheriff's office. Lots of lawyers in the movement. Train us in our rights. Constitutional law. Need search warrants to search private property. You ever try searching a 300-acre farm for one five-foot sister? And nobody in these towns ever talks to the law."

"They still got the power," I said.

"Some of us, with clean records, we join those sheriff's offices up there," he went on. "The pretty sisters become secretaries, hear all the inside information, get the deputies' home addresses and become our undercovers. Tell us everything."

"Don't care for those Germans hurting non-violent protesters," the Hammer Lady said.

"Couldn't be helped," he said. "This is revolution."

"That's what they always say," I said.

Saying that felt stupid on my part. Some of the tougher ones fixed on me again, for a beat-down. They did not care who I was.

I was an outsider,

"Why we wear these," a Latina woman on my left said. She looked like someone's grandmother, in her fifties, sweet-faced, thickening under the chin and in the hips.

She took out her own black ski mask and unrolled it just like the Skateboarder had done. The eye-holes were covered by plastic, to keep out tear-gas.

Maybe lots of Angelenos carried these ski masks. There was no law against it.

"McKissick had the FBI following her everywhere," the Actor interjected. Losing center stage pained him. He was struggling to regain his audience. "At the start, she was just a walk-on player in the Civil Rights group. FBI wire-tapped her phone. Illegally, people. Saying that we needed it for our 'National Security.' McKissick shouting Blacks down South should be able, vote, live like they want."

"Absolutely," I said.

They looked puzzled now, trying to figure out if they were going to slug me or listen to the Actor some more.

"And I got some warrants on me for traffic," I lied. "That cop couldn't check me for them. Radio too busy, that's why."

"Man, then you better scoot out of here," the Actor said. Like I thought, he was holding center stage. "He comes back, maybe check you again. Get going."

"You talked me into it," I said.

Somehow, they were letting me drift, since I was now their revolutionary comrade.

"See you at the barricades," I said as my body shifted away from them.

Chapter 23.

Scouting Locations
or
Los Angeles Is a Movie Town

The ticket in my hand had the name "Samissal 26512" scribbled on the bottom line. Stress had made me forget to look at the Latino cop's uniform name-tag,

That last LAPD encounter was fast sapping my strength.

Going back to my motel and curling up on the bed sounded wonderful. But it was not my bed anymore. Some sweaty joker who ran porn movie houses in rural Ohio would be slumbering in the bed by now. The movie convention crowd was mobbing Los Angeles motels.

❧

"Help you, boss?" a Latino waiter asked at another restaurant. He had wrist tattoos, a full moustache and quick, droopy eyes that took in everything,.

The dive looked like an afterthought beanery with saggy chairs and plastic yellow menus taped to the walls. A picture of a bullfighter who looked like he was planning to lose to the bull completed the image.

"Do you have a dance floor?" I asked, feeling silly as usual.

"Negative, boss."

"Partner, I ain't nobody's boss," I said. "Just a drifter and a dinosaur, wondering what these kids will do next."

"That's the LA talk, boss," he said. "Us Latinos respect you Whites like that 'cause you all ran California for so long."

"We did?" I asked. "I didn't know that. Thought that LA is more than half Latino now. Hispanic mayor."

"You guys still run it, boss. Behind closed doors and all that there. Check it out."

"LA looks like it got complicated politics," I said.

"Most *gringos* don't wanna live near us wetbacks, illegals, beaners. Whatever you wanna call us. You think we all narcos. And we can't stand living near the blacks. Us Mex work. No welfare. We live better than our daddies did. The brothers don't. They love that gangsta mess."

"Seems like nobody in LA gets along," I said. "And the cops got to keep it from blowing up into another riot."

"Cops, man! Don't talk to me about them. They the biggest gang going."

The chicken with *mole* chocolate sauce warmed and cheered me. Mexican spices in the sauce burned my tongue and surprised me. It was an ancient Aztec recipe that had survived to this day in Mexico and Los Angeles.

❧

In neighborhood terms, Hollywood seemed to dip between seedy and dull. My feet kept turning down blocks of both.

Some dogged instinct pulled me back to the death scene on Gower and Sunset.

Across Sunset, some buildings had been fixed up to look like the Old West, with dried timber and wagon wheels against the storefronts. A wooden sign read "Gower Gulch." It might remind Californians of their cowboy roots, before every strip mall in the world had cut up their land into parcels and parking lots.

License plates read "California – the Golden State." The Western buildings clashed with the cookie cutter modern ones nearby, and I wondered why I had not noticed the jarring discrepancy before. If policing was a memory test, I'd fail it every time.

The blues were starting to pull me down like a raincoat on a muggy day, so I went into the doorway for Florida's dance school, hoping that he might be there.

∽

My luck held. Florida was there and teaching a class of both men and women, dressed in California casual and trying to get the American Waltz steps down.

His dozen students ranged in age from about forty to seventy, the same as most ballroom classes across the country. They hung back against the walls, looking shy or lazy. A clump of Asian women who seemed to know each other clustered together.

Florida did not look happy to see me, but he was enough of a showman to carry it off. Nobody would notice a thing.

"Looky here," he said to his class. "We have an extra man. That is always a good thing. We usually have more women than men."

"Because we live longer," a blocky woman in a foreign accent said, moving sideways inside her green sequin dress.

The women nearby giggled.

"Hollywood never sleeps, right?" I said. "Every time I check in here, there's a class going on."

"I gotta work hard right now," Florida said. "Gotta get my name out there, in front of the dancing public."

"Then, afterwards," I said, "you can goof off like the rest of Hollywood."

"Goof off?" he said. "I never worked so hard in my life."

Nobody seemed sure what to make of Florida and me tossing words back and forth like this. His students nodded and kept dancing.

Florida watched them, weight on his left foot.

"You keep coming back in here at the weirdest times," he muttered. "It's a bit creepy. Why?"

"Told you," I said. "I'm Max and dancing is my life. The harrier things get, the more I need to dance. Life is pretty hairy right now."

– 110 –

"I told you," Florida said. "Didn't see anything about the woman dying. Can't help you."

"You can help me by staying open," I said. "Don't close up your dance school until I'm safely out of this goat rodeo."

"Could you dance with Glynnis here?" he asked. "The woman in that lovely red dress there. How's your waltz?"

The Asian women remained in a pack as they copied Florida.

"Everyone, change partners," Florida said. "Move to your left, please."

"Yessir," I said, moving left to Glynnis. "My name's Max. Teacher wants us to dance together. Let's obey Teacher."

"Good to have a tall partner," Glynnis said. "You're not crooked over yet, like some of them. Sorry, but I don't know the waltz yet."

"You will," I said. "It's fun."

"Florida gives so many classes per day," she said. "We all do just like you did, drop in without a reservation."

"That's my theory," I said. "Florida could open up a dance studio twenty-four hours a day, seven days a week, and it would never be empty. Dancers will get off work after midnight and want to dance a slow foxtrot somewhere. They could be like 7-11 stores, never closed. I would go there and so would you."

"You are a talker," she said.

"Is that good or bad?"

"I don't think that I've ever seen you dancing here," she said.

A white streak showed in her reddish hair, over her round face.

"Strangers always show up in ballroom," I said. "Regulars might form around a good teacher like Florida but newcomers still drift in."

"What do you mean?" she asked.

Many Angelenos seemed to ask me that question.

"Dancers like us got used to these unknowns," I went on.

Somehow, pontificating calmed me down. And I wanted them all to remember me in case I came back for another class.

"In ballroom, a mystery person will arrive, dance and talk about life over drinks of water," I said. "Some are sitting out unhappy love affairs and looking for reasons to stay or go. Others test the market by seeing who likes their looks. Often, we never see them again. So they remain a mystery. We always remember them."

"You're a mystery, all right," she said.

"I came running in from the riots outside," I said.

"Oh, that's so sad. Dead woman. I live near here and used to see her on the street all the time. She was always writing things down in a notebook."

My feet stopped.

"What kinds of things?" I asked.

"God only knows. I mean, wasn't she crazy? You have to be crazy to live on the streets, right?"

"Not necessarily," I said. "Just homeless. Did you ever speak to her?"

"Why would I?"

"You're right. No reason. Do most of you live nearby?"

"Oh, yes. We love Hollywood. Some of us were in the Industry, you know. And who can afford to move?"

"You're right," I said. "You can look for me dancing regularly here. It suits me."

"That's nice."

More than nice, I thought. Maybe I will find another eyewitness to McKissick's death here on this dance-floor. Dancing and being everyone's ear was the best way to dig up a witness here.

After a half hour of dance lesson, I felt relaxed and loose.

Everything looked better. Dancing usually did that for me.

This time, I paid Florida forty bucks and took a flyer for more classes. He looked glad to see me go. Maybe he figured out my scheme to pump his dancers about McKissick.

✦

My legs tingled and tightened some, walking the quieter, tree-lined Hollywood streets and alleys. It was the area where regular, square-John citizens who did not work in showbiz, shuffled through junk mail at the door and their own lives.

My thoughts went to my Showbizzer pals, Zygolt and her group, struggling to flower in the arts in the desert town of Basta, about 120 miles from LA.

After too much walking, I called Yan. It felt necessary to remind myself that Koy, my beloved was on her way to China and had given me my freedom.

My breath shortened. The curtain was going up, and I was stepping out onstage.

"Yes?" Yan answered.

This was not an eloquent invitation to speak.

"This is Max Royster," I began. "You asked me to call you today."

"Yes?" she said again.

"And I thought that you might care to join me for lunch," I said. "Just found a good place on Willoughby."

"Uh, I don't know."

This seemed to be getting difficult.

My lips formed the word "please." But I was not about to say it aloud. Not yet, anyway.

The City of the Angels might be going up in flames and here I was, stammering like an eighth-grader back at Saint Blaise's School for Young Men.

"Okay," she said. Finally. "I guess I can do that."

"Ah, such enthusiasm," I mouthed into the phone.

"Excuse me?"

"Little bit of wind there," I said, louder this time. "Distorts the phone terribly. Now, where and when may we meet? Remembering that I am carless in speed-racer LA."

"Near my place," she said. "Highland and Santa Monica Boulevard at one. Be on the corner, okay? I don't like people knowing where I live."

CHAPTER 24.

Wishing and Hoping
or
The Basic Steps

Once again, I met Yan on the anonymous Los Angeles corner and fell into her eyes and aura.

A scent of patchouli and clean cotton wafted from her.

Over her protests, I brought her to another faceless restaurant that smelled of Crisco cooking oil and French fries. Framed pictures of old cowboys with six-shooters looked down on us from the chipped wooden walls. Two dusty windows nearby made me think about jumping through them and to escape. Mexico lay just two hours to the south.

I ordered food, more to pay rent than to eat it.

Afterwards, we danced with Yan to the Latino music on the jukebox.

The tanned, biracial waiter, a gold front tooth and dyed blue hair in a pompadour, slammed his hand down. Salt, pepper, Tabasco and jalapeño sauce bottles rattled on the counter.

"No dancing here, ace!" he hollered.

"I'm afraid that I must insist," I said, over my shoulder while holding Yan in the ballroom dance frame.

"No dancing here," the waiter repeated.

"Why not?" I asked. "Is this cafe owned by the Taliban?"

"Ace," he said, his voice rising and hardening. "You saying I'm a terrorist?"

My feet stepped back from his anger.

"Hardly."

"Just 'cause my folks come from Surinam, you say that I'm a terrorist?"

"Surinam got terrorists?" I said. "That's news to me."

"I gotta leave," Yan said, wriggling out of my arms and backing away. "I can't help you."

"Ah, but you can," I said. "I need a place to sleep for a few days. All the hotels are chock-full around here."

"No way that could be," she said. "This is Los Angeles."

"Yes, way," I said. "Have to live close to Hollywood Station of the vaunted LAPD. Because that is where they and the whiz-bang DA's office want me to report until this case goes to the Grand Jury. They seem to need me there. I'm their blue blanket, their se-curity, like Linus with his blanket in the *Peanuts* comic strip."

"Just rent a car and drive to the police station."

"I hate driving," I said. "And don't have the cash to start roving this California landscape in a rental car. Plus, that leaves a trail for the cops or FBI to track me."

"Why does the FBI care about you?"

"Because this mess about McKissick could slide into a civil rights smorgasbord kind of case."

"But both of them are Black women? Can't be no Civil Rights deal, that way."

"One blue, the other Black and dead. That means civil rights violation, and the FBI gobbles those cases up for dinner and publicity. So they will be watching all credit card records with my name. Try renting a car without a credit card today. But we're skirting the issue here. C'mere."

I restored her into my embrace. She accepted, dragging her feet but she accepted.

"Yup," Yan said. Her head bobbed as we danced.

"You can't dance in here!" the waiter said, even louder. "Told you already."

Ignoring him, I pressed closer to Yan.

"As I am trying very hard to say," I said to Yan. "I need a floor to sleep on for a few days. And I can pay cash."

She pulled away from my dance hold a little, then settled back down.

"You won't tell anyone where you are?" she said. "'cause I don't want trouble with my apartment manager."

"Nobody."

"Not even the police or FBI?"

"I can forget an address with the best of them," I said. "Or anything else that I have to."

"You better. 'cause I need the money."

That eased me. Yan seemed to be going for my hustle.

We talked prices. She accepted my offer. The price hurt me. But I had no time for comparison shopping.

"So, I can move in tonight?" I asked. "Otherwise, it's some park bench for me at sundown."

My gut sucked in and out.

If she said "No," Our Hero would be in sorrow's clutch.

"Yeah, okay," she said. "Whatever."

Chapter 25.

Subtext
or
This Means What?

Yan's body kept moving through the dance.

"Man, you can't dance in here," the waiter repeated.

We danced.

The waiter came from around the counter and shoved plates of tacos at us.

"Here!" he snapped.

Tacos in hand, we sat down and ate.

"How is yours?" she asked me.

"We might have done better staying on the dance floor," I said. "And maybe eating that instead."

Her mouth pulled down.

"It will keep us from starving, anyway," I said. "May we dance some more?"

Her darkish head inclined. I hoped that it meant That probably meant "Yes."

The music wrapped around us.

My eyes closed. Inside their pinkish dark, my body relaxed. Maybe this McKissick death would blow away.

"Can we go now?" Yan asked me. "Think those tacos upset my stomach."

"It's that kind of place."

"Whatever."

"It'll be tough tearing me away from my new friend the waiter," I said. "Not to mention his dance floor."

"What dance floor?"

"I said not to mention that."

"You're kind of wacko," Yan said. "Do I really want you sharing my place?"

"Passionately," I said. "Because I'm cute and fun."

"Yeah?"

"And generous with cash," I lied.

That was impossible.

"Look at our waiter's face when he sees the tip I left him. The charge for dancing."

She watched.

"His face ain't changing," she said.

"Can't help that," I said. "I did my part."

‽

We left that cafe of joy and dancing and moved along the sidewalk. Yan's eyes and cheekbones excited me in the darkness.

Step by step, we were drawing closer to her home.

My phone buzzed.

I hesitated. I was on the knife-edge with Yan. The slightest act out of the ordinary might send her skittering. But at last I took the phone out of my pocket.

The display read "Private Number."

I took the risk and answered it as Yan stared at me with that ambiguous tilt of her head.

The display read "Private Number."

I took the risk and answered it as Yan stared at me with that ambiguous tilt of her head.

"Yes?" I said.

"This is Deputy District Attorney Brookings," the tiny voice said in my ear. "And I think that we can push through a hotel room voucher for you."

Something pinged inside my head.

"Swell," I said, using the slang term to tell myself that something felt wrong here. Glancing around to get my bearings bought me some time. "I'm at North Orange Street and Sunset Boulevard."

"By Hollywood High School?"

My head swiveled around. Staircases yawned upwards around us, to a squat structure with luxurious large trees and bushes around it.

"I guess so," I said. "Big sandy building with some bushes."

"That's it," Brookings said. "Just wait there, okay? I'm leaving Hollywood Station now with hotel vouchers. Be there in a tick."

"Tick this," I said.

But he had hung up.

Yan cocked her head to stare at me.

"Howzit?" she asked.

"There's a trout in the milk," I said. "Get up these stairs, please, and behind the trees. Don't say or anything until I give you the word."

"Men!" she spat. "Why do you have to play master and commander all the time?"

"No time for radical feminist politics now," I said. "Just please do this, for both of us."

My voice climbed and broke. That was a sure sign that nerves were taking over.

Brookings might be tricking me.

I slid behind some brush near the Hollywood High School front. Nobody could see me now unless they stepped on me.

My friend in the Transit cops back in New York, Jacky Maple, used to hide this way behind subway dumpsters and trash cans. He stopped doing it when a drunk relieved himself all over Jacky on a dark platform.

"This is all juvie delinquent stuff, man!" Yan said. "You got me in trouble, for sure."

"By dancing?"

"What you say?"

"It starts with the dancing," I muttered.

"Huh?"

"Never mind," I said. "Please be patient. Waiting is the hardest part."

Chapter 26.

Tailing
or
Documenting Failure

Yan stood a few feet away up the stairs, behind a shrub.

"Is this some kind of cute trick to get me alone?" she asked,

"I wish," I whispered. "You look lovely but I don't want to lose my sleeping deal."

"What you say, my cranky kid?"

"No matter," I said. "Natives speak with garbled tongue."

"Keep slamming us LA people. Act like a New York wise-acre. See where it gets you."

"You're right," I said. "Sorry about that. Being scared turns me silly."

"More and more," she said. "Bet you're divorced."

"Getting married was the silliest thing of all," I said. "Which is why I am scrambling under trees tonight with you and liking you more with each tree."

A violet SUV came barreling down Sunset, headlights from oncoming cars lighting up lots of chrome and custom design. It figured that Brookings would sport a showboat kind of car.

His actor's balanced and even face showed over the dashboard. He looked over the intersection like the young man in a hurry that he was.

But the cars behind him drew my eye. Two were moving slower than the mad sluice of Los Angeles traffic that never seemed to stop,

"Brookings got company," I said. "A nice loose tail, watching him."

"Huh?" Yan whispered.

"Maybe he can't see it. Doesn't know about it. Might be innocent."

"How come you can see it and he doesn't?"

"Because they don't teach all that slop in law school," I said. "Because I'm a mess who knows some tricks."

The two cars, a dark green Toyota Prius and a tan Ford Escort, jockeyed to hang back from Brookings.

When Brookings swerved around the school looking for me, they followed him.

Brookings squared the block again.

My feet twitched, like they used to at Saint Blaise's School for Young Men, when I would gack up an easy soccer pass. Nobody had ever called me athletic.

When Brookings came around again, he stopped his SUV.

He moved his head, looking around for me.

The two cars tailing him stopped. They were about forty feet away from him. Doors eased open and men slid out.

The men walked towards Brookings and me.

Brookings did not see them yet. They moved without noise, on soft shoes.

"Trouble coming every day," I whispered.

Brookings stayed put. But the men kept coming closer. Clean-cut, youngish, moving like runners, with loose casual clothes. The clothes could cover handguns and radios.

They moved well. Brookings still did not see them.

He was looking for someone older and wider and less hopeful. He was looking for me.

One man stopped and crouched.

"FBI!" he shouted. "You in the bushes! Freeze!"

"Aww!" I shouted.

Brookings swung his head around. He saw them. The FBI agents trotted towards me now.

"What's this?" Brookings shouted. "What's going on here?"

"FBI!" another one shouted. "Stay where you are, Mr. Brookings!"

The FBI knew Brookings. They were watching him to get something.

I was that something.

Both car headlights switched on. I felt like a bunny rabbit caught for Easter dinner.

The cars moved up closer. Their engines gunned.

Behind me, another car stopped.

"Trapping Our Hero," I said.

My legs pumped.

"You, girl!" I shouted. "RUN!"

"What are you saying?" she demanded.

"Take off!" I bellowed. "Run home,"

Yan darted out of hiding. Her feet flew.

More cars roared towards us.

I ran after Yan. She moved much better than I did.

"You there!" one agent shouted. "Freeze!"

Fear flooded me, but I kept running.

Chapter 27.

I Stand My Ground, Sort Of
or
Running

"Why are they doing this?" Yan gasped.

"Just run," I said. My voice struggled to break wild.

She moved out far ahead of my steak-and-eggs-and-bourbon belly.

Tires cawed, chasing us.

"If they call in more cars, we are gacked," I panted.

Something sharp cut my ribs from running.

"Get into this alley!"

My arms screamed as I dragged a huge cardboard box, one that might block a car, across the alley mouth.

Rolling a plastic trash barrel beside the box, I pointed to a gate leading onto someone's front lawn. We stepped onto the barrel. My shoes slipped. An awful word came from my lips. Somehow, we jumped the gate.

A car swerved into the alley and braked. It turned to avoid the box.

Whipping my head back, I saw figures jump out of the car and try shoving the box back.

Movies always showed Los Angeles homeowners drowning their lawns with water cannons. It was not Hollywood mythology, but current events. The grass wet my toes.

"Why are they doing this?" she repeated.

"For that Government pension," I wheezed. "Which looks better to them every day."

We made it onto the street. Yan turned towards the corner. My hand stopped her.

"Dunno why I'm obeying your crazy orders," she said. "I must be I'm as crazy as you are."

"Don't think like the FBI does," I said. "Be creative. Let's head to the next street over and then corner away."

"Why?"

"To duck jail," I said. "Running from the FBI makes it a federal crime."

"What?"

"But I didn't hear anyone shouting," I said. "Please remember that."

By now, we were creating across more lawns and zigzagging towards the alleys. The loud car sounds faded.

"What happened?" Yan asked.

There was no point in telling her too much.

"That was someone going to score me a motel room tonight," I said. "Sure that it is a charming place. Because nobody else wanted the room."

"Stop acting completely off-the-wall, big belly. Try being mature."

"Wounded am I. The FBI heard of this room. Maybe they wiretapped him under the Patriot Act or something. So they figured to tail him and scoop me up. It was their last chance to get me."

"Why?"

"Because I'm going to vanish underground. Right now."

❧

Looking behind us and freezing whenever a car flashed lights nearby, we made it to shelter.

Underground was Yan's building, a smooth reddish-brown brick place with four apartments per floor. Two doors opened onto the street and one into the alley. That eased me a bit. Covering this place to catch me would come hard to my friends in the FBI.

Outside, a beery-looking gangster type walked a liver-colored pit bull on a rope leash. The creature looked solid and feisty, and probably weighed at least seventy pounds.

The pit bull gave me a hard look over. That was enough to scare me.

I hoped that the pit bull did not live in Yan's building.

We walked up five flights of wooden stairs reeking with curry smell.

"My palace," she muttered, unlocking a steel door at the head of the stairs.

Oyster-colored walls lay over gummy wooden floors. Neglect darkened the corners. Paint chips littered the floor next to heaped paperbacks, movie magazines and opened boxes of crackers. Maybe Yan munched while she looked at Hollywood starlets.

Everything would happen in this one room. The bed dominated the place. It lay just ten feet or so from the hall door.

A large wooden bookcase, about seven feet tall, choked with hardcover books, some looking old, stood near the bed. Like me, she probably read herself to sleep and needed to have her books close at hand.

A stool near the bookcase would let her stretch to the top shelf.

My hand touched the bookcase and it rocked forward. Yan lived an unbalanced life on the edge. If she put too many books on it, the bookcase might topple over someday and crush the reader unaware.

Her kitchenette with a sink and stove was an afterthought off to the left. The painted pink door to the bathroom sagged on its hinges.

It looked like the place where the owner read a lot more than she cleaned house. But I was the same way.

"You're still breathing hard. When was the last time you went running, Max?"

"When Lazarus woke up from his nap," I said.

"That's jacked. You should run. Everyone runs. You're getting a gut on you, you know?"

"Just show me your sofa," I said.

"Who said anything about a sofa? My last one broke apart, and I can't afford a new one. You get the floor, dude."

This was getting up to be The-Moment-of-Truth.

We were both rolling the Universe into one big ball of a question, so I stepped in and kissed her. For one long scary second, it felt like she was pulling away, but then she eased her body into mine and relaxed.

Everything in Hollywood seemed to hush.

Whatever disasters we faced, we were somehow needing to clutch at each other.

She stared at me, her eyes all of a dark question and shook her head.

"The floor," she said. "You darn well better get to sleep on that floor now."

Chapter 28.

See All the Instant Experts
or
Nobody Knows Nothing

"Splintery and smelling of dust," I whispered to myself, "All night."

That's how Our Hero would describe this Fair Maiden's floor.

A noise that sounded like a truck tire being stripped issued from the boudoir.

"And the Fair Maiden does snore," I muttered. "That makes me feel superior. Nobody says that I snore."

Some more minutes sloughed past like mourners trailing a hearse on foot.

My feet padded to the kitchenette sink where I washed the armpits and crotch of my clothes with hot water and soap. Then I squeezed them dry and draped them on a chair near the bookcase. The warm LA air should dry them during the night. Or else I would get pretty aromatic over the next few days.

DDA Brookings and the FBI had plans to handle my laundry problems in another way.

As I stepped past the bookcase, my left arm brushed it. The bookcase rocked back and then settled.

Someday, that bookcase might avalanche.

Yan snored again.

The noise ripped through the apartment again.

"But, then, nobody is in a position to know whether I snore or not," I whispered. "These months, I am a man alone."

Yan subsided.

My body eased.

Time floated.

"RRRRIP!"

She snored again.

"Romantic evening," I muttered.

This cycle kept on the entire night.

This love-nest was fast turning me into a cranky old copper.

❧

"Sleep okay?" she asked me the next morning.

She stood at ease over me, one hand on her hip like a modern dancer. She wore fresh white jeans and a green T-shirt that showed her wiry build.

She seemed to dominate me by standing above me. From my teenage years, I remembered stories of homeless people turned into sex slaves for room and board.

With her door closed and in this apartment, Yan might see herself as an evil queen, wanting to satisfy all her hungers.

"Huh?" I said.

"I said 'Did you sleep okay?'"

"Like you wouldn't believe."

"That's cool, then. I've been up for a while. You were out like a light."

"Making up for lost time."

"There isn't much to eat now. Gotta hit Ralphs pretty quick. Got candy bars, some honey."

"Coffee, maybe?"

"Instant coffee. Just black, ya know."

"Mankind is persecuted," I muttered.

"Huh?"

"That'll be ducky," I said. "Would love a cup. Thank you."

"Got some taco chips but they're kinda old. TV's warming up."

Her apartment had four windows looking out onto the famous Los Angeles blue sky. A tan icebox and a chipped white stove fought for space in the kitchenette. The place smelled of cigar smoke.

Yan boiled water and switched on a tummy-sized TV set with a wire coat hangar for an antenna. The picture came on fuzzy and blue and I watched the tube show LAPD chiefs with much gold braid and harsh faces talking to reporters.

Maybe some Hollywood director used this place as his own little love nest to smoke and relax with Yan. It seemed like anything was possible in Los Angeles. A cigar scent was okay. It could have been something worse.

"I see young reporters with much teeth and hair coming into focus," I said. "Let me shower while they explain the world to us."

❧

The water blasted out hot from the shower and stung me. It felt needed, after that Dostoevsky white night.

My spare duds were still at the gracious American Motel.

My travel toothbrush scraped across my teeth and the bristles stung.

Toweling myself off and getting into my only clothes again, I heard a familiar voice from Yan's TV set: Alwer.

She stood before a modern gray steel building, LAPD headquarters.

"I approached the suspect to effect an arrest," Alwer said on the TV.

"That's all that we have to say at this time," Alwer's lawyer said. He seemed to have aged since I'd last seen him. His shoulders drooped and his face frozen into some kind of judicial mask. His suit hung on him and his tie knot was off-center. He was trying to shield Alwer from a lynch mob. Different paralegal and assistant types were escorting Alwer away.

Disorganized, scattered losers roved near the TV camera. My Patrol instincts did not like that. No LAPD blue suits monitored the crowd.

Things could get hairy, even at LAPD Headquarters.

"Look at those losers mobbing up around Alwer," I muttered to Yan. "Like I said before, every fool is an instant expert on police brutality."

"Officer Alwer," a model-thin, Black woman reporter with a foxy face and teased reddish hair said. "What do your arrestees say about your brutality? Haven't you got the reputation of a bully? Someone who abuses the helpless ones?"

Alwer's head bobbed like someone was walloping her. Watching her, my gut felt sick.

"We saw your personnel package at PAB," the reporter went on. "Bully, bully, bully!"

"Lets go!" Alwer's lawyer said. He sounded like he was losing control.

"Bully, bully!" a blonde woman hollered.

"She was hiding a sign under her shirt!" Alwer sputtered. "I ordered her to show me her hands. She grabbed my gun."

"Nobody believes you!" a man shouted off camera.

"LAPD kills our children!" an Asian woman with red and blonde streaks in her black hair said. "So what if she got a sign? That a crime or something?"

"Here comes the experts," I said.

The Actor pushed through the crowd.

"They all lie in Traffic Court!" the Actor said. He covered his face with one wide hand.

Others shouted, covering the talk with noise.

"Look at Alwer's face," I said. "She's torn now. She's trying to Make It Right."

"She should," Yan said.

"Sometimes, you just got to move on while you're still bleeding," I said. "Trying to Make It Right often makes it worse."

On the TV, the camera zoomed in to a close-up of Alwer's face.

"You're sure that she grabbed your gun?" the woman reporter asked.

"We're not speaking!" her lawyer said. "Keeping us on camera puts your ethics in question."

Something wet hit the TV camera. It smeared the lens.

"Listen!" the Actor said. "I was Ms. McKissick's neighbor and appreciated her onscreen work. And she could not grab anything. Her hands weren't strong enough.

"She tried to write letters or something every day. Maybe her memoirs. She loved writing but couldn't do it. Age and drugs had atrophied her grip. She could barely hold a pen."

"The Blood of Jesus is on Stupid!" a man with a Slavic accent shouted.

"Blood of Jesus!" the crowd chanted.

"Huh?" Alwer said.

My lips repeated that same brilliant expression.

"She could not open her own mail!" the Actor shouted. "You killed her for no reason!"

Rocks flew at Alwer. One hit her in the shoulder.

A bottle smashed.

"THE BLOOD OF JESUS!" the crowd chanted.

The TV screen blacked out.

CHAPTER 29.

Calm
or
Maybe Not

The TV screen gave off sounds but no picture.

Inside Yan's apartment, the noise of the impending riot made the TV shake. The din ached my ears.

The picture came back on, wobbly. Maybe the cameraman was running.

The Actor heaved something that looked like a bottle at Alwer.

"The Blood of Jesus is on Stupid!" he cried out.

He skittered away.

"He sounds in fine dramatic form," I said. "His voice coach should pet him gently on his handsome head."

"What does he mean by that 'Jesus' stuff?" Yan asked.

"It means that he wants to be fashionable," I said. "Because everyone else is saying that same thing."

"That's totally dummy, man."

"But popular," I said. "I predict 'the Blood of Jesus is on Stupid!' will become the next catch-phrase of Angelenos who dislike their police. Which is to say, almost everybody."

On the TV, another car blossomed in orange fire. A smirky White kid with a grin that he could not seem to swallow hurled a clump of burning garbage at the camera.

Cops ran out from the building lobby. One drew his baton from his belt.

The camera hobbled.

The White kid smirked again.

A body blotted out the screen.

Yan went into her bathroom and closed the door. Running water splashed in the sink.

Slouching down in a chipped wooden chair, I punched in a number from my cellphone.

"Hello?" a woman's sleepy voice said. Zygolt, a dancer and one of my Showbizzer pals from my days in the desert town of Basta.

"This is Max, Zygolt. Big trouble in Hollywood here. Need help at 1283 Willoughby Street. Can you get here?"

"No way. Why?"

"For a thousand bucks. And I've got a sneaky plan."

Keeping my voice low, I whispered my plot to her.

Yan came out of the bathroom. She looked at me.

"Remember those numbers?" I asked Zygolt on my phone. "Can you wait for me outside there at eight tomorrow morning? Be outside the front windows there so I can see you without leaving the place. If you get here early, just wait for me."

Everything hung while she thought it over.

My eyes squeezed shut.

This long shot, this Hail-Mary pass, was something that I needed now. Or else, nothing else would work.

"You're lucky that I'm bored," Zygolt said. "And broke. Otherwise, forget it. 1283 Willoughby, yeah. And a thousand. In cash. But not tomorrow."

"When, then? I'm jammed up here, Zygolt, my dear. A thousand buys you a lot of time, paying off bills. Keeping yourself intact. You know that you need it. These are parlous times, financially speaking."

"Check outside that address, day after tomorrow," she said. "Or maybe the day after. Can't say now. But eight a.m. is the curtain time. Okay? I never missed a performance."

"That the best you can do?" I asked.

"Get pushy and I'll drop the whole nutty idea," she said.

"Thank you, my dear. I'll check outside each day at eight, sharp."

Zygolt clicked off. Somehow, I kept making people angry.

I knocked on the bathroom door. Yan answered, drying her face with a red hand-towel.

"Phone interval," I told Yan. "Be off in a second."

Yan was going to be busy for a bit. So I had time.

Stepping away from the bathroom door, I called Brookings on my cell.

"Hello?" he said.

"You sound a bit impatient," I said. "That's just fine. Because I feel that way, too. I'm a trifle impatient when Learned Counsel such as yourself decides to hand me over to the FBI, the 'Famous But Incompetent'."

"I don't have time for this," he said.

"Ah, but you do. Or else, make time. Did you know that you were leading the FBI precisely to me? Because they're experts at stealing wits to make their own cases."

Brookings said something foul.

I was wrong about Yan. She came out of the bathroom and smirked when she heard my words. There was no fooling her this morning. She was sharper than I had thought.

"That sounds a bit harshish," I said. "Perhaps Learned Counsel must needs temper his dialectic."

Yan smirked. She knew that I was telling off Authority and she liked it. Now, we were partners.

She twisted her face and shook her head. Her body eased near mine. My knees bent.

"Royster, you're wasting my precious time with your own problems with authority. Now, I'm busy. Got beaucoup things to do."

"'Busy' is the new four-letter word," I said. Fatigue croaked my voice. "Maybe you got things to do but you only got one witness. And that's me. And if you keep dragging the FBI to my tail, you won't even have me anymore. The Feds will grab me and pull me into Federal Limbo like the Supreme Being yanking the Virgin Mary into Heaven."

Yan put her hand on me. Pleasure burned me at her touch.

"What d'you want, Royster?" Brookings asked.

"I'll set up a spot for us to meet," I said.

Yan's hand moved more. It made me wiggle.

"Just you and me and a video gizmo for my statement. You can ask your questions and I'll answer them. I'll pick a spot where not even the FBI can tail you."

"You think that you're pretty hot, don't you, Royster?"

"You all haven't snagged me yet."

"Why don't you just run?"

"Because Alwer needs a square deal. Which she may not get from any other wits that scrape themselves off the walls to you and tell lies. Lies are real popular in this case. Everyone parrots them. So, I'm sticking. But not locked down as a material witness."

"Call me back this afternoon," he said. "I need to clear this with upstairs."

"You and upstairs may go to the Deuce, to use a literary expression, and I don't mean 42nd Street, but the Devil himself," I said. "I'll call you back in one hour."

"Oh, no, you won't call," Yan whispered.

She made goo-goo eyes and moved her hand around on me more.

"I got plans for today, you and me. No more phone calls."

Something was changing in Yan's face and voice. She moved differently now, sluggish. Her eyelids shuttered and then opened. My breath caught. Maybe she used drugs. I wanted to make sure that she was rational.

"Are you okay?" I asked her. "Clear in the head and everything?"

"I'm okay, Max. Doctor prescribed some stuff for my condition. Don't ask about my condition. Medicine slows me down sometimes. But I know what I'm doing. You're not going to call anyone for a while."

She was right.

Her hands grabbed me more and would not let go. Her dark eyes swam closer to me. My own breath sharpened in my ears. There would be time to call Brookings later.

∾

Hours later, I woke up next to Yan.
"It's dark outside," I said.
"Hmmmm," she said.
"Night," I said. "We fell asleep exploring some unknown avenues in Sex-Land."
"Yeah."
"And I didn't call Brookings," I said. "Just like a damn fool."
"Told you that you wouldn't call," she said.
The dark made her eyes glow.
"I enslaved you. I didn't want you to leave," she whispered.

CHAPTER 30.

Civil Un-Resting
or
The Voice of the People

"I saw McKissick's movie *Truck Stop Trouble* years and years ago," Yan said the next morning.

Gray mist hung outside the windows. It might have been natural fog rolling in from the Pacific, just a few miles away.

She sat up in bed without clothing. The half-light from outside dappled her. Her body showed muscled flanks and a ridged flat belly. She looked like a gymnast a few years past her prime.

"Even then, it was way old," she said. "Like, something my parents would watch."

"I prefer the quaintly-titled film '*You've Got One Comin'*,'" I said.

"Cinema tastes vary."

"Didn't you see her in *Risa, Queen of Jungle Love*, Mister Smarty-Pants?"

"Los Angeles remains a company town," I said. "And the company makes movies. When somebody dies in a Technicolor way, movie moguls sweat to cash in."

"You think you're so sharp and cool!"

"Not this week," I said. "Or else, I wouldn't be sleeping on your floor."

"You're not. On the floor, I mean. You're snoring along-side me. D'you know how much you snore, dude?"

"Even as a wee babe," I said. "Grandma Royster stated that I was a real window-rattler."

My shoulder muscle cracked as I reached for my phone inside my pants on the floor. Both our clothes lay tossed aside.

Just to be on the safe side, I looked through the front window to the street outside for Zygolt's car.

She had said that she would not be here today but she lived an unpredictable life and acted without thinking sometimes. She was unreliable but she was all that I had.

Her car was not outside. Tomorrow, I would have to check again at eight a.m.

My shoulders slumped. There was no rescue today.

"What are you doing?" she asked.

"I bet you put that question to all naked millionaire roustabouts in your bed. I'm calling on the halls of power."

My hand speared the phone and punched in Brookings' number.

"6125, please hold," a woman operator's voice said.

"My life on hold," I said.

"These coppers are so fascist," Yan said. "I kind of hope that they have another riot. Just to make a statement."

"Everyone loses with a riot," I said. "And from what I know of your LA euphemisms, you don't have riots here. You just have 'civil unrest.'"

Yan rose and switched on her TV set.

Traffic noise clashed outside as the TV came on. Cartoons played on the screen.

Yan switched channels.

A softly fat Black man stuffed into a dark blue police uniform swung a club at a clown lying limp on the floor sidewalk?

The club hit the clown.

Dust exploded from him.

"Stop resisting!" the police comedian hollered. "You under legal-type arrest for Conspiracy to Put a 'For Sale' Sign on Your Motor Vehicle!"

The television audience hooted and hollered.

"Stop it, Jesus!" a teenaged girl's voice shouted. "The Blood of Jesus is on Stupid!"

"There's that phrase again. Trailer-trash talk," I said. "It must mean something to somebody."

"You rambling, Max. Again and again."

"Police brutality," I said. "Everyone is an instant expert."

Yan cut off the TV and said a colorful word.

Brooking shouted from my cellphone.

"Royster, you didn't call me yesterday!"

"Glad we agree," I said. "I overslept."

"You planning to oversleep the Grand Jury?"

"Are you going to be at Hollywood Station today?"

"That can't matter to you. I'm calling you an 'unreliable witness'," Brookings said.

"For oversleeping?"

"For everything. NYPD sent me your file."

"My, oh, my," I said. "Did those Irish choirboy Budweiser Tribesmen stab me in the back? Again?"

"Lt. Lenny Hundshamer says that you're an unreliable witness."

"So is his mother," I said. "Everyone at her kennel says so. Brookings, I got a witness statement to put into your grand jury. And I'm going to do it. Why are you trying to block me?"

"I'm not."

"Then put me down on paper, shove me into testifying and let me get out of this nutty LA where everyone seems to hate everyone else."

"Anytime a lawyer produces a friendly witness, he's vouching for that witness to be honest and of good character," Brookings said. "So, how can I use you?"

"Try making up your own mind. Forget what the NYPD said."

"Royster, I'm trying to put together a complex case ending in someone's death," Brookings said. His voice climbed. "No case is more difficult than this one. We both know that these stakes are high. Have to do a balancing act between what people call justice and what justice really is.

"I already had to deal with Sgt. Poole and his nonsense. He's in big trouble. You're someone messing up a clear presentation to the Grand Jury. D'you think that I want this kind of case?"

My head ducked down like someone was swinging at me.

"Guess not," I said.

"The only thing sure about a prosecution like this is that nobody's gonna agree with what I do," he said. "Everyone's running to second-guess me already. If I wobble, they'll replace me. Some of this evidence, the kind that I cannot write down without the defense getting it, will get lost."

"I remember that from my cop days," I said. "Anything the D.A. writes down on paper has to go to the defense. That's why you prosecutors don't want to take too many notes."

"About time that you remembered that. If another DDA takes this case, and I forget some details, they are lost forever."

"And truth loses," I said. "I get you."

"Then stop fighting me."

"I'm not."

"You're just trying to get to Miami," he said. "That's clear to me. But you've got some responsibility right here. You're exactly the kind of clown that the material witness law was written for. And, if I get a chance, I'm going to have you in a cell until the trial comes around."

I wondered if anyone was listening to Brookings.

My eyes hop-scotched around Yan's apartment.

Daylight gave it the blues.

"Sound like you're losing control, Brookings," I said.

"I'm just realizing something now," he said. "You're a wild card. Don't know if you'll tell the truth or not. Don't know if I want you in my case."

"Dream on," I said. Temper thinned my voice. Hurling the phone felt like a good idea. "You're getting me whether you want me or not. But on my terms, not yours. Just look over your shoulder."

He hung up.

"You better not think about leaving here," Yan said.

She sprawled on the bed again.

"I mean, why would you leave me like this?" she asked.

"America."

"You can't leave me here."

"I'm sorry but I must," I said. "Please try to understand."

"You leave here now, you're not coming back!"

My ribs heaved. More shouting might weaken my will. Or it could bring on my good friends from the LAPD Hollywood Station.

"Then, I'll stay," I said. "For a little while."

CHAPTER 31.

Puttin' Up With It
or
All Kinds of Courage

Yan and I kept watching *Los Angeles Today- The Real Story of Civil Unrest* on the TV.

"We pulled over this Dee-Wee, what we call a drunk driver. 'Driving-While-Intoxicated,' in our radio slang," an officer said to an off-screen interviewer.

The officer was a frail Anglo woman with azure eyes over a peachy-cream complexion She blinked, once, maybe fighting shyness. Her eyes glowed in the child-like face. Under her left cheekbone, a round lump of skin bulged. Her chrome nameplate read "Seabrook" against her dark blue uniform shirt.

"Just a routine stop. But like they teach us in the academy, no traffic stop is ever routine. It's always an unknown stop."

Yan moved closer to me. Again I could sense the animal tang from her skin.

"Like a lot of folks," I said, "the police fascinate you. Ya may hate them or love them. But they won't bore you. For a woman like you, living alone in a 'hood like this, good cops are what you need to survive. Without them, your daily routine is much more risky."

"That's the kind of crud that gets me mad," she said.

"Perhaps," I said. "But it's realistic. Try getting through a day without any cops to protect you. D'you think that these TV radicals and instant experts will do it? Think that they got the heart and the dedication for that?"

On the TV screen, the officer squinted and blew out a long breath.

"Guy looked okay, normal," she said on the screen.

Her face twisted with feeling.

"And he was way drunk, at ten in the morning. He started to get out of the car. Talking 'bout his *medicina* and *pastilles*. That means 'pills'. We learn that much Spanish, one way or another.

"So, I told him, 'Sir, stay in the car. *Senor, no te meuves del coche.* More Academy Spanish. He was all cooperative, you know? Even weepy, some. I figured, Oh, wow, another sad drunk.

"Then, in one second. he changed to a monster. Cussed something and jumped me, knocked me down and covered me with his body. All his weight. Pinned me. Couldn't get anything free to hit him.

"Then he bit me. I could feel his teeth ripping my face, chewing it like you would a tough, gristly steak. Back and forth. His jaws chomp-chomp-chomping. Like someone who liked the taste so much that he didn't wanna swallow.

"Ya seen drunks come shaky out of a bar and tear into a roast beef hero. We have a lot of officers from different cultures in our ranks. Some get too romantic or bossy with their female partners. That can be tough to change. The Department was way scared about more sexual harassment charges, so they paired up women on patrol.

"This drunk's hands were all over my Sam Browne belt, like he was trying to grab my gun. Maybe he was. Nobody could tell, that's for sure.

"Now, I see this Officer Alwer case that everyone's screaming about. My partner, Becky, could have shot this drunk when he bit me."

"Maybe," I said to TV screen. "Maybe not."

"Because I couldn't defend my gun against a grab," the cop on the TV screen said. "Couldn't do anything. And if he gets my gun, the first thing he'll do is shoot Becky. Felt way mad at myself for letting this happen, even while it was going on. He was so violent, took me right by surprise.

"Becky hit the drunk again. Blood squirted, and his head went back. I hit him with my elbow. Smack in his eye. Detached his retina, we found out later.

"We can't use a baton to the head unless it's a life-or-death deal. But he was reaching for my gun and that sure qualifies. Otherwise, Becky would be in trouble with the brass. Get fired or prosecuted, even. Coppers get jailed for stuff like that. Like I said, we both could have shot him. So, what's happening to Officer Alwer could happen to me or any other cop.

"Becky hit him. Didn't stop him. But I saw this homeless guy run up and kick the drunk. Skinny Black guy, white-gray whiskers, pushing seventy, but he sure could kick.

"The drunk screamed. He got kicked again. The homeless guy kept kicking and shouting 'Get off that lady, man!' BAM! This homeless dude was like the ones we jack up every day. Some mutual bad feelings, sure. But not today. 'Get off that lady!' WHAM!

"Becky's trying to get the Taser, out of our car. But it was hung up under the seat.

"People came running up. They sat on the drunk so he couldn't get away. My backup got there way fast. Lights and sirens, Code Three.

"The locals put wet towels on my face, told me not to worry until the ambulance came. Wouldn't tell me how bad I looked. And I lost it. Kept begging them to show me a mirror so I could see the damage. Had to know. Doesn't make sense but that's how it was.

"And these beer-drinkers, card-players, old-time, old - school veterano gangster types from the 1970's, they were so great with me

"You think that all civilians hate you and then something like this shows up, and you realize how many good folks live in crap neighborhoods."

"We agree," I said, to the TV set. "On that, anyway."

In the hallway, a dog barked heavily. Maybe it was the pit bull I'd seen before.

"Dude got four years for driving drunk, felony ADW on a PO and Resisting. Turns out that he had cut another copper in Denver three years before and did an insanity plea. Claimed a back injury from the homeless guy kicking him. Sicced Internal Affairs on me for letting it happen. Can you believe that?"

"No way!" Yan said.

"That day changed me, too. I work more careful now. But I saw the good that people can do, surprising you.

"The doctors, facial surgeons, said to let my bite all heal natural. No stitches or anything. Cleaned it out and kept it clean. You can see the scar, right? Not a big deal. Little lumpy there. Makeup covers it. But I learned a lot that day, about how people really are, and I never forget that. Had a great career with the LAPD and want to keep protecting and serving as long as I can.

"But I worry about Officer Alwer and what this will do to her head. Public opinion is the real killer. Nobody understands it until they've been through it. "

CHAPTER 32

**Real Truth
or
Is This Just Pillow Talk?**

Somewhere in the middle of the night, we lay bundled up on Yan's bed.

"This is the quiet time in any big city," I said. "When traffic noise dies down. You can hear the water drip from the faucet. And you walk the floor, thinking."

"Thinking about what?" Yan asked.

"About the cops. And what happened here with Alwer and McKissick. I know what I saw happen there."

"You haven't told me what you saw."

"Yan, I'm saving that for the Grand Jury," I lied.

What I saw would not matter much. But I had to deal with it, somehow.

"Can't talk about it beforehand."

"But you're in my bed, now. And you're still not telling me."

"What does your bed have to do with me going to jail for perjury? Or contempt of court?"

"Sweetcakes, my bed and what I do in it, gotta, like, to do with everything."

"How so?"

"Bed's awesome. Happiest place. Nobody can get to you, like, mess with you there."

"You kids, overuse that word 'like,'" I said. "Have you noticed that? I have. After a while, the word 'like' grates a bit."

"Sweet-talker, you stalling?"

"Yan, I'll talk it up for the grand jury. Until that time, I'm holding my mud."

She wound her body against mine and my legs clenched.

"That's giving me a charley horse in my left leg," I said. "Same leg where I had knee surgery. Very romantic."

"*Brah* —"

"What's more important, Yan, is what this death joins hands with. The other police killings on videos. Most cop shootings are justified. I think so, anyway. But, some videos show us cops shooting people for little or no reason. "

"Nothing new there, *brah*. That always happened before. For years."

"That's what my Black friends say."

"And you?"

"I'm in a fix. I'm trying to figure out where the truth lies."

"You say 'us cops'. Still figure you're one of the gang, huh?"

"The gang might disagree," I said. "They're always trying to lock me down in Bellevue for life. While I was suffering through my two years of rocky, heartbreaking service, they kept suspending me.

"Little things like being ten feet off my foot post, trying to get warm in a January doorway. Ducking the wind blowing in off the East River. Not giving out the required number of public urination summonses. Leaving my apartment while on Sick Call."

"And you never saw any brutality?"

"Never. Maybe they knew enough not to break bad and do it in front of me. I told everyone up front that I wouldn't stand for that stuff. Wouldn't pretend that I didn't see it. Because, I would see it, all right. And step right in."

"Now what do you think?"

"When I watch some of these shootings on video, I see horrible policing and thoughtless murder. Some of the victims have no weapon. Not a can opener. Not a pocket-knife. This kind of shooting kicked off all those race riots in '67."

"Oh, here we go again!" she said. "Back to those race riots of '67! Who cares anymore?"

"Me, for one. I get the wild theory that the summer riots gashed a wound open and that wound never healed."

"Listen up, Mister History Channel," she said.

"There is no memory of it now," I answered.

"Like you said."

"Darn near no mention on the Internet. Which means that nobody under sixty years old will know much about it. I remember, reading on board that ship, that even Hartford, Connecticut, suffered a riot that summer. Hartford, insurance capital of the Free World."

"*Brah*, you keep running on about this," she said. "Way boring. Maybe you should write letters about of your ideas and not talk so much. Write a letter every day, like that actress did."

This was something new. Breathing hard, I tried to sound normal.

"How did you know that McKissick wrote letters all the time?" I asked.

Her head dipped down.

"I don't know," she said. "Guess they said so on TV or something. They talk about her 24/7."

Yan knew something more than she was saying. To learn what it was, I would have to stay close to her and ignore Brookings and his machinery.

To keep her unaware that she had just slipped, I went back to my lecture tone. These days, I seemed to be lecturing too much. Maybe I did that because nobody in Los Angeles seemed over-brimming with book knowledge.

"Their Senator Dodd called it a civil race war against Whites and I quote 'done by Black extremists controlled by Red China and Fidel Castro'."

"Senator baby sounds simple upstairs."

"Well, he HAD been an FBI agent, chasing Dillinger in the Thirties."

"Who's Dillinger?"

"Oh, he's just a name that I use to remind myself that I'm getting older. Remember names that nobody else does remembers."

"Boy, oh, boy!" Yan said. "That book. Did you read it or didja inhale it?"

"It is worth remembering. Milwaukee, Wisconsin, hit the fan with one dead cop, three dead civvies and 1,500 busted. Buffalo, New York, didn't do much better."

"Boyfriend, this is such a downer. Blood and death and stuff. Why does it matter?"

"Look outside the window tonight and you'll see," I said. "That's why. Why is everyone here so angry with everyone else?"

"Dudes come to LA to make money and then split. That's what I did. Why else would anyone leave Hawaii where I had my family and all? California, 'The Golden State,' like it says on our license plates. I dig the money you can make here. Real cash. Rents are cheaper here. Can save for the future. Living too long without bucks, winding up in someone's alley, homeless and wrinkled and old, that really scares me. and stuff and then go. Moved away and come back twice.

"Hawaii don't do racism on color, but watch out, tourists! Here in LA nobody mixes. Ya gotta know your street.

"*Haoles* like me run from Blacks and Latinos and don't try talking to them too much. Those guys keep hitting on me so I run clear. Zip up the windows, hit the AC and zoom away. Me, I don't feel like I know LA much, just my walking-around blocks here in Hollywood."

"So, LA is still a gold-rush mess, filled with money-grubbing nerved-up jokers speeding through life and crashing into each other in mammoth traffic jams?" I asked.

"Guess so."

"Then I give up on trying to understand this place," I said. "Better I should just fly."

"But you can't, Max. Cops and stuff. I heard you on the phone. FBI's ready to shoot you on sight."

"LA needs to change," I said.

"You can't do it. Got other stuff to worry about. Like those riots."

"Call me paranoid. "But I get the feeling that cities like Syracuse, New York, and Grand Rapids, Michigan, covered up and tried to sweep away the riots that they lived through in '67. But, more important, what are these cops doing, shooting innocents for running away, no weapons in their hands? That is way wrong. Maybe I should listen to these radicals more carefully."

BOP! BOP! BOP! blasted outside.

Nerves screamed.

My body slewed across hers. We dragged each other to floor. Scared made me feel sick.

"Shots fired!" I yelled. "Don't move!"

Chapter 33.

In the Middle Of the Night
or
Swapping Philosophies

"You all jacked, man," Yan said. "It's only firecrackers."

My breathing cut me. The left side of my chest ached. That was no good. This was bad timing to need the heart doc again.

"Maybe," I panted. "But I knew a guy, once. He heard noise like that, said it was firecrackers, too. Then he fell down. Bleeding, like. And he didn't get up again. Or talk."

"In that case, I'm calling the cops," she said, spearing her cellphone. "911, baby. Enough talk, now."

"Don't do that," I said. "Call the Man, I mean."

"You think that I wanna get shot? Nutso."

"You're like all the other civilians," I said. Everything felt like I was playing for time. "Slam the police when you're feeling fat and safe and comfortable. But, when the tragic thing never comes to pass, you forget all about needing us."

"Ain't that how we are?" she asked.

"Please stay off your phone," I said.

"You fricking nuts or something?"

"Realistically, the cops can't catch that enterprising young nimrod shooting off his hope-and-dream firearm. They're way too swamped to respond. But they might use their system to find me."

"With my phone?"

"Call me paranoid. But your phone just might get pin-pointed by communication towers to this address. And I don't the Blue Meanies sitting on my lap just as yet."

"They can't find you through my phone."

"Maybe not. But I run from risks."

"Maybe you're just afraid to call the cops about the shots or firecrackers or whatever they were."

"Naw. The mopes'll stop shooting. Run out of bullets. Some other taxpayer will call."

She kept moving against me.

"Somehow," I said, "this feels more comfortable, chatting and fussing with you. Like I belong here."

"Yeah. Funny, huh?"

"Hilarious," I said.

"And I'm supposed to be unstable," she said. "Shrinks say so."

"NYPD said the same thing about me," I said. "Let's ignore them together."

Hugging each other, we slipped back into comfort. This felt so rare.

"I said I like it that you told me about your girlfriend in China," she said.

"Not my girlfriend," I said. "My life."

"Your life in China," she said. "Not Hollywood. Good that you can feel that way about someone. When did you last see her?"

"She had a dog-show in New York last year," I said. "Not since then."

"Rough stuff, dude."

Another helicopter zoomed overhead.

"This hasn't happened to me for a long time," I murmured.

"Gunshots?"

"You know what I mean."

"Yeah."

Her eyes seemed to probe mine. They looked innocent. There was no way that she could suffer trouble or need doctors for her feelings. Somebody medical had messed up and read the wrong chart.

We drifted back into hugging and kissing, like a warm bath-tub full of clear water.

"You're lots older than me," she said. "But I dig you somehow. Don't know why. Maybe looking for my Daddy."

"Who was he?"

"Hippie type who would dress up, take a straight job and then quit after he saved enough loot. Take us up into the woods, live in a cabin, chop wood, grow veggies and bow-hunt game for food. Sometimes it worked out. Other times, we went hungry. He and my mother never planned jack, man."

"Did they run out of cash?"

"Every time, guy. At six, I could see it happening before they did. Said that I was never going hungry again, those headaches and growly feeling inside. Always have a stash of loot somewhere nearby."

"But you don't know why you like me."

"Never figure that one out, man. So I just roll with it."

"Roll away," I murmured.

We seized each other, kissed and dozed some more.

"Penny for your thoughts?" she asked some time later.

"Nothing right now," I fibbed. Ruining the mood would be crass. "Just drifting."

"Been married, Max?"

"Once. It didn't flourish."

"Why?"

"Like most messed-up marriages, both of us helped spoil the dance. We cooperated."

"Marrying a copper would feel all creepy."

"Wasn't a cop when we spliced together. Just a fat happy chef. Friends scattered everywhere."

"But you had the cop dream."

"Never," I said. "Had the dream of getting a soft city job and a pension. Lady Yan, I lasted barely two years as a cop. Suspended all the damn time."

"Why?"

"Sergeants."

"What did you do?"

"I spoke truth to power."

"And what happened?"

"Power didn't much care for it."

Outside, on the street, some fool triggered more shots.

The sound made us clutch each other.

"As a rookie cop," I said, "everyone treats you like you're five years old. A punishment-centered bureaucracy. You can't decide anything for yourself. And nothing stays clear.

"Everything that you do can get you punished by the bosses, sued by the clients or shot by some thug. Every rule gets bent every day. It's a mess."

"For instance?"

"Instance: a man can't evict his girlfriend out of his apartment if she has established residency there. With street people, what is residency? Is it her name on the lease? Her clothes in his closet? How much clothing? Mail addressed to her there?"

"Why not just let her stay there, Max?"

"Because, with all that anger bubbling around, both guy and gal are in danger. They argue. Nobody is happy. For cash reasons or other reasons, nobody can leave. But they should. Just to keep the peace."

"But the cops should just leave them alone," she said. "Let them work out their own problems."

"That's well-meaning amateurs talk," I said. "And it's dangerous. Because experts show us time and time again, that when people feel trapped, one of them will reach for the rolling pin, the knife or the pot of boiling water.

"They'll tell themselves 'Well, I called the cops, and they couldn't do anything. I can't take this anymore, even after some drinks or blow to settle myself. So, I gotta do something.' And, they do. Believe me, Yan, they do."

"That is so screwed up, your thinking," Yan said. "What about the arguments between sex partners where they talk things out, promise to do better and go to sleep holding each other? And they never need cops. How about those?"

"If a cop gambles that it will turn out that way and loses," I said, "then someone gets hurt. Burned, slashed, killed. How many times would you want to gamble that, based on guessing?"

CHAPTER 34.

Facing the Day
or
How Much Longer Can We Cuddle?

"So, why does establishing residency matter so fricking much?" Yan asked me.

"Because, if the person renting the place has their name on the lease, they can have a guest. And said renter can ask the guest to leave. So can the cops. But if that guest has 'established residency', to wear out the phrase, in that apartment, you can only sling him or her out through legit formal eviction notices. Which are a pain."

"And if a cop forces some tenant due to leave without the law?"

"The cop gets suspended, loses vacation days and the city refuses to defend him in civil court. So the wronged party can sue the cop for cash and win without hardly trying. The cop might get fired, lose his pension, no college for his kids. That's why residency matters.

"And each sergeant on Patrol has his own ideas on what is 'residency'. That's the trouble with policing. Society tells us, 'Judge what can't be judged.'

"Working street patrol, you never knew how the bosses were going to react. That's why so many good cops run to get off patrol."

"You're stretching."

"No, I'm not," I said. "How many times do you see a gray-haired street cop? Wise cops, older cops, they get off Patrol and get away from all these questions that nobody wants to answer."

"Think anyone cares?"

"Only when you want your new lover or boyfriend tossed out of your bed and apartment by the cops. Like most civilians, you want your life back. Wonder why this dumb cop is asking all these wombat questions about who has keys, and how long he has been wallowing in your bed. Then it's not so dull."

"Crazy stuff, man."

"That's just one rule that patrol cops have to remember to protect themselves. Many, many others. The world, the civilized, white-bread, nine-to-five jokers, by the office water-cooler, want cops to solve society's toughest problems. And be polite and thorough and soft-spoken while doing so."

"You're just griping, Max. You knew what the job was when you took it."

"When I took the job, I knew nothing about it except that New York cops looked pudgy and angry. Then I learned why."

"Just feeling sorry for yourself."

"With good reason. The average American man lives seventy-four winters But the average cop only makes it to fifty-nine. We feel cheated."

"Blame that on doughnuts."

"Blame it on sergeants. And the public."

By now, Yan's face felt familiar to me, as if we had known each other for years. Looking into her eyes, I couldn't see any hint of lying or any mark of illness. She had thrown out comments about her head problems. But nothing showed.

Her talk about McKissick came back to me. Something felt wrong there and I was going to learn what it was.

"I guess that I'm starting to trust you," she said. "So, here's a spare key to this place. And the street door key. You deserve your freedom, come and go like you want. Call me crazy but you're not going to steal my bookcase or something."

"Thanks," I said.

"Don't thank me," she said. "Maybe I'm doing something dumb, the key and all."

"These helicopters zooming overhead keep lighting up your street," I said. "Beautiful palm trees you got here on the corner. Some corners here, you can see mountains. I just wish this beautiful land was matched by the jokers living here."

"So you calling us 'jokers'?"

"There's some funny stuff going on when Angelenos try talking to each other about anything. I never sense much real communication. Even that lawyer Brookings. Can't tell what he really wants. Maybe he doesn't even know."

"Does that matter?"

"Not to be melancholy. but if folks can't communicate, riots like the ones after Rodney King will happen again. Or those 1967 riots all over again."

Outside, more guns fired. They sounded like small calibers, close by. By habit, ducked.

"Hear those other shots now?" she asked.

"Let's not have that debate again. No cops, okay?"

We drifted back to sleep.

❦

Helicopters roared back over us again. White spotlights hit Yan's windows and walked across her dingy floors and heaps of movie magazines, paperback and boxes of crackers. Like before, the engines sounded like they were punishing Angelenos for living here.

"I never get used to these cops here," she said. "No matter how long I stay here in this nuthouse city."

"Every cop agency reflects their city in some way," I said. "That's the problem here."

"Their helicopters keep buzzing over my block, Max. Look now. Shining the spotlight into everyone's fricking apartment. Lighting up everything. Scaring kids. Scaring ME. Can they do that? That legal?"

"Can't hear you."

"Too loud, man. They do that stuff all the time. Mean, I want them to save my butt and all. But they don't have to make me deaf doing it.

"Other places, they just send a car and cruise the area. Think that they got some big plan to punish anyone who calls 911. They get off on waking up the world with their engines and their spotlights."

"Like I said before, you're thinking loose," I said.

Maybe she was feeling the drugs that she took now. They might muddy up her head.

"You want them to save you by your way, not by theirs," I said. "Maybe they're establishing order. Telling us who is boss. Domination. Young angry cops love to remind everyone that the cops are in charge. They're new and tense, and they figure that without their bodies, hands, guns and shouts, everything will fall apart."

"Were you like that when you were a young cop? Angry?"

"Joined at forty-two, Yan. Just wanted the medical benefits and the pension. The city could have hired me as a zookeeper, pedicuring wallabies or manicuring kangaroos, for all of me."

"Can't be a cop when you're forty-two, *brah*."

"You can try. I took the test at twenty-three and the city lost my papers for nineteen years. Acting as my own lawyer, I danced into court, put on a great tearjerker performance and threatened to sue them."

She wrapped her arms around me and rested her head on my chest. It made me feel like a teenager again.

"Judge was a fat old ward-heeler, political clown, kept falling asleep. Finally granted my motion. Probably so he could take another nap. The Department let me join."

More helicopter noise chopped the night apart and broke it over our heads.

"Does scare me," I said. "Loud, loud, loud. Makes me feel like I'm caught in their infernal hellish machine."

"Huh?"

"Caught, Yan. Like you. Like everyone else in this lovely city. 'We got you, sucker.' It's not a true feeling. There are great cops here. I see how well they work.

But the fear rides with me, just the same. Everything makes me feel like I gotta apologize to the cops for breathing. Because some of them are angry and unpredictable. I'm caught in their white-hot spotlights and head-breaking noise machines. And I can't get out."

CHAPTER 35.

Getting Close to the People
or
Why Some Cops Don't

Somewhere in the middle of the night, we woke up, holding each other.

"Some reason, can't sleep," Yan murmured.

"Me neither," I said. "Nerves."

Yan sighed. She clicked on her laptop. It buzzed and warmed a bluish light. She put on a local TV news station.

"Love can't conquer all," I muttered. "Even, with all this chaos going on and I should want to know about it, TV news still makes these li'l red hairs on the back of my neck stand up."

"You always talking too much nutty stuff," Yan said.

"Even so," I said. "TV news can put me back into the Land of Nod."

"Land of Nod?"

"Sleep."

The feeling of tired came back over me again and stretched out my body.

Maybe I drooled some. True elegance.

Yan talking woke me up again.

"Check this out, homeboy," she said.

"Aughhh?" I asked.

"Just check it."

"What?"

"This You Tube video just went viral," she said. When she was sleepy, she lisped a bit. It made her seem innocent and child-like.

Her eye pupils looked dilated now. That told me that she may have taken some drugs. Grass, coke or amphetamines would do that to her eyes.

Yan was not the traditional homespun woman type. Staying with her might wreck me.

But somehow being with her felt right to me. Maybe I was losing my perspective. Perhaps this was the year when I would start using people.

"It just happened," she said.

She pointed a nail painted mauve at her laptop computer screen.

The screen showed an alley driveway near some palm trees. Far away, the white Hollywood sign showed on a hillside.

Angelenos in casual clothes drifted in front of the camera. Some sucked canned beers. They were Latino, Asian, Black, White and everyone else. Kids skittered next to seniors, headphones on and metal bits showing in their lips and cheeks.

"Maybe that's their lawbreaking civil disobedience," I mumbled. "The right to pound down some suds in public view whenever they wanna."

On the laptop screen, the crowd started talking.

"Stuff just ain't right," a man's scratchy voice said off-camera. "What they do, people –"

"Not only that," another man said. "Yeah. Righteous. I read this book…"

"Video-speak," I said. "A new low in communication."

A black-and-white lurched into the camera's view.

"Read this book…" the same man's voice kept saying.

The group shied away from the patrol car. They looked like guilty school kids about to play a prank on teacher.

"Afternoon, everybody," the cop said from inside the car. He sounded loose and friendly.

"Cop's working solo," I said to Yan. "Even with all this riot talk bouncing around. He's either mad confident or got a wild kind of Tombstone courage."

"What's 'Tombstone courage'?" Yan asked me.

"That's a quality that dumb brave cops get," I said. "They believe that they are Wyatt Earp , taming the Wild West town of Tombstone gunslingers and that nothing can hurt them. They're wrong."

Yan's apartment had turned cooler. Some chill brushed against my skin. Los Angeles was a desert city, with only irrigation and sprinklers keeping it green.

Like most deserts, sundown took the heat away and the nights felt cold. Yan's blanket felt good against the chill.

Daybreak would bring the sun and the cheery LA weather. But that was far off.

On the screen, Mexican mariachi music played somewhere. The trumpet shrilled and climbed. It sounded like a melancholy dirge.

The cop lurched out of his car, burly, with a bald head and a gleaming black leather holster holding a long-barreled revolver against the dark blue uniform.

A traditionalist would carry that revolver. Some trusted the balance and reliability of the revolver over the newer, quick-shooting semi-automatic pistols.

With a bump, I recognized the cop as Taus, the same one who had talked with me in Tiny's sandwich shop.

The music changed. Now the trumpet blared out rapid notes.

Helicopter noise buzzed overhead.

"What's happening here?" Taus asked. "What can I do for you folks?"

A White guy, standing shorter than Taus, wearing rimless glasses and wispy blond hair going fast, hunched closer to the car. Glasses bobbled on his pug nose.

"Son, I say, son," the man with the bobbling glasses said. "I just can't understand it."

"Can't understand what?" Taus asked.

Taus stepped closer to the man.

Others drifted in behind Taus.

"That woman dying," Bobbles drawled. He spoke with the timing of someone comfortable speaking in public.

Maybe he was a stand-up comic in between gigs. He sported a Puckish, mischievous look about him and held a smile that he could not swallow. On the screen, his delivery sounded rehearsed.

"Hurt me bad, son," Bobbles said.

"Hurts everyone, Mr. Willis," Taus said. "Nobody normal wants to kill anyone."

"Yeah, but," Bobbles said.

Hunger spiraled through my gut, but I wanted to see what would happen on the video.

On the screen, more blue jean locals got between Taus and his car.

A White woman, reedy and dapper in a gold polo shirt and tailored hip-huggers, took off her wristwatch and made a fist.

Another man, pudgy and sunburned, with bristling black curls, slipped a bandanna from his shorts pocket and tied a knot in it. He yanked the bandanna tight in his hands.

"TAUS, GET OUT OF THERE!" I hissed.

"Know that cop?" Yan asked me. Surprise lifted her voice.

On the screen, more shapes drifted by Taus.

They said things that I could not hear.

Then another shape barged into the camera's view.

Bobbles was still speaking with Taus. Taus' smile shone against the blue uniform.

His belt radio kept talking.

"Any unit in the vicinity," the belt radio said with a woman's nasal voice. "6A-17, 6A-17, see the woman at 496 Selma Avenue in Hollywood Division. Domestic violence dispute. All units, use caution. Suspect has an attack canine on the premises. No suspect description, no further."

"Now!" Bobbles shouted.

Fists slugged into Taus. Taus shook his head like some-one in shock and hit back. A kick smashed into the radio on his belt. The radio flew out of the leather holder and onto the sidewalk. It squealed.

The man with the bandanna wrapped it around Taus' neck and yanked it tight. Taus choked. Someone grabbed Taus' baton and slid it from his middle. The baton flashed and hit Taus.

"Murderer!" a woman cawed.

Bobbles pinned Taus' arms from behind.

Taus head-butted backwards.

Bobbles ducked.

Another fist hit Taus, and he howled.

Taus kicked out.

Another man dropped.

"Get back!" Taus choked.

More fists hit him. The baton swung into his crotch.

Taus crumpled.

The camera shook.

Taus strained against Bobbles' arms holding him.

More bodies slammed into Taus.

"Blood of Jesus!" a man shouted.

Another body blotted out the camera.

Bobbles' glasses sideways.

"Yech!" Bobbles shouted to the woman in the gold polo shirt. "You hit me!"

Taus went to the ground.

The bandanna fell.

Feet stomped Taus.

The baton swung again.

Taus covered his holster and curled up.

His knees went up.

"Break him down!" the woman shouted. "Make him pay! Punk him!"

"Blood of Jesus!" Bobbles shouted.

"Get his knees!" the woman shouted. "So he can't walk no more!"

Someone screamed.

Maybe it was Taus.

"Look!" Bobbles shouted. "Officer Taus cracking up!"

The camera found Taus, who was crying.

"Stop it!" Taus wailed. "Stop hurting me!"

"You're nothing!" Bobbles shouted. "None of you cops! Your day is dead! Right?"

Taus' face, red, bruised and blooded, showed again.

"Right," Taus whimpered. "What you say. Just stop hurting me."

His bald head vanished under the bodies.

The screen went to black.

Yan looked at me.

"What they say," she said. "Thousands of viewers already saw this clip."

"And millions more will see it," I said.

Chapter 36.

Crude Awakening
or
Real Life

By morning, Yan wrenched me in two ways at once, but I rolled up from her bed and reached for my clothes.

I looked through the window outside but did not spot Zygolt's station wagon. It was a Buick Roadmaster with wooden panels, the kind you rarely see anymore, and I would never forget it

For another day, I would have to wing it.

"*Brah*, you going somewhere, seems like?" Yan asked. "I got you all restless or something?"

"Didn't want to wake you?"

"You such a airhead sometimes. How I'm gonna feel, wake up later and you gonna feel, bed all empty?"

"I'll be back, Yan."

"You do that. And just maybe I don't let you back in."

Stung by that, I footed downstairs away from her bed.

℘

A warning clicked in my head about Yan, a feeling that something is hacked up, and I couldn't figure out exactly what it was.

Outside on Willoughby, I heard glass smashing to my left. So, I stepped right, forcing myself to walk and not run.

My eyes swept along the street, looking for any signs of surveillance. The cars along the curb looked empty, without any coffee cups on the dashboards or cigarette piles outside the driver's window.

Believe it or not, some stakeouts were still that obvious. Detectives playing the lazy game. Stakeouts could make you that way.

BASH!

Something broke near me. Glass sparkled.

BAM! went something else.

Someone was winging bottles at me from the rooftop.

My feet hopped me up onto my toes.

My heart hammered.

SMASH!

Another bottle rained down from above.

My head jerked around.

I could not see the glassware-slinging fools.

More bottles smashed around me.

I ran.

The pavement smacked my feet.

"Party time!" a man's voice shouted from high above me.

I looked up.

Three White losers with doo-rags on their head were throwing bottles at me.

Zigzagging, I dodged the incoming glass.

My body slammed into someone heavy on the street and spun around, and I sprawled onto my bad left knee.

Pain corkscrewed through me.

The someone reached down and yanked me to my feet. My knee screamed again.

"Man, they crazy!" the someone shouted.

A husky Black guy with a vain pencil moustache dusted me off.

"Kill some sucker that way!"

The White doo-rag losers broke and scattered across the rooftops.

Another knot of men, Latinos in stiff black cowboy hats and boots under blue jeans, came around the corner. They circled a parked gray van. They used their boots to kick in the windows and ravage the van.

"What are Latinos rioting for?" I asked. "Ain't no Latinos involved in this mess. Why are Whites throwing bottles at me? Or were they aiming at you?"

Pencil Moustache shrugged. Now, he looked older, pushing seventy.

"Maybe LA gone crazy," he said.

"Who could tell?" I asked.

"I hear you," he said.

"Black police kills a Black homeless lady," I rattle on. "Then why do Latinos and pink folks feel that they GOTTA throw anything loose lying around? Is that supposed to fix things?"

He shrugged.

Something burst bright lights in my head. My sight went.

Pain burned.

I felt myself dragged somewhere.

Then I was falling downstairs. Stone steps barked my kneecaps.

Being scared turned me to a sweaty mess.

My sight came back.

A foot had kicked me down the steps. I did not know whose it was. Not Pencil Moustache who kicked me. My head turned to see him throwing combination punches at a group surrounding him. His fists pumped.

At the bottom of the steps, my back slammed against metal doors.

A body smelling of onions smashed into me.

Knuckles hit my jaw.

A door opened, and I fell backwards.

Now I was inside a basement. I could not see. Another fist smacked me.

My jaw numbed. Another blow one hit me.

"Party! Party!" A nasal voice shouted. Feet hit my spine.

I sagged.

They kept kicking me.

CHAPTER 37.

Shelter?
or
Hide Me In Plain Sight

More bodies slammed into me.

Street people pushed me deeper into the basement. No light hit here.

Arms scissored around my neck and squeezed. Someone's mouth smelled of rum.

"Awrk," I croaked.

"Stomp him!" someone behind me said with a giggle.

"Awrk," I repeated. My usual war cry.

My foot lashed out, hit something hard, but my bones felt broken. Trying to ignore the pain, I kicked again into the dark.

"Aww, we got us a tough guy!" a Southern drawl twanged.

"Toughest guy in my ballet class," I said.

I found Southern Drawl's leg with my kick. He cussed. My next kick pushed him back. Someone hit my forehead. But the dark worked against them. They could not see me terrified of their hands and feet,

I dropped to the floor. It smelled like a mop. I spun onto my back and kicked low. Both my feet flew out. They hit legs.

"Stomp that chump!" Southern Drawl said.

"This chump de-parting," I whispered. "Tout de suite."

"You dying here, ace!" a woman's voice shouted in my ear. She came from nowhere.

More bodies crowded me. My feet kicked out again and hit a wall. The shock stunned my legs.

"Gonna cut you throat right here!" the woman shouted again.

Stay here, die here, I thought,

My elbows and knees swung everywhere. I felt wet things on my skin. Nerves screamed at me. I felt like crying for Mommy.

"Teach him not to walk here!" a man hollered off to my left. "Don't know nobody here!"

Stay here, die here, I told myself again.

I bolted back out the doorway and up the steps. The feet felt like they belonged to some other joker. I could not move them faster.

&

On the street, everything smelled of burning rubber. Glass shattered. The gray buildings with shut windows looked down on me. I felt like I was wandering around in some nutty nightmare, without any plan or logic to it.

No cars moved down the Hollywood streets. That was a bad sign in Los Angeles, where everyone lived behind the wheel. Some Bad Elements roved over the corners up ahead.

In a hardware store that also sold Mexican food in front, I copied the keys that Yan had given me.

My legs ached. They carried me past the death scene at Gower. The fake cowboy stores in the Gower Gulch looked shut. Fear was keeping us Americans from shopping. Another bad sign.

For once, the door to Florida's dance studio was closed. Florida might be inside sleeping on his sofa. Dance studio entrepreneurs sometimes lived in their studios when they were starting out.

I hammered on the door with my fist. Hollywood fell more quiet. Nothing stirred inside. No Florida to shelter me. The street nuts could still find me.

LA does not have a riot now, I thought. Not yet. But they are making progress that way.

The nearby Bad Element did not look like any charmers that I wanted to forge a relationship with. I pushed myself faster along the pavements and back into Yan's apartment building.

Her door was unlocked. She must have forgotten to turn the key. Marijuana smell told me why.

My hand pushed in her door. She was placing a cream-colored photo album under the kitchen sink cabinet. When she saw me, she froze. Her eyes said she was riding high on something.

"It's Max," I panted. "Did you miss me?"

❧

Some time later, we woke up in bed. Getting hit guaranteed deep sleep, like whiskey used to do. I could go under sleep's tide, turn over and never hit bottom.

My skin and nerves recalled the fists and feet that had slammed me, and I swore once again to get into shape and learn to fight better. But life never worked like the movies. The street people who had slugged me had probably been born and raised fist-fighting the whole world.

My middle-class childhood slowed me too much to enjoy fights. I would always lose and the other side, the scrappers, would always win.

The burning rubber smell still wafted through the apartment. Tangled music grated from the street. Naked, she rose and moved to bend and drink water from the kitchen sink tap.

"Keep things quiet," she said. "'cause I'm scared."

"YOU'RE scared?" I rolled over, sleep fleeing me. "However do you think I feel?"

"You say that it's not just Blacks fighting Whites outside? No race stuff?"

"Just fools cutting up normals," I said. "So far, I'm a normal. But that could change any minute and I become like the rest of them."

"See what happens when you go outside? Stay here, Max."

"Because I'm so strong and healthy?"

She shot me a look. Her face twisted, but I had no idea why. The silence hung.

"What is it?" I said. "What are you not telling me?"

"Oh, no mind games? We gonna play policeman now?"

"Don't give me any more mysteries," I said. "I'm still scared by that mob outside. Those wastrels in that basement could stomp me into fresh farm scrapple. The LAPD would not find my body down there for months. If ever."

Something smashed below us. Yan grabbed my arm.

"Don't make any noise," she whispered. "Think they smashed in my front door. They in the building now."

CHAPTER 38.

Here Comes Company
or
Home Invasion

Down below, feet ran through the halls.

Nobody shouted. That scared me more. The characters downstairs might be planning home invasions and not wanting anyone to hear their voices.

"How strong is your apartment door here?" I whispered.

"Way, mad strong. That's one thing the owner's good for. Nobody's kicking that monster in. Go back to sleep."

"Are you serious?" I asked. "Jesus H. Christ on little rubber crutches, how d'you know that nothing's gonna happen."

We wrapped arms around each other.

Somehow, I slept again. Maybe the worries dulled the pain and bruises until they knocked me out.

⓾

"Because I'm so strong and healthy?" I repeated later that morning in Yan's bed. Hours ago, I had said that phrase to Yan.

Her beauteous face had shot me a strange twisted and angry look from my words.

The beating made me feel like a skeleton hit by a jet. Everything hurt. Some morning, I might wake up and not be able to wiggle my ears.

My thoughts needed to get clear about her. There was not much strong and healthy about me. She could find better, younger and stronger men than I was. So she was doing this for some hidden reason. There was something that I had and she wanted it.

The only way to discover that was to spend more time with her. If I left and stayed away, I would never know.

And, somehow, McKissick's death was tied into this Hollywood love-nest with Yan.

Koy seemed very far away from me on her way to China right now and I missed her more than I wanted to say.

Outside, the city lay still. It felt as if there had never been fools torching cars or trying to stomp me.

"Maybe it was all in good, clean fun," I whispered. "Them mischievous carefree Angelenos."

As if she heard me, Yan murmured something in her sleep. That sucked my breath in. Turning back on my side, I nuzzled her neck and slipped back into sleep like a canoe gliding out from the shore.

❧

Later on, we woke and whispered soft words to each other.

She swallowed some pills with more tap water.

Outside was still quiet. I still felt scared.

"Yeah," she whispered. "Whatever happens, just go with it for the moment."

Maybe her drugs were talking.

Later, stealing up from Yan's bed, I heard a car engine rev up and sputter.

Checking the time, I saw that it was after eight a.m. Maybe Zygolt had kept her word and gotten here.

Carefully, I drew the curtain blinds. A wood-trimmed Buick Roadmaster bumped past my apartment. At this distance, with my contacts out, the driver's face blurred. I used the trick of pulling the skin near my right eye with my index finger. That always strengthened the eye.

Now I could see Zygolt, my Showbizzer boss-lady, at the wheel. Her white curls showed. Relieved, I sank back to sleep. My Showbizzers were outside, sneaking around, waiting to help me.

∽

Half an hour later, I showered and dressed in the clothes hand-washed and air-dried yesterday. It was time for a wardrobe change.

The American Motel staff was probably selling off my clothes from my room in a yard sale.

The basement smell still followed me and my bones creaked and fought back against moving.

"Today, I must away, my love," I said to Yan.

"Don't clear out of here like this," she murmured.

Again, something clicked inside me. Her answer sounded fake. Why would she want me to stay here? Nobody could call me movie-star handsome. Maybe, under her slangy talk, she was as scared as I was.

"Don't hurl flowery compliments at me," I said. "Bipeds will say we're in love."

She sighed. Her body moved.

"All right," she said. "Can you get back here when you finish your business? Whatever it is."

"Yes, I can."

"Then, later," she said.

She gave me a hug and a quick kiss.

∽

My feet brought me downstairs.

The street door sagged to one side. It lay useless. The hoodlums had smashed the lock out. Wood splinters lay everywhere. That was not my problem anymore. Being a civilian could feel very liberating.

Before going out, my eyes swept the streets for more groups.

There were none, but the lingering burning smell still made my tongue curl up.

I ventured outside.

Zygolt was parked in at the curb, fifty yards away.

Moving slowly, I walked to the station wagon and slid into the back seat.

Zygolt kept facing front. An aging dancer, she showed the rewards of dieting and discipline in her long slim frame. Age only showed in the lines near the eyes and on her neck.

"Boss-man looks a bit shot to hell," Zygolt said.

"How true," I said. My hand took out my wallet and handed her some cash.

"Lot of money, boss-man," she said.

"What's with the pidgin English, Zygolt?" I asked. "Showing off your rebel streak again?"

"This serf thinks for herself, boss-man. How did you ever decide that you could give us orders? 'Hey, you, Zygolt, drive on into war-zone Los Angeles on a hush-hush mission for me. If you're not busy, that is.'"

"Some of that money is for you. Aren't Showbizzers usually broke?"

"Been happy at home and now you got me driving through the desert from Basta," she said. "Don't like driving at night. Can't see enough. Landed here too early. And then playing gal detective, waiting for you way too long."

"Just like I trained you and the others on surveillance. Good job putting the car where I could see it from that address."

"No flattery, boss-man. Now that I got this money, I'm heading for an old lover's apartment to take a hot bath and get some sleep. And nobody can stop me. What's your scheme? Why do you need me?"

Slouched down so that nobody could see me, I told Zygolt my plan.

She blew out a breath and shook her white curls.

"Won't work," she said. "Where d'you come up with these crazy half-baked ideas?"

"Let's try anyway, okay?" I asked. "Right now, I need you to drive me over to LAPD Hollywood Station."

"More Hardy Boys-type plans?"

Behind us, a siren screeched, then stopped. I heard a shotgun's RACK-RACK!

"Police!" a voice shouted over the loudspeaker. "Put your hands outside the windows!"

CHAPTER 39.

Control
or
Community Relations

My hands went out the window and stretched, showing all my fingers. Nervous LAPD cops and shotguns made a very bad combination.

"Don't reach for anything," the loudspeaker voice said.

"Why?" Zygolt said. "We're not doing anything wrong. This is so unfair."

"So is double-ought buckshot," I said.

"Driver!" the steel voice behind us said.

My eyes flew through the alley. There were no doorways to duck into. A steel dumpster squatted ten feet away.

"With your left hand, take the keys out of the ignition and throw them on the ground. Outside the vehicle."

"What did I do?" Zygolt cawed.

"Zygolt, don't ask that," I said. "Stop thinking like a dancer. They got a shotgun pointed at us. Talking time is done."

"Driver!" the LAPD voice rang out. "Do it now!"

"Don't move, whatever you do," I said to Zygolt. "If they check me, they'll pull me in as a Material Witness for that DDA Brookings character. You play dumb. I got to run."

One LAPD car growled behind us. More would come soon. My foot kicked open the passenger door, and I sprang out, aiming for the dumpster.

KRUUMP!

My ears blew out.

"Awwww!" I croaked.

My head hit the dumpster. That hurt, too. The cop had fired the shotgun but missed me.

He had no reason for it. My jumping made him nervous. Maybe it was an accident. Warning shots like that were prohibited.

"Police officer!" I shouted.

It came out bad.

A second blast would kill. My head felt numb from hitting the dumpster.

Zygolt floored her Buick. It fishtailed, straightened out and tore away.

"Don't blame you," I whispered. "Wish I could run."

So did the cops. Their car lurched and went hurtling down an alley, away from Zygolt.

Shooting like that was illegal. So the cops would stay off the radio, hide themselves, re-load the shotgun and persuade each to forget about it. In true cop tradition, they would get their stories straight. This reminded me of my Patrol years again.

If nobody took down their car number, they were in the clear. Or they would gamble it that way.

The cop car WHOOSHED! Turned the corner and was gone.

My head still rang from pain but I forced myself up and moving. Taxpayers might hear that shotgun blast and call it in. And the LAPD would roll on it and find bruised me staggering about.

Or maybe nobody would care enough.

Two streets passed under my feet. It felt like the morning after of a whiskey weekend. My fingertips felt my face. My right eye seemed have skin bulging out just beneath.

If anyone back in Manhattan asked about my black eye, I could tell that I got in Los Angeles dumpster-diving.

❧

Putting distance between my body and the shotgunned dumpster felt wise. So I did it as fast as I could, down the Hollywood streets. My gut said that something bad might happen there.

Nobody was walking the street. My watch had stopped around three a.m. that morning, so I felt disoriented.

The morning sky looked pearl-white now, with none of that famous California sun. This was not Manhattan, with clocks everywhere for nervous sidewalk striders to keep an eye on the time. LA did not have that many public clocks, and this looked like a neighborhood of homes and stubby apartment buildings. The struggle wore on.

"Hey, you!" a voice shouted from behind me. "Hold up, there, senior!"

My feet stopped. This old body betrayed me again. Resting felt good. A Black LAPD cop emerged from a black-and-white. He was short and slim with horn-rimmed glasses on a neck-chain. He held a slim Beretta pointed at the ground. His nameplate read "Throckmorton."

"Going somewhere, senior?" the man, Throckmorton, asked. "You look kinda suspicious to me walking around in this area now. Might be that you fit a few descriptions of crime suspects that I got on the radio. What do you have to say?"

"What's with this 'senior' stuff?" I said. "I'm leaving this riot. That's just common sense, Officer."

His partner eased out of the car. She was a wiry, redheaded woman who looked like a runway model strapped inside the tight dark blue uniform and gleaming black gun leather. Her nameplate read 'Chi.' Perhaps she had married an Asian named Mister Chi.

"Show me your hands!" Throckmorton hollered.

"Why are you shouting, officer?" I asked. "I'm right here."

"Who clobbered you in the face? You're all swole up."

Like lightning, my hands went up. The cop moved in on me, the Beretta pointed at my belly button. Panic whirl-agigged through me. Too many cops were scaring me today. This would be a dandy time for that first heart attack.

Like a pro, he angled his body and patted me down, playing it close under my belt. Most cops avoided that area and missed derringers, daggers and handcuff keys.

"Break out some ID," the woman said.

That scared me more. Brookings or the FBI might have paper out on me by now. These two would sling me into a holding pen.

"I'm just running from the riot, Officer," I managed to say.

"What riot?" the woman cop snapped. "There's no riot here. LA doesn't have riots."

That set me back on my heels. It made it easier to play dumb.

"Whatever you call it," I said, like a dry wit at the Yale University Hasty Pudding Club. "Your nomenclature, I'm running from it."

"Listen, senior," she said. "You not amusing us. Get it?"

"Like Queen Victoria," I said.

"Refusing to answer and hiding from us is illegal," the man said. "For right now. Temporary. We gotta give this area extra patrol. Dangerous here."

"You like repeating yourself," I said. "Let's see what the courts say about that. I'm shaken to the sweetbreads and can hardly wait."

"What's your name?" the woman asked. They were closing in on me.

CHAPTER 40.

Squiggle Room
or
Tank of Wet Sweat

"You want my name?" I asked the LAPD cops. It was time for a show. But I was getting an idea. "No, you don't want my name."

"Why not?"

"Because one of yours just stopped me before and fired his shotgun at me!" I shouted.

"Cripes," Throckmorton said. "We heard that. Went out over the air as '415 group with a gun.' Not us."

"Well, it was one of you," I said. "I'm sure that your PSB will ask you which cops are working near you today. What calls you both responded to. Computer has it, right? If I go formal now, PSB WILL find that cop. And that officer had no reason to shoot."

Both cops looked at each other. My Patrol days swam back to me in memory. There might be a way out.

"That officer needs retraining," I said.

This was the time for truth. Lying or exaggerating would blow my chance here. Fighting the urge to stretch it, I kept my voice level.

"My friend witnessed the whole thing. Buckshot hit our car. I can show you where it peppered a dumpster. I remember exactly what he looked like. And I want to report his negligence."

"Whoa, whoa," the woman said. "You're going too fast, sir. I can't understand a word that you're saying."

Chi was playing it this way in case someone was videotaping our little talk.

"I can figure it out," Throckmorton said. "And it sounds like BS. You must have done something, get him shooting at you."

Her partner did not understand Chi's trick.

"I get it now," I said. "Officer Throckmorton. I hope that you're not trying to cover this up. Because I need to report this."

"You could wind up arrested yourself. Felony fleeing —"

"He fled from ME!"

"Could be other charges. You could find yourself locked down for a few years."

Knowing that he was right chilled me. But my plan was blossoming. LAPD vocabulary echoed from old movies.

"Maybe I should speak to your Watch Commander," I said.

Throckmorton shook his head. Light glinted on his glasses.

"Leave now, senior," he said. "No harm, no foul."

This talk felt weird to me, as screwy as Los Angeles was. Alice in Wonderland held the lease on this city, for sure.

My head shook. My voice was going to shake as well.

"Watch Commander," I said. "Now, I'm repeating myself. You two got me doing it."

"You gotta lot of bad habits," Chi said.

She stepped in and speed-cuffed me like someone putting on bedtime slippers.

"Where you're going, we can help you break them," she said.

"What's the charge now?" I asked.

"No criminal charge, sir," she said. "But you seem disoriented."

"Do I? To whom?"

"Under the California Health and Safety Code of 51.50, we're bringing you in for a mental evaluation at the station. Then, maybe the hospital. But, right now, you cannot care for yourself. No arrest. Just evaluation."

"It's a distinction without a difference," I said.

"See?" she said. "Disoriented."

They frisked and then jammed Our Hero onto a hard plastic back seat with the metal biting onto the wrists and a floor smelling of spilled soda. No fresh air reached back here. It felt like being in an aquarium tank filled with sweat.

Chi drove. Trios of black-and-whites parked at corners. Shotgun barrels bristled in some. We turned corners, getting me lost. My back teeth crunched from stress. Maybe my scheme would fail.

Then my smile came back.

☙

We pulled up outside Hollywood Station.

Demonstrators crowded in front. McKissick's face glowered like a sacrificed angel from posters at the end of sticks.

"No asking to loosen the cuffs or give you a break or put on air conditioning," Throckmorton said. His Black scholar's face worked. "Are you some kind of real tough guy?"

I blew him a kiss. He frowned.

They frog-marched me into the Watch Commander's office. A slim Asian woman with white frosting her hair and a chipped front tooth scanned me. The name "Ling" rode on her nameplate under the gold-and-silver badge. She tried quizzing me in her Midwestern accent.

"Do you know what you were detained for?" Ling asked.

"51.50 H & S" I recited from memory.

I shook my head and asked for a sheet of paper and a pen.

"Why?" she said.

"To explain fully, lieutenant," I said.

Cops and civilians and street people milled around the hallway outside the Watch Commander's office door.

I had to time it just right.

"We don't work that way," she said. "Talk first, then we write."

"I don't work for you, Lieutenant. Uncuff me so that I can write. You'll be glad you did."

She considered this.

"He been searched?" she asked.

"Real good," Chi said.

"Okay, give the baby his bottle," she said.

More bodies filed past his door. A familiar voice lectured someone.

The handcuffs clicked off, and my wrists felt alive again. Chi lifted a sheet of paper from an opened ream on the shelf and, sneering, put it in front of me.

"Please, let me sit here, Lieutenant," I said. "Otherwise, my paper might get lost somehow."

"Whatever," she sighed.

Chi gave me a pen from her uniform pocket. Now she was mothering me with a wistful look.

I wrote like the devil was jogging behind me and filled two pages.

Both Throckmorton and Chi watched me and tried to peer over my shoulder, but I was careful to keep what I wrote covered with my left hand.

I finished and signed the paper with a flourish.

A tallish gray suit strode near the office doorway.

I lunged up and stretched out the hand with the paper and tapped the gray suit on the elbow with it.

Chi grabbed me but it was too late.

The gray suit stopped.

Brookings, the Deputy District Attorney, looked at me from inside the gray suit.

His face froze in shock,

"DDA Brookings," I panted. "Here's my written statement on Ms. McKissick's death. Everything that I saw. So witnessed by Lt. Ling and Officers Chi and Throckmorton. Now try keeping that out of your Grand Jury."

CHAPTER 41.

LAPD Humor
or
"You're Not Funny."

Brookings' eyes shuddered wide open when he recognized me. They hooded again.

"Royster!" he said. "What are you doing here?"

"Annoying adults," I said. "My only job skill."

"What gives?" Lt. Ling asked.

"DDA Brookings is playing tricky with me," I said. "Like the Laplanders say, 'He has a fox behind his ear.'"

Ling, Chi, Throckmorton and other LAPD cops in tailored blue-black uniforms and shining leather clenched around us. I could feel tension grip us all.

"This all comes from a perversion," I said. "Rodney King and Ferguson, Missouri. Nobody can look at cops and Blacks without feeling guilty about something."

"You're a psycho, Royster," Brookings said. "I can't use you as a witness."

"Who are you to judge?" I asked. "Does law school teach you psychiatry as an elective? I'm taking out my cellphone now, slowly. I been searched, remember? This may take some broken-field running, but I'm going to yell to the media about your tricks to keep me from testifying."

Taking care to move slow, I drew out my cellphone and flipped it open.

"Lieutenant, stop him," Brookings said.

The LAPD group around me tightened. I could smell the pressed wool uniforms hair gel.

"Why?" Ling asked. "Need a reason to put hands on him."

"He's disrespecting you all," Brookings said.

"That's my right, Brookings," I said. "I'm a taxpayer. Calling the press is no crime. Not yet. Neither is disrespecting you in your elegant suit and slippery ethics."

"Right," Ling said.

My head whipped around in surprise. The other cops nodded their heads. LAPD Officer Quizal came in from the hall and scrutinized us.

"What I saw may clear Alwer," I said. "Maybe not. Because you won't work with me, I can't say. But I did not see her do anything wrong."

"I'll decide that," Brookings said.

"Another expert," I said.

"Stop wisecracking," Ling said.

"Show some maturity," another cop, Black, with graying sideburns, said.

"How?" I asked. "By shutting up?"

Brookings made a low noise in his throat.

"We all pretty edgy after seeing our own Officer Taus get done up," the Black cop went on. "So, you just kind of walk slow there, player. Catch my drift?"

"Okay to take something else out of my pocket?" I asked. "Everybody, all right?"

Everyone stared at me.

"Officer Quizal," I said. "You're looking at me funny."

"You're NOT funny," she said. "Told you that before."

"What's in your pocket, you?" Ling asked.

This was getting to be my big moment with the audience.

"Stuff that screams are made of," I said. "Like 'The Blood of Jesus is on Stupid.' Whatever that means. This is my two-page essay on what I saw betwixt Alwer and McKissick. I'm giving it to you before witnesses."

"Stop trying to impress us," Brookings said.

"It's now written discovery material," I said, making noises like a lawyer, even an exhausted one. "You must turn it over to the defense."

"Who says?" asked a cop with a gremlin tattooed on his thumb.

"The United States Supreme Court, you jackass," Ling said. "Why don't you try reading something once in a while?"

"I'm not accepting this," Brookings said.

"Oh, yes, you are," I said.

I took a deep breath, leaned closer and shoved my essay into the breast pocket of his jacket.

"Now, put that into your precious sacrosanct file. Or else, you lose any chance of trying this case."

"What's the authority for that?" Gremlin asked.

"The same United States Supreme Court," Ling said.

"You sound like you're returning a tennis serve," I said, "from a dumb opponent."

"You know, Royster," Brookings said. "Maybe I pre-judged you. That might have clouded my judgment."

"Prejudice is a terrible thing."

"Ha-ha," Brookings responded.

"Decent of you, admitting it," I said. "But, to repeat myself, you have to depose me. I insist."

Brookings considered that.

"Okay," he said at last. "Lieutenant, can we use one of your private rooms?"

"Give me the room where you interview kids," I said. "You got toys there for me to play with."

"Royster –"

"Or do you want me to play with myself?" I asked.

"Come on," Brookings said. "Let's get this over with."

☙

Ling led us into a room painted in pink and baby blue colors with pictures of happy hippos and crocodiles dancing together on the walls. The pictures made me feel better and wonder if I could start a ballroom dance program in county jail.

Brookings kept twitching. Ling watched him like a kid who might misbehave again if she left him alone.

"This is taking too long," Brookings said.

"Truth and justice do," I said. "They're very inconvenient."

"Royster," Ling said in warning.

"Lieutenant," I said. "This is important enough for you, the Watch Commander, to sit in with us. Tomorrow, deputy chiefs will grill you about this scenario. They'll tell you how they would have handled it better. That's the way of police supervision."

"Anyone ever say that you're a windbag?" Ling asked.

"Three times a day, after meals," I said.

"You proved a crazy way to show that you're not disoriented," Ling said. "I support my officers' decision to haul you in."

"Ling, stop fretting," I said. "Not planning to sue anyone. Not yet."

CHAPTER 42.

Out of the Shadows
or
Your Federal Taxes at Work

"Sure," I said. "Let me rest now because I'm beat down."

"But, before you grill him," a new voice said, "I would speak with Mr. Royster."

Everyone spun to look at the stranger. He stood about three inches over my six feet with long hair the color of chalk tied into a ponytail behind his well-shaped head. Wire-rimmed glasses, faded gold, sat on his aristocrat's nose.

He stepped closer to me, tossing back his head and examining me the way a horse doctor might look at an ailing palomino pony. There was something old-fashioned and scholarly about him, a hint of the Benjamin Franklin in old wood-carvings.

At the same time, he looked ageless. No fat clogged his mug or body. His face showed tight sunburned skin against the white ponytail.

"Gentlemen," he said in a precise tone, "I would speak with this man in conference."

English did not sound like his first language. He sounded like someone who had worked to master it better than the natives.

"Dream on," Ling said.

"That's impossible," Brookings huffed. "This is an ongoing death case that is shaking up all those folks outside."

"The ones throwing the bricks and bottles," I said. "Those folks."

"I understand," the older man said. "But my people have an urgent need as well. If you would just take a minute to glance at this letter. It will answer your questions."

Brookings pouted. His good-looking face twisted.

He grasped the letter from the man's open hand, scanned it and pouted some more. Then he looked at the cops, eyes sparking, holding himself in.

"Gotta do it," Brookings said. "Give these two some privacy. Make it quick, sir."

"As long as it takes," the man said. "That's up to Mr. Royster."

"God help us," Brookings said.

"She better," I said.

"I don't get this," the Lieutenant Ling opined.

"I don't like any of this myself," I said. "I was just crossing a Hollywood street when I lost my freedom."

"We'll be down the hall, sir," Brookings said.

Brookings and the entourage left, shrugging their shoulders.

They all made faces while the mystery man and I scrutinized each other.

"Well, damn," I said. "You can get DDA Brookings to call you 'sir'. Must be someone important."

"Some say so," he said.

"Who are you? Mister Softee?"

"Xeous is my name," he said. "It was another name, in another country, in a place where nobody kept records after the Serbian assassins came in. So, I have seen, first-hand, what you call months of hell, gang rape as a weapon of terror and all that genocide brings."

"Sorry that you went through all that," I said. "But Daddy here ain't talking without no lawyer."

"I'm not a policeman," he said.

"Then, I'm gonna slide on out."

"The policemen are down the hall. THEY are the ones who will hold you. Not I."

"Held is held is held. What's that letter you showed them? Making them back water and clear out of here."

"Perhaps, we will regard that letter later. But not now. For the moment, I concern myself with radical elements in the arts."

My body jackknifed from surprise.

"Sounds like another witch-hunt from the Senator Joe McCarthy hearings in the Cold War," I said. "Useless waste of my federal tax dollars."

"Do you believe so, sir?" Xeous asked. "Years ago, an actor was performing before a politician and spat out his lines whilst glaring at the politician.

"The politician's wife said 'He looks as if he meant that mad speech for you.'

"And the politician responded, 'Well, he does look at me kind of sharpish, don't he?'"

"Well, Mr. Royster, I do sincerely wish that we had done a bit of what you call 'witch-hunting' at that time. Because the actor was a known radical named John Wilkes Booth, a super-star at twenty-five. The politician in this small vignette was Lincoln."

"And you think that grilling me will prevent another assassination?" I asked. "Other than that, Mrs. Lincoln, how did you enjoy the play?"

"There is no time for your cocktail party witticisms," Xeous said. "The New York police and federal government have the opinion that you are frivolous. For example, you upset the FBI on a sensitive case of a millionaire's young daughter kidnapped in a blizzard. You caused many problems."

He bit off the words like a diamond cutter with his instruments.

"As you know, the deceased actress used her last name McKissick to identify herself. Never her full name once she became famous."

"Like Capuccine or Topol," I said. "Just another show-bizzer gimmick. Hollywood's full of them."

"Quite true. But what we want to know is, when did you first meet her? And what were you doing with her?"

"I never met her," I said.

Shock crackled my voice.

"Oh, no? This picture says that you did."

Chapter 43.

Do the Suits Really Believe This?
or
You're Jerkin' My Gherkin, Right?

"Look at this picture," Xeous said inside the room, his words clipping off again.

"There's McKissick. There's a burning American flag. And there is you."

"That seedy-eyed character in the Army field jacket? He don't favor me in the face," I said, trying to dumb down my talk.

"Please stop clowning. This situation is grave."

"For suits like you, it always is."

"Are you denying that is you, Mr. Royster?"

"'Denying?' Is this a court of law? If so, I've never seen one like this."

"This talk determines your future, Mr. Royster."

"And yours, too, champ. Come toe-dancing in here with your Star Chamber secret jury routine, wave the flag and threaten me with veiled hints on my future. Don't even know who you are. For all I know, you're a line worker in a dog food factory. Let's break out some paper on you."

"Mr. Royster, you saw how the police reacted to me. Isn't that sufficient?"

"Not to this registered Manhattan Independent."

"Pardon me?"

"So, give."

"Here is something for your perusal," he said. "Please do not touch the letter. Just look at it, please."

"'Congress Of the United States,'" I read from the letter in his mitt. "Nice lettering. Gold seal and crest at the bottom. 'The bearer is authorized to make any investigations, as directed by the Congress,' blah, blah, blah. This is Bolshoi, champ. When was this sneaky-pete picture taken?"

"Perhaps you should tell us," Xeous said.

"No can do. Because it's not me."

"Are you so sure? How many rallies have you attended when someone burned the flag?"

"On the edge of a crowd? Fifty yards away, judging by your picture here? Nobody my age can answer that question with honesty."

"And why not?"

"Because we've seen too much. Too many rallies. Because that was the only way to get attention in the past. And justice."

"And riots," he said. "And shootings. Arson destroying entire neighborhoods. Crowds turn to mobs, Mr. Royster. And mobs have no brains. Or compassion. I would wager that, like most Americans, you have never seen what a mob can do. But I have. And it created change in me."

"Think it turned your brain."

"During the Cold War, I studied and learned from your own counterintelligence people. They would infiltrate so-called peace and civil rights rallies and perform operations that seem ridiculous to us today."

"Such as?" I asked.

"They would listen to the anti-war speakers and count how many words they would use in an average sentence. Twelve words or twenty-one. Whatever was the average."

"Why?" I asked.

"Because our opposite numbers, especially in the FBI, believed that most radicals had been seduced, or if you prefer, brainwashed, by Moscow or Peking. And that they were controlled by them."

"By using word counts?" I said. "That doesn't make sense."

"If you are an anti-Communist, it does. Because Karl Marx's *Das Kapital* has an average of sixteen words per sentence. Eldridge Cleaver's *Soul On Ice* has nineteen. So, if you concede that the radical leaders had been brainwashed, their own speeches will reflect those and other radical books. We, in the intelligence community –"

"Do you suits truly believe this fantasy?" I asked. "You can't. You're playing with me. You're jerkin' my gherkin."

"Such a crudity. in Intelligence work, we have to consider all what we term 'capabilities'. Look at your own history. Intelligence officers or spies, dating back to your own Revolution, pulling off incredible acts of bravery and skill.

"In 1776, John Honeyman worked as an agent for General Washington and convinced the Hessians soldier that Washington was too weak to attack them. So Washington crossed the Delaware River and surprised the drunken Hessians, full of Christmas food and spirits. He and smashed their Army.

"A Tory traitor in New York, Thomas Hickey, came within inches of killing General George Washington in 1776. With Washington dead, the American Revolution would have withered and died that month.

"Russia's spy Richard Sorge, prevented Hitler from conquering Russia. Most historians say that if not for Sorge, Hitler would have ruled the world."

"Every little schoolboy knows that spying is vital," I said. "So, stop showing off."

"Showing off, indeed," he said. "You're one to talk, Mr. Royster. It seems that you wrote the book on that."

"Just copying my betters," I said. "These side-bars of pique may distract you from your mission."

"My mission is to de-brief you and get you to Mr. Juan Bria in Miami for your cruise ship job."

He recited a Miami number for my benefit.

"Or else, the industry will blacklist you for not taking the position that you had committed yourself to."

Surprise cranked my head back.

"Xeous, you're the one person around here older than I am. Must be pushing eighty, by the look of you. I mean, aren't you getting a bit long in the tooth for this sort of thing?"

"Aren't you, Mr. Royster? Try leaving this room now and I can promise you that you shall never work in the cruise industry or hold any other meaningful job again."

Chill crept over me.

"The ones before weren't too meaningful," I managed to say. Jolly to the end, that I am.

Now we both knew that I could not leave.

"So we'll continue your education here," he said. "And look further, to the power of a mob. No police agency can kill or stop every rioter. The government just fights back as best it can, hunkers down behind barricades and prays for bad weather. They know that nothing stops a mob. The French Revolution proved that."

"Stow the history lesson, Xeous. It's today that interests me."

He ignored me and kept speaking.

"In 1907, Romanian peasants killed 11,000 landowners in a week. Burma, now Myanmar, killed 3,000 of its own in 1988. France, 20,000 in 1871. Taiwan lost 28,000 in riots where Chinese troops butchered them and imposed a dictatorship until just 28 years ago, crushing all freedoms."

"So, what does this have to do with McKissick dying in LAPD clutches?"

"You saw what that mob did to Officer Taus here. You Tube showed the world that atrocity. You should remember the riots in Ferguson, Missouri, and the LA riots after the Rodney King beating here. Complete breakdown of order. Like many Americans, you look at the large movements of governments.

"But what about the secret operations that never reach the media? The private wars? Where brothers-in-arms over the years, develop trust with each other, lie low and perfect their skills to strike out against their foes. I postulate that McKissick and yourself formed such a bond decades ago. And now you are planning to use your witnessing her death to advance some operation against America's best interests."

CHAPTER 44.

Let Me Tell You A Story
or
Would You Believe?

"McKissick did not come up through the customary Black American actress route," Xeous said. "Her parents were actually middle-class and were college professors who lived in rather a good Boston neighborhood.

"They taught her excellent handwriting skills, and for her entire life, she was a poetess and a compulsive letter-writer. A quaint talent something in today's computer age. Like her mother, she wrote to friends and acquaintances throughout her life. She wrote to the President often. The Secret Service saw her as dangerous, opened a file on her and notified my people when she wrote those letters. When she died, we knew that somewhere, somehow, she had already written the reason why."

Just to test him, I moved towards the door.

"Tell me something worth hearing," I said. "Or else, I'm leaving."

"No, you're not," he said. "You're too involved."

He was right. I stopped.

"She was to the manor born. Her parents and schools taught her the gentler aspects of life. She saw different cultures in

Boston: White, Irish, Italian and Portuguese. That made her descent into jobs like cleaner and dishwasher all the more difficult.

"Then, chance happened when she was seventeen. She and a friend, planned a day of shopping at Caldor's near Fenway Park. First, her friend had to try out for a part in a play in Roxbury. It was a light comedy frothy piece of time-passing that called for a few Black roles. Could McKissick accompany her to this audition and then continue on to their planned shopping?

"The friend read for the part but did not get it. The director saw McKissick and asked if she wanted to try out for the part. You may surmise what happened."

"What happened is, like I said, you're boring me," I said. "Thinking about knocking you down just to shut you up."

"I wish that you would try," he said.

We measured each other.

I shoved the chair back.

He raised his hands and slipped out of the corner, like a pro boxer.

His chin tucked down.

There was no way that I could take him bare-handed, in my shape.

"Stay where you are," he said. "Don't be a fool with a broken kneecap."

I slammed my fist against the wall but stayed in the chair.

The cops outside would think that he was slugging me and ignore any noise as long as they could.

"What does this have to do with Police Officer Alwer and Actress McKissick fifty years later?" I asked, trying to save face.

"For some reason that only artists can ever fathom, she looked around in her teenage years and probed at becoming an actress. The color and variety and fame probably drew her. She was tall for her age, five feet ten inches and weighed only about 125 pounds at that time.

"Her parents read leather-covered books after dinner. They did not want their only daughter showing her face and body on stage. They argued. But her parents thought that the demanding hard life of a working actress would stop her. McKissick took the part.

"By a fluke, the play, *Lynch's Narrowbacks*, caught on. Critics and audiences liked it. The play opened on Broadway.

"McKissick never suffered from stage-fright. Many did. She looked like a professional from the very start. In Manhattan, she discovered sex and saw that she enjoyed it. She enjoyed more than most. This was pre-AIDS, when having a child out of wedlock was a much greater concern than sexually transmitted diseases.

"During this time, she found many men to teach her and she learned many actions."

"Makes a fella stop and dream," I said. "But you're just trying to distract me, get me thinking about sexy fleshy delights."

"When the play continued, her parents screamed for her to consider college. But she refused. By now, she was of legal age and could do as she pleased."

"As always happens, the play ended. McKissick had not saved her wages. Nobody else in the play had. So she needed funds. As a Black woman with a GED from high school, she had limited options. She began with modeling, then slid down to food catering and then to dishwasher.

"Men kept taking her out for drinks and dinner and paying the bill afterwards with her body.

"Our people learned this from the letters that she wrote. Patriotic people surrendered those letters to us.

"Again, I say that the answer to all this lies in some letter that she wrote. We just have to find that letter.

"Even in New York then, cops would harass interracial couples. They did this to McKissick, daughter of a Black businessman and college teacher. It shocked her. She joined civil rights groups and first came to the attention of those of us in the Intelligence Community."

"You do historical head-shrinking on her?" I asked.

"Never before had McKissick seen where the kitchen help labored, sweated, cursed and died before this."

"You understand. It shocked her. Much like the young Charles Dickens, whose father, mother and younger children were cast into debtor's prison and Dickens was forced to work in a blacking factory. It only lasted for six weeks but it made Dickens a social critic championing the under-dog, through his books, for the rest of his life."

"Did the same trick on McKissick, too?" I asked.

"Mr. Xeous, this really doesn't engage my interest."

"However, this will," he said.

He slid out a fat Manila envelope from his inside pocket and slapped it down on the table.

"This is a GTR, a Government Travel Request, putting you on the next first class flight to Miami with any civilian commercial carrier."

"Doesn't have to be first class," I said. "Could be business class. That way, I don't have to tip so well."

Everything I had wanted was in that GTR envelope. It could be my ticket out of this SoCal mess.

"Forget about signing any statement," Xeous said. "We know that McKissick left her letters with different friends. They formed a kind of a diary for her."

It was time to lie my way out of this.

"I think that I know who has the letters," I said.

That was my first lie. All I had was a detective's hunch.

"And who has them," I said, still lying. "But why are they so important?"

"Because when we make the letters public and convince everyone that they are genuine, they will see that she was mentally deranged. And this martyr talk will die. LA will not suffer a riot."

"Big stuff," I said.

His hands twitched.

"LA doesn't have riots," I reminded him.

"Get me those letters and the ticket is yours, and you can leave with me for the airport. No policemen will accompany us."

"Off the record," I said. "And I have your word on this?"

"Absolutely. You see your own name already on the GTR?"

"DDA Brookings and the cops here won't let me leave," I said.

"They will if I promise to bring you back in two hours," he said.

"So, you'll lie to them?"

He shrugged a shoulder of the suit.

"They are policemen," he said.

"That says it all?"

"They are interested in one death, Mr. Royster. But I am concerned with stopping mob violence that could cause dozens more. Which do you think is more important?"

Something in words made my senses ping. He was lying about something. That made two of us.

He shrugged his high shoulders and put the GTR envelope back in his jacket pocket. My eyes followed him.

Something still rang wrong.

"How did McKissick wind up homeless?" I asked, to gain time. I needed to plot my next move.

"She took to Blaxploitation films. And they to her. Audiences liked her looks. For her roles, she studied karate and made it look good on the screen. With her height and that karate, she stood up for battered women in her films and fought the male abusers.

"Audiences in Europe liked her, as well. She did a Blaxploitation film shot in Spain and one in Italy. She gave talks against the Vietnam War and the repressive regimes in Spain and Greece. She met a Greek yachtsman named Spyros and they fell in love, according to the movie tabloids. Spyros was a traitor to the current Greek regime and a known Communist, in exile from his country."

"If I remember rightly from my reading," I said. "Greece was ruled by a military dictatorship at that time. Army colonels had hijacked the government there and seized power for themselves."

"Nevertheless, a traitor and a Communist. That heightened our attention to her even more."

"This was decades ago, Xeous," I said. "How is it you knew this, and you're still running around, chasing people whose politics frighten you?"

CHAPTER 45.

Fair Exchange
or
Blow Me

Xeous blew out a breath that seemed to fill our room.

"I know all this because I have been involved in such matters ever since I was a boy, in Albania," he said. "And because all good intelligence officers read voraciously."

"Could spend your time better, reading Gomorrah comics," I said. "Or pulp fiction, like Captain Billie's Whiz-Bang. Instead, you're looking for things that may not exist."

"She and Spyros the Greek yachtsman married and lived in Capri. She kept flying back to the States for work. They had two boys very soon. McKissick also had good comic timing, when the bullets and karate chops were flying."

"Didn't she make *Forbidden Foxy Love?*" I asked.

"With most of the cast into the Black revolutionary movement, too. This was a frightening time of dissent."

"Frightening, partly because of control freaks like you," I said. "And you were still in Albania, I take it?"

He shrugged. "Back and forth."

"Inside Albania, you sure couldn't get much in-depth news about civil Rights," I said. "You only ate from the dishes our Government cooked for you."

"For about five years," he said, "from 1970 to 1975, I fully believed that America would have a physical, bloody and shooting revolution. Blacks against Whites, pro-war types versus anti-war hippies, even young against old. Your young peoples' speeches, your films and your music said so."

"You watched too many movies," I said.

"McKissick obtained another part in a Blaxploitation film, this one in Morocco," Xeous said. "The genre was moving out of Watts and Detroit by now. Morocco promised the viewers something new. She wanted to go. Spyros did not want her to go. They quarreled in public, in a café. She walked out. The paparazzi enjoyed that tremendously.

"She flew to Morocco. Spyros became intoxicated and angry and took friends and his sons on a cruise just beyond the harbor. A squall struck and their boat broke up on the rocks. Spyros and the boys drowned, along with some of the Beautiful People.

"After that, McKissick threw herself into more violent protests. Like the Black Panthers, she called for all prisoners of color to be released because they had not received a fair trial.

"Most groups saw her anger and shied away from her. So did directors. She started drugging on the set. Everyone gossiped about her.

"Her letter-writing grew more frenzied. Our mental health friends say that she needed to justify her life through letters. She felt guilt about her dead family and letters helped ease it. It is something hard for a layman to grasp.

"Her looks went, as did her fans. Other actresses came up. You know the situation when that happens, I am sure."

"There's only four stages in the life of an actress," I said. "One: Who is McKissick? Two: Get me McKissick! Three: Get me a young McKissick! Four: Who was McKissick?"

Xeous moved his hands inside the jacket pocket, where the envelope with my GTR still lay. Now I turned sure that something was going wrong. My danger grew the longer that I was in this room.

"If I show you where to find her letters, do I get the GTR ticket to Miami?" I asked.

"Immediately. But please hide the envelope in your pocket. The officers should not see it. I will tell them that I am driving you to the Federal Building on Wilshire Boulevard. My car has weapons in it so you will pose no danger to me. Do not try anything. En route, I will drive you to where the letters are. After that, the LAX Airport."

Trying to look greedy came easy to me now, and I did my best.

He handed me the envelope and moved to open the door.

"Officers!" he said. "Please come in here."

I ripped the envelope open, saw the grainy powder inside and flung it onto his open mouth.

"Aww!" he shouted. The stuff went right in. Powder covered his face. His tongue came out, spitting out frothy white powder.

Ling and the others filled the doorway.

"I'll kill you!" Xeous shouted.

He jumped at me. I could feel the floor vibrate. I bobbed and weaved away from his big hands, skipping backwards like boxing had taught me to do.

Ling and her cops wrestled him onto the table. The table SCREECHED! and moved back against the wall.

They waited, bellies heaving.

Xeous shouted in some foreign language. It might have been Albanian. It sounded rough and scratchy.

"Slow down," Ling said. "This loudmouth isn't worth it."

"Thanks," I said.

The cops used their bodies to block me from his view. They scanned him, looking for signs of madness.

"Sure, you wanna shut him up," Ling went on. "We all do. Talks too much."

"You should listen to him for a while," I said. "Lectures longer than a runaway bishop at the Easter service."

"Just let it go," Ling said to Xeous. "You represent Washington, right? Forget Royster."

Xeous kept shouting.

They released Xeous. He slumped into a chair. His chest heaved. He looked much older now, and I started to feel sorry for him.

Then he giggled.

"Fast-acting stuff," I said.

"Guess that he didn't want me able to talk after he dusted me."

The cops stared at him. Brookings put a hand to his own head.

"I don't know," Xeous said.

He giggled some more. His eyes bugged out.

"Halloo! Whoop!" Xeous shouted.

His face cracked into more laughing.

"Maybe Xeous was planning to plant some drugs on somebody," I said. "But he opened the envelope too quick and inhaled some of it by accident. That meant that he was trying to use the LAPD. Bad idea, right?"

"You're talking very irrationally," Brookings said.

"He's all drugged up," Ling said. "Has a bad bundle in his system."

"Royster, you do this?" Brookings asked.

"Do what?" I asked. "Come on. Get this poor schlub an ambulance for possible narcotic poisoning."

"Then we have to pinch him for Being-Under-the-Influence-in-Public," Ling said.

"Better him than me," I said. "He's no relative of mine."

"What did he take?" a burly Latino cop asked from the hallway.

"Nënë! Nënë!" Xeous shouted.

"Take him," I said. "Teach Washington not to waste our taxpayers' cash on his paranoia."

"Royster, you better stop playing with us!" Ling said.

CHAPTER 46.

Law Talk
Or
What I Stepped In

"Playing with truth and justice?" I said. "All depends on your point of view."

"Come on," Brookings said. "Let's get this over with."

"Tell the Ambulance Johnnies to be gentle with Brother Xeous," I said. "He's important. He told me so hisself."

"Come on, senior," Ling said to Xeous.

Xeous made a clown face with pop eyes.

"You're an amazing pain, childish and dangerous," Brookings said as he led me into another steel-gray-and linoleum room. "No wonder the NYPD tossed you out. But it seems, as I said before, that you're my best witness."

"I agree," I said. "So, let's get an objective-type person taking this all down now."

Brookings hoisted himself up and busied in the hallway.

"Lieutenant," Brookings said to someone I couldn't see. "I need a Police Service Rep to take down a statement here. When can we get one?"

"That's over-time," some woman said in a foreign accent. "Somebody'll want it for sure."

"Marva will," another woman said. "She's the original overtime slut."

A siren burped outside. Brakes squealed. Radios kept buzzing near me.

Xeous giggled more in the hallway. By now, I knew his voice, and I always would.

Brookings returned.

"What did that silly old man talk to you about?" Brookings asked me.

"Cabbage and kings," I said. "And how he protects America against chaos. And he's not silly."

"Don't like any Government interference, my case, my little part of the pie," he said. Anger ran a syrup through his words. "Who does he think he is, anyway?"

"You government jokers are all alike," I said. "Need I say more?"

A pale, White lady, red face like a turkey-cock's wattles, blondish hair paling with age, pushed open the door and settled herself at the conference table. She held a flat gray machine under one tired arm. She set it down, clicked it on, and settled herself in front of it.

"Thanks, Marva," Brookings said. "It's working now? We're taking this down?"

"Okey-dokey," Marva said.

"Now, Mr. Royster," Brookings said. "Please tell me what you remember of this incident. Everything, please, sir. Where you were coming from, what you were doing and who else was near you at that time?"

Leaning back, I could feel and hear the bones in my body rattle like pool balls breaking apart. Eyes shuttered, the scene with Alwer and McKissick came back to me.

I reached back and talked.

Marva's fingers danced over the keys of the transcriber, her expression bored attentiveness. That seemed to be a requirement for a court reporter job.

I recounted everything that I recalled.

Brookings quizzed me, going back and forth in time.

"When did you first see them fighting?" he asked.

"They were already fighting when I first saw them," I said. "Just like some of these world-famous Internet videos circling about. Nobody could tell who started the mess."

"Since Alwer is a law enforcement officer," he said, "there is the presumption that she was acting legally."

"Not any more," I said.

"That presumption can be overcome by new facts," he said.

"Or lynch-mob psychology," I snapped back. "A grand jury finding 'no true bill' for murder in this case would probably rupture your career. But a conviction would paint you as a fearless brutality fighter who took on the LAPD. Next step up that golden ladder. To a judgeship, maybe. Or Congress. Not having to deal with hairy issues and childish talkers like me."

"So, from what you saw, Alwer may be telling the truth?" he asked.

"From what I saw, we may never know. Like most of these cases. That's why they linger on, in street-corner talk around a trash-can fire, a few pals and a bottle of wallop. For years and years. Because most don't trust you Government truth jockeys."

"If you stopped giving speeches, that would help," he said.

"How many good witnesses you got?" I asked.

"That's my worry. Not yours."

"If you had better ones than me, you wouldn't be nursemaiding me like you are," I said. "So I am it. The Numero Uno Senor Garçon Monsieur."

Brookings made another of his faces, scrunching his eyes shut. Fear was aging him.

"Tell me again what you saw," he said. "Every detail, no matter how small."

The interrogation showed Brookings' skill. Someone making up a story would have trouble keeping it straight when he skipped around like that.

"Thank you, Marva," Brookings said after all his questions. "Please get this to me as soon as possible."

"S'okay," Marva said.

She gathered her machine and left us alone again.

"So, you didn't really see much of anything, did you?" he said.

"Don't tell me. Tell Los Angeles."

"You saw a struggle. Not much beforehand."

"That's right," I said. "But nobody else saw much, either, before the wrestling started."

"Nobody credible."

"So, as this layman sees it," I said, "it goes to Alwer's and McKissick's mental states when the deal went down. Did Alwer want to kill someone? Did Alwer overreact and panic and kill someone without cause? What about McKissick? Was she looking for a lawsuit cash award? Did she want to try suicide-by-cop? For someone homeless, with mental problems, I feel for her. But, objectively, you have to ask those questions."

"Suicide-by-cop sounds like wishful thinking on your part, as an ex-cop," he said.

"Is it? I remember reading that psychologists analyzed fatal cop shootings across America. Thirty-six percent were suicide-by-cop. That's a big percentage."

"I'm sure that's an exaggeration," he said. "I'm too busy with my own cases to read the tabloid media like you seem to do."

"That's because you never walked a beat in a gunny neighborhood," I said. "Lot of times, I would stop a client running from a crime, and he would put his hand under his shirt and say 'Go ahead and shoot me, man! I don't care!'

"And it took me months to see that they were telling the truth. They did not care. Mama and Daddy Royster raised me as a White, middle-class kid, aimed at college, career and some straight-limbed offspring in the suburbs. Nothing prepared me for hearing that."

"Police use-of-force experts sometimes testify to that," Brookings said. "But I have trouble believing them."

"Believe them. There's a lot of self-hatred out there on the street. Some just don't care."

Brooking's cellphone buzzed. He put it to his ear and listened while I tried devising any hustle that might get me to Miami and my new life.

"That's a surprise," he said to me, tucking the phone away. "Alwer's here in the station with her lawyer. She wants a sit-down with me. To explain her state of mind."

"Her lawyer must be nuts."

"Or very subtle. We won't know until trial. Can you sit with us? Having an ex-cop at the table might help. And I can't use any LAPD without them leaking to the press. The cops are all enraged over what happened to their Officer Taus. You probably saw the video about Taus. Objectivity goes right out the window. So, sit down with us. What do you say?"

"No time to get anyone normal," I said. "So Royster was invented. But why are you letting me sit in on this talk? I'm a witness in her case."

"There's an old California statute that permits it," he said. "I remember it from law school. It struck me as silly but useful. I can permit it because she is not going to talk about what happened at the death. This is just what they call deep background. It does not address what took place."

"Still seems kooky, letting me in."

"You've already given a written statement, Royster. There is not much that can change that. You're locked into your statement."

"Never heard of this kind of sit-down," I said. "But it's your case."

"You're a bag of loose talk, Royster."

"I never heard of this kind of talk, on a case like this," I said. "You and Alwer."

"Rare, but it happens. I think she's trying for some mercy."

"We all need it," I said.

❧

Alwer was the first through the door and into the steel-gray and linoleum room. Brookings was smart to keep this room. If we moved anywhere, we might lose our territory. Cops were moving through the halls and slamming doors to have private war talks.

That day, Alwer sported a pink business suit that showed off how small she was. Black curls escaped from either side of her head, framing her heart-shaped face.

Her lawyer was the counselor that been on TV with her. He shook hands with all, mumbled something and sat down away from us.

It looked like he wanted us to see Alwer as making her own statement, without riding piggyback on learned counsel.

"The Department, they run all these tests before they hire us," Alwer said in a soft measured cadence. "Parking tickets. What your neighbors say about you. Credit check, References. High school teachers. all your past jobs.

"The, first day of the Academy, we recruits go into the gymnasium alone and line up on a black streak on the floor. It's dark, this gym. Some of us whisper.

"'Don't talk,' the others say. 'They don't want you talking. Their folks had been police and drilled them how to get through the Academy.

"We're standing there, in our best clothes, waiting. Waiting and waiting. Seemed like time stopped. I started getting more nervous. Everyone told us that this Academy was no joke. Especially when you're Black, they look at you more careful.

"We keep waiting in line. Nobody moving.

"Then they come screaming at us out of nowhere. Wearing their full-dress blue uniforms with the long sleeves, those Class-A's, with all their medals, colored ribbons, shiny, shiny, shoes. Like soldiers on parade.

"'What's the matter with you? Can't you stand in line? Where you get that gang-banger haircut?'"

"Keys! I hear loose keys! Who got loose keys?"

"Loose keys get you killed!' another trainer shouts. "Too much noise!"

"All of you run back here!' another one says. "Drop those keys and get back in formation! Move, move, move!"

"Skinny blonde lady cop, all her medals on, shouts at us 'This class is starting to really hack me off!'"

"Now I'm really scared," Alwer said.

Chapter 47.

**Cane the Boys, Cane Them,
Damn Their Hides!
or
This Is Discipline?**

Brookings coughed.

He twisted his face as if he thought Alwer was lying.

"I can't see where this is going," he said.

"I do," I said. "Just listen. Okay, counselor? And stop sulking."

Brookings kept sulking.

"There was some funny stuff in the Academy," Alwer said. "Like, later that day, we were getting through our first Ethics class. Some of us were just twenty-one years old. Somebody was arguing with the female trainer, forgot himself and said, 'But, Mom —'"

"Forgot himself, all right," Brookings said. "Used to arguing with his momma."

"That first day, they screamed at us all day," Alwer said. Her voice dipped. "Found out later, they call it 'Black Line Monday', 'cause they make all the recruits toe that black line. Some trainers who lived far away, they take motel rooms, stay overnight, bring all their medals and best pressed uniforms. Just to scream at us at six in the morning."

"Knowing cops like I do," I said, "maybe those cops use those rooms for a bit of slap-and-tickle with somebody's wife. Black Line Monday makes a great excuse."

"Probably," Alwer said.

"Depend on it," I said.

"So, they running us crazy for hours," Alwer said. "Kept saying that we were worst they had ever seen. Calling us 'Unsat'. For 'Unsatisfactory', I guess. They talk they own lingo.

"They kept shouting at us. I felt like that damn day would never end. Felt like throwing up. One boy shows up three minutes late for assembly, and they nearly threw him off the job right there. But I remember one trainer came up next to me and whispered 'It's okay. Take it easy.' All he said. Guess because I looked so scared, and he could tell. Showed me that they – the trainers – were human, too."

"You probably needed that reminder," I said. "Maybe that trainer did, too."

"They kept saying that we need to be tough for the street," Alwer went on. "So they kept yelling at us."

"That's just an excuse for bullying you," I said. "Very convenient for distorted personalities."

"A lot of that went on through the Academy," Alwer said. "Sometimes, in a good mood, they would joke with us and all, but we always knew that they could do whatever they wanted to with us.

"The class ahead of us failed their inspection. So this lieutenant decides to punish US as a warning. Hollered at us, made us do push-ups and more push-ups. Push-ups on asphalt roadway. Hot day, too. My palms got burned, pushing up. Our sweatshirts had our names printed on them, front and back, so they could ID us. Criticize us. Looked down at the asphalt, saw the letters of my name ALWER spelled backways on the asphalt from where my sweatshirt kept dropping on to it. Cause you have to go all the way down for an Academy-approved pushup. My arms felt like I was gonna die."

"This sounds hellish," Alwer's lawyer said. "Tell us why you didn't quit."

"Quit to what? Where could I go? Already resigned my old job. Most of us had good- paying jobs before this. Lotta teachers."

"Teachers become LAPD?" Brookings asked. "Join this crazed department. Why?"

"Because teachers, like cops, enjoy interaction with an unruly public," I said. "Both have to think on their feet and persuade people, take risks and change lives. And both groups struggle against politically motivated administrators who stopped caring long ago. They both get death or firing threats if they do their jobs too well."

"That same lieutenant sewed up the pockets on his own pants so he couldn't put his hands in them," Alwer said. "He was born here but whenever he got mad, shout at us in German. Don't know why.

"He saw some other recruit, hands in his pockets, and made him carry around this big rock for the whole day. As punishment."

"That was to make a man out of him," I said. "Or something like that."

"I finally get my Academy diploma, my hands be shaky and stuff," Alwer said. "The veteranos warned us that probation would be worse. They were right."

"How so?" I asked.

"Royster, let her talk," Brookings said.

"'cause my Training Officer, P-3 Kossano, like he always acted angry with everyone. Stated that I should never write the word 'home' on a report. It's unprofessional, he said. How do I know that the person really lives there? They could be lying. Instead, I should write the word 'residence.' Then, half hour later, he switches it back to 'home.' Just to mess up my head."

"When he corrected your reports like that," I asked, "was he on overtime?"

"Sure. We both were."

"There's your answer," I said. "How much did a Training Officer, what you call 'a P-3?' make per hour?"

"About forty-four bucks."

"Yep," I said. "At over-time, for correcting your report, he pockets roughly sixty-three per hour. Then, does he slam you for writing the report too slowly?"

"How'd you know?"

"Sixty-three an hour is cheaper than him looking for a second job. He's got his own little rat-farm going on here. Why should he help you? He can't afford to."

"Then, he wrote me up for not having my gun leg back," Alwer said. "'cept he was lying. Always kept my gun leg back."

"Explain that, please," her lawyer said.

"Academy trains us to get into an interview stance, facing a suspect. You turn your body, blade it, so your weak side is forward. So you're a smaller target,-"

"Just like boxing," I said. "Keep your strong side back, to throw the heavier punch."

"Keep your gun leg back, it harder for the suspect to grab your gun," Alwer said. "Give you more time to react, hit him with your baton. Training Officer sees you forgetting that, he's gonna pencil-screw you and put it on paper. 'cause if the suspect get your gun, he gonna shoot your Training Officer first, since he already got YOUR gun. Lotta Hollywood Training Officers do that, mess with their rookies and get 'em fired while rookie's on that one-year probation."

"Again, why?" Brookings asked.

"Firing rookies, 'boots' they call us, that's a Hollywood tradition," Alwer said. "They proud of it. Hollywood doesn't get much real violent crime. Mostly thefts from tourists. So, the senior officers make a game out of getting they boots fired. Things like the gun leg."

"I get this image," I said. "Rookies hopping about Hollywood, switching gun legs back or forward, until it looks like some kind of dance, when they consider everyone around them a suspect. The mind boggles."

"I can't believe this kind of nonsense still goes on," Brookings said.

"One of my classmates was a gay lady," Alwer said. "Department is real modern about that. They make us call it 'Alternate Life-Style.' We not allowed to call it 'gay' in public. If you gay and your partner in law enforcement, they let your partner sit with you in their uniform at graduation. Out in the open. Way up front.

"But this girl's Training Officer didn't like that she was gay. Harassed her about, said the Department didn't need gay police ladies. She HAD to report him."

"Why HAD to?"

"Because that's misconduct. She don't report him for that, when she's on probation, she gets fired and the Training Officer just gets suspended. So, she reports it. He gets suspended, drunk off-duty, shoots up her house, kills her cat but misses her."

"I can't believe that," Brookings said.

"Here, sir," Alwer's lawyer said. "Written up in *The LA* Times."

He withdrew a clipping from his mover-and-shaker briefcase and passed it to Brookings. He scanned it.

"Let Academy trainers bully twenty-one-year-old recruits," I said. "That sends a message that it's okay to push someone around. So, when they hit the streets, they're already programmed to abuse innocents, with words, hands or batons."

"Ain't making excuses," Alwer said. "But we all act nervous when we work the street. Some of us stress out. If the suspects don't get you, the Department will. So, maybe, we over-react sometimes."

A landline buzzed.

Brookings picked it, grunted and sat back.

He looked at me and looked away.

My insides curled up and went cold.

"Be right down," Brookings said into the phone.

He stood up and massaged his suit jacket chest.

"Excuse me a minute," he said. "Be right back."

He went out into the hallway.

GET OUT! my body screamed. All the bells inside me rang.

Brookings was getting some kind of material witness order on me. He was coming back with some cops to handcuff me and put me in civil jail under that order.

It was time to move.

"Good timing," I said. "Tell Mr. Brookings I need a restroom break."

Getting up, I kept a dumb grin on my mug, like I was thinking of a funny story somewhere.

My luck ran good. The hallway was empty.

Moving like I had been there before, I strode down the hall.

Two uniforms, both Anglos and youngish, came out of an office.

On the staircase behind me, I could hear Brookings speaking. He was coming back up and getting closer.

I nodded to the cops,

Neither nodded back.

I stepped past them.

A gray door marked Men loomed up on my right. Going down the stairs was out. Brookings was huffing up that way. He would snag me.

My palms pushed the door open. Luck was still running good. Three windows looked out onto an alley. Far away, the famous white HOLLYWOOD sign nestled on a green mountainside.

Hysteria helped me push the first window open.

"Royster!" Brookings shouted. "Where's Royster?"

Feet pounded in the hall.

The window wrenched up. It looked out over the cop parking lot and an alley. Some cop might see me and shoot. But I had to take the chance.

Fifteen feet to the concrete.

Squeezing through the window, I hung by my hands and let myself fall.

Chapter 48.

Alley Ghosts
or
Cross-Country

Heights always scared me. Aging did not help.

I forced my knees to bend and wrapped my arms around my head. Paratroopers did that to break their falls and duck injuries.

My feet aimed for the alley next to the cop parking lot.

When my feet hit the ground, I felt an obscene THWOCK! Shock jarred my shins. Everything jolted.

"Bad," I whispered. "Real bad. Something broke."

Keep rolling like a high-school jock, I thought. Full of pep for the home team, Rolling, rolling. Stopping makes me a quitter, a weak sister.

Reality hammered me.

"Stop rolling and you fall apart like a condo made of toothpicks," I whispered.

So the condo kept rolling. Something stopped me. I lay flat. My heels felt like they were on fire but I could move them all right.

Once again, I thought, the skeleton fingers of death reach out for Our Hero but Max Royster eludes them yet again.

My wind left me and I gasped for air. Maybe it was stress doing it. That happened more and more. Aging, the old reliable.

Crisscrossing Hollywood, it felt like the LA cops were riding piggyback on my collarbones and I kept tossing glances back behind me.

An abandoned house showed up on my left. Some trees gathered in the back, above bushes. From the street, nobody could see inside the bushes. So I wedged myself through a wire fence, walked to the back, looked around and rolled underneath the biggest bush.

If Brookings put out an All Points Bulletin on me, right now was the dangerous time. In a few hours, the cops would assume that I was long gone. They would stop looking for me near Hollywood Station. And I knew that street cops had short attention spans. They would find something else, some other minor tragedy, and stop looking for Royster.

Stress knocked me out. Dozing felt good.

Waking up, it was dark under the bush.

My cop job mentor, Sgt. Al Lipkin, and his words came back to me, from somewhere in my way-back machine memory. That was in Manhattan, in another culture, and painful years ago.

"Royster, you'll never work another kill case near me again," Lipkin had said years ago. "Bigmouth show-off. No discipline. But if you ever do, somewhere else, a murder case that ya can't figger, check the site again," he had cackled on his high-pitched Queens accent. "And again. Again. Eye-balling the scene builds ya theories as to what happened."

Hearing Lipkin's words in my head again, I rolled up from my backyard bush and through the fence to the street. My whole body felt stiff. The night chill was hitting Los Angeles again. By memory, I found Gower Street and ankled to the death scene, looking for a stoop to sit somewhere.

Hollywood was not Manhattan. There were no stoops here to sit and think deep thoughts and it made me realize again that I needed to flee LA and get to Miami.

Maybe Hollywood architects did not like Easterners like me coming here to squat on their stoops and New Yorkify the landscape.

A green industrial van lay parked on Gower. After feeling the hood cool to the touch, I leaned my hips against it and rested somewhat, scanning the death scene again. A cool engine meant that the owner had parked it here a while ago and would not be returning soon.

Angelenos probably did not enjoy vagrants such as I leaning up against their prized chariots.

On the street, cars ripped past me in the never-ending chain of cream white lights and big motors announcing inadequate personalities.

Perhaps if I rented a small foreign sports car, I could to sign, tool around Hollywood long enough to find a stoop to hunker down on.

Across Gower, in Van Florida's storefront, headlights showed his sign, done in royal blue: Hollywood Dance Rendezvous Club.

Florida had a plastic container holding his flyers next to the door. Florida understood marketing. Anyone walking by could pocket a flyer and daydream about dressing elegantly next

Friday night and dream of holding their next true love's body in a close tango hold.

A light showed inside Florida's dance club. Then it moved.

All the scenes and words from Callie McKissick death crowded me. Then my head dropped and I dozed.

Gently, I seated myself against the van's front wheel. Sleep slipped over me again.

When I woke, it felt much later. My watch had stopped at three yesterday afternoon and my cell phone was dead from over-use. Hollywood did not have the public clocks that Manhattan boasted but it felt late to me.

My head snapped up.

Sleep felt like a rich country of treasure right now. My whole frame hungered for more of it.

Inside Florida's club, the light moved again.

So, it was Florida in there now, with a moving light, like a flashlight.

Why?

My thought pushed me up off my van and towards Florida's studio and I knuckled his door.

The buzzer alongside the door was too formal. To work this right, I had to shake him up.

Florida's face appeared at the storefront windows, saw me and the front door opened a crack.

"What the hell do you want?" Florida asked. He looked furious. "I was sleeping!"

That clicked. My idea was right. I had him.

"Lie number one," I said. "You weren't sleeping. Why're you lying to me about it? I'm nobody, right?"

"Leave me alone," he said.

"Saw your flashlight moving around," I said. "Ex-cop in me thought about burglars. But, no deal. What burglar cracks into a dance school storefront? For what?"

"You think that you're hot stuff, don't you?"

"So, it's you. Why not turn on your lights? Use that flashlight? Might be. Maybe because you didn't want anyone to know that you were up and moving around-"

"You better leave-"

"Something that you said to me came back tonight," I went on. My voice climbed from excitement. It was the old cop feeling of catching someone in a lie and moving in for the kill. "You said 'I never worked so hard in my life.' So, why can't you sleep? With all that hard work?"

"That concerns you?"

"Mistake number two," I said. My voice still climbed.

"You're talking to me like it's three in the afternoon. But it's night. Way after hours. That doesn't make sense."

"Stop this!" he barked.

Nothing was stopping me now.

"Middle of the night, I boom your sacred door," I said.

"Anything else, you ignore or call 911. But you know that I'm trying to dig up witnesses. Why don't you threaten me with the cops? Anybody would."

He tried cooling himself, shaking his head.

"You're not making any sense, Royster!"

"Making my kind of sense. You don't want police here here because of what the locals will think, at America's most famous crime scene, street people WILL figure out that you're talking to the cops about Callie McKissick. And what I will tell the cops, that worries you, too. I'll tell them that you saw Alwer and Callie McKissick. And you won't talk-"

He slammed the door.

That left me outside. As usual.

Slumping my shoulders like a Method actor being rejected at an audition, I turned and trudged away.

A doorway thirty feet away looked kind of clean so I folded myself into it and waited.

This was a gamble, I told myself. A real long shot.

Traffic kept a-trafficking.

I waited.

The door opened and Florida zipped out, checked the street and locked the door.

He could not see me inside the doorway.

He wore a shoulder bag, kneepads and heavy-looking roller skates on his feet. That figured. A dance teacher would want to protect his knees from the trauma that running brought to his kneecaps. So he would chose skating.

Florida glided down the street, skates noising a bit and saw me. I got up and blocked him.

"The dance school is your dream, right?" I shouted. "Come into the DA's office, talk some and they'll protect your dream."

"Against mobs?" Florida said. "Right now, LA can't even protect itself. Watch it happen like before. If I ever say what I saw, my school here is finished."

"There are lives at stake," I said.

"Whose?"

"Yours," I said. "If you don't come in, I tell the DA.

Then, maybe I go public. Your face in dance photos on the news. Some law will spot you and subpoena you-"

He spun and skated away. I blew it, talking too much, as always. My bluff failed. There was no way that I could tell this to Brookings, without Florida's body there.

My feet pounded after him.

He looked back at me and put on a burst of speed. I tried to run. My guts and bouncing body screamed against it.

If I could reach him, I would slug him down and call the cops somehow. Some bystander would call 911. The cops would lock us both us for Disorderly Conduct and I would call Brookings to keep Florida inside until the Grand Jury.

Florida crested across the avenue in a long graceful swerve. He made it look easy.

I felt like I was dying.

Pain knifed my lungs.

My wind went out.

Florida went down another street and was gone.

℟

Limping, I charted a course through Hollywood's grassy squares and parking lots to reach Yan's place. The LAPD would not be prowling those places.

They might be looking for me near the bus stops or freeway entrances. Maybe Brookings could put paper out on me. He might have gathered up enough for a Material Witness order.

With that, they could bust me. But, first, they had to find me. So I made myself hard to find.

My body slumped onto a longish street with trashcans overturned and broken glass spackling the sidewalk.

A black-and-white LAPD car nosed out of an alley.

Everything in me froze.

The driver got out, shaved-headed, black wrap-around sunglasses, pale white skin, knotty arms with gray gloves covering his hands. The gloves were called 'Gliders' for searching crackheads or dead bodies, without their germs killing you. I used to wear them on Patrol.

"Boot!" called out a cop in the passenger seat. "Where you going?"

"Sir," the driver said. "Be right back, sir."

The passenger cop looked about fifty, grizzled frown lines cut into his face and two stripes on the sleeve hanging out the window. He had called the driver 'Boot'. That made him the

Training Officer, the P-3. The driver must be a Probationer, new to the Department. The Probationer had to obey his Training Officer or risk getting fired.

The driver turned his body and stooped into a doorway.

Something in the doorway moved. My own skin jumped.

The something was a Black man, dressed in rags and two shoes, broken through the toes. Dirt crusted his face. He rolled on a lump of thrown-out carpet, surrounded by tied-up plastic bags. He tried raising his head up and it flopped back down. He could have been 20 or 90. Nobody could tell unless they got close to him, and nobody would want to.

From where I crouched, the cops could not see me. If I moved, that would change. I had to watch them.

"Rupert," the Probationer said. "What do I always tell you?"

"I know, Officer Zito," said the man in the doorway.

"To you, my name is Stan. Remember?"

"Yeah, Stan. And you always tell me, 'Rupert, don't scare the tourists.' That's what you always say."

"Rupert, how d'you think you look today, huh?"

"Pretty scary?"

"I'm disappointed with you, Rupert. Saw you last week, all cleaned up, and just out of Weingarten De-Tox Center. Now, you're messing up our deal."

"Yessuh."

"We had agreed that both of us would make Hollywood look better. Starting with this alley. So did I keep up my bargain?"

"Yeah. But my legs, got no feeling. Can't walk. Lost my meds."

"BOOT!" the Training Officer bellowed from the car. He sounded furious not just with his probationer but with life itself. "What the hell you doing wasting time here?"

"Negative, sir," Zito, the Probationer, said. "Got a sick man here, sir."

"He's just drunk. All maggoted up old bum. You want me to give you an Unsat?"

"Negative, sir," Zito said.

"Well, you're getting one, for this BS! You hear me?"

His tone made me cringe. I wanted to slug him.

"Yessir," Zito said.

He lifted up his hip radio and spoke into it.

"Seven-B-15, requesting a Rescue Ambulance, alley off Melrose and North Detroit Avenue," Zito said. "For a male Black, conscious and breathing, about fifty years of age, unknown physical illness, unable to walk. History of schizophrenia and bipolar episodes."

"Seven-B-15, do you need an additional unit with a Taser?" the radio asked.

My knees bent more.

"Negative, Dispatch," Zito said. "Non-combative at this time. No additional, repeat, no additional unit required."

"Zito!" the Training Officer shouted. "Your stuff is weak, you know that?"

"Yessir."

"We wasting time here, Boot! We could be doing real work out there, instead of nursemaiding this bozo. He'll be back here next week. Know that? why you doing this, dummy?"

"Sir, to keep him alive."

"You think that's police work?"

The Training Officer hopped out and slammed the car door. He lit up a forbidden cigar. An ambulance siren blurted around the corner. The ambulance blocked the Training Officer. and Zito from seeing me move away. From about thirty feet away, the Training Officer's voice still carried.

My insides pounded as I cut through more Hollywood alleys. The sirens and helicopters far behind me and moving east were not so loud now. Maybe things were cooling down.

Youngsters slithered out of doorways and roved the streets. They flashed guilty looks at me, like none of us should be outside now. White, Black, Latino and Asian. Everyone lived in Hollywood.

"Need my smokes, dude," a scruffy-looking rascal, in his twenties, baseball hat turned backwards said across a street to his scruffy-looking pals. "Do without food, beer, no sweat but need those butts."

Others moved around and hid in doorways.

Yan's street showed no signs of police occupying army stuff. I scrunched down in a doorway about eighty feet from her place.

The art of the stakeout, I thought.

Time oozed past.

The day was winding down and so was I. The famous Hollywood sun crested over rooftops for a Technicolor sunset.

My body cramped more.

A garbage truck slipped past me, ripping my ears with noise. It stopped ten feet away. Someone threw a soda cup onto the sidewalk. It sprayed out. Soda splashed onto my face.

"Art isn't easy," I said.

Ways grew darkened along the Hollywood earth, to misquote Homer.

Trying to get comfortable I felt my bones creak, like a Museum of Natural History dinosaur.

The evening passed. Sometimes I dozed. The streets stayed quiet.

A black-and-white passed. The cops inside didn't see me.

All night long, I kept waking and slipping back to sleep.

❧

Dawn came gray and damp. Smog chilled the day. Early workers clambered into their cars with coffee cups and sour expressions.

Then the Buick Roadmaster station wagon bumped in front of Yan's place. Zygolt got out, carrying a large shoulder bag. Her pale hair, frizzed out in curls over her wire-rim glasses and serious face gave her the look of a guerilla journalist about to take on the Big Boys.

My pulse pounded. Breath came in short. This was my big gamble. She found the street door key where I had stashed it outside under a city garbage can. She entered Yan's building and propped the door open for me.

My bones and nerves and tendons click-clacked in agony when I pushed myself out of the doorway to creep across the street

Almost everything could go wrong now. That chilled me more as I went into the building after Zygolt,

Cigarette and marijuana butts dotted the floor. Two broken mailbox doors swung open. Someone had taken advantage of the reduction in patrolling cops. That always happened in times of unrest like those now, when the cow-flop hit the fan.

Hours ago, someone had been smoking a cigarette and eating popcorn. Both odors lingered. I did my best to ignore the smells as I watched Zygolt.

Following our plan, she moved with care up the stairs until she came to Yan's door.

My feet followed her up the stairs and onto the landing. The hallway turned a right-angle corner and shielded me from anyone at Yan's door.

Yan could not see me from there but I could watch everything.

Zygolt knocked on the door, ignoring the buzzer. Our only hope was to get Yan rattled.

This hustle would never work on anyone grounded in logic. But it was the only one that I could scheme.

"Who?" Yan shouted from inside the apartment.

"This is Trish Van der Camp," Zygolt shouted back, "from *Twilight Magazine* and I need to interview you about this death of Ms. McKissick."

"Stick your magazine up your ass!" Yan hollered.

From where I stood, I could hear Yan click the peephole open.

"I need to learn more about Ms. McKissick for my article in the next month's edition," Zygolt ran on.

"Stop hassling me!"

"My magazine is willing to reimburse you for your time," Zygolt said. As I had coached her, she took out cash and showed it to Yan. "Right now, in your hand."

This was a con. No legit magazine would pay up front for this kind of interview.

"Get out of here!" Yan shouted. "Or else, I'm coming at you with a knife!"

Zygolt's shoes squealed.

Startled, I watched her turn and run from the door to the stairs.

Panic flooded me.

"Don't run, Zygolt!" I hissed. "You're the last hope for truth and justice."

CHAPTER 49.

Interrupt
or
Meet Have Pity

Zygolt ran.

Yan opened the door.

I stayed hidden from her from her down the hall. If she looked my way, she might see me. But Yan was way distracted.

She stood in the doorway and waved a blocky big Bowie knife with a leather grip.

With a happy look, she stalked back into her apartment and slammed the door.

Zygolt kept running down the stairs. I did not blame her. My own fear-sweat sponged back across my skin. Years ago, on Patrol, a maniac had razor-cut me, and I felt the shock all over again now.

I needed Zygolt now, but she had already clambered past me and was skittering down the stairs.

"Don't come back!" Yan shouted and slammed the door.

Zygolt's feet did not touch the steps. My body hustled down the stairs after her.

The vestibule loomed dark and large.

Zygolt stopped at the street door. Her chest heaved. She was a stage-dancer, not a street fighter. Her eyes danced all over.

A noise clicked behind me, like metal snicking on stone. Then, it sounded again. Breathing hard, I tried to ignore it.

"Zygolt, I need you back there," I said.

"Sure, boss-man Max! You try it! You see the size of that knife? She'll kill me!"

"Yan's street people," I said. "She ain't gonna kill nothing but her own good chances."

"I'm splitting!"

"Split this in your head," I said, like a rhymester. "Don't you want bread?"

"Huh?"

"You always need cash, Zygolt. Today, I'm the man with the plan. A cool grand for you to go back and play act two with Little Miss Bowie knife."

"She's nuts!"

"No," I said. "Just very private."

Behind us, that same noise clicked again.

"How can you ask that of me? Don't you care?"

"Zygolt, I trained you and your Showbiz pals in interviewing. Remember? It's the most important skill a cop can have. 'cause a cop does it every day. And everyone – witness, client, victim – has a key. The cop just has to find it."

"And just what is Yan's key?"

"Money. Like most of us. You, too, today. So, get back on stage and turn it."

"Max, you also taught us that nobody nowhere no-how can defend themselves against a damn knife. Karate, MMA, judo, nothing works! A knifer can kill a karate expert, no problem."

"Please, keep your voice low," I whispered. "You're right. You can only run, shoot or talk them down. You can play this scene and talk Yan down. I know you can."

"How come you don't have a weapon?"

She was right. Yan had surprised me with her anger.

"A pro never fights bare-handed, you said," Zygolt said.

"Because we don't need it," I lied. "You can control her."

That noise clicked louder. Something stood behind me.

"Zygolt," I said. "Routine Three."

Her eyes widened.

Routine Three meant go left. She sprang left.

I went right.

Yan must be here, behind me.

My hands up, edges ready to strike, I whipped around to face Yan's knife.

Something hard as a cannonball hit my belt buckle.

The liver-colored pit bull bit at my shirt. The rope was still tied to his collar, the end frayed where he had chewed through it.

His teeth ripped through my shirt. Then my flesh.

"Have pity!" I shouted. His teeth flashed. His jaws ground.

It was the same pit bull that I had seen before, outside on the street. He looked bigger now.

Zygolt's head snapped up.

"Max, don't panic!"

His teeth worked more.

"Awwww!" I shouted. "Easy for you to say!"

The pit bull squirmed. He tried to get a better grip on my gut. He snarled. My knee struck him in the stomach. It did nothing.

"ARGHH!" he growled. Sounded like he was gargling blood. My blood.

"Zygolt!" I hollered. "Get a stick! Something. Anything!"

My hands reached under his belly and heaved. He went backwards, landed on his tail and sprang up. His teeth flashed again.

I hammered him on the head.

"I christen thee 'Have Pity'," I panted. Gabbing always calmed me, no matter what. "Right now. And I wish you would."

Have Pity did not care to listen.

He lunged.

My body whipped to one side. He staggered me back.

We went down. He was on top.

"Bad," I hissed. It was.

My body was underneath him. He had the power here. His teeth caught my sleeve. I had to do something fast.

It was hard. But I dropped down to the floor, covered my head and neck with my forearms and tucked my legs up into the fetal pose. Teeth poked my skin.

Have Pity kept snarling. The noise drowned everything else out. I felt like I was inside a Waring blender, becoming meat puree.

More teeth probed me. Then he straddled me. The rank smell choked me.

Then he moved off, probing with his teeth. He was trying to find an entry. Then he would gash my veins.

The snarls changed. Garbage smell hit me. Something bumped us from behind. He stopped. It bumped us again.

Then he squeaked, like a trumpet hitting high C.

He did it again.

Then something got between us. It wedged him away.

Wetness covered us both, a tropical mix of pineapple and rotting bananas.

My body clenched and shook. The shakes hit me bad. My heart hammered. Something pulpy rose in my throat.

His nails scraped the floor. For some doggy reason, he was bolting away. Maybe he scented some other oldster to terrify.

"Max, he's gone," Zygolt said.

"Me, too. To the Land of the Shades."

"Max?"

"Where'd that puppy come from?"

"Dunno."

"What did you dump on us? Smells like garbage."

"Max, there weren't any sticks or pipes or anything to hit him with. Except this."

A metal garbage can lay on the floor near us. Trash covered me. Some stuck to my hair.

"I'm grateful, Zygolt," I panted. "Even if you did dump last month's garbage on me."

"Wasn't nothing else."

"Said I'm grateful. He hits an artery, and I would bleed out like some hemophiliac Roman Senator trying to do the honorable thing and die by exsanguinating in his private bath. I owe you my life."

"Back in Basta, you taught all us Showbizzers those routines," she said. "And I remembered that Routine Three means 'Go Left.' Routine One was 'Drop Flat.' And Routine Two was 'Go Right.'"

"Borrowed that from the Bowery Boys," I said.

"Who are the Bowery Boys?"

"Never mind. I guess that pit bulls don't like showers of garbage any more than we humans do. Am I bleeding too badly anywhere?"

"Not that I can see. Your shirt's ripped in the back."

"They'll only notice that when I'm leaving," I said. "Not approaching."

"Dropping, rolling into a ball. Is that the best way to handle a dog attack?"

"Second best. When the dog's facing you like he was, you should gouge his eyes with your thumb."

"Why didn't you do that?"

The vestibule got quiet again.

"I couldn't," I said.

"Why not?"

"Dog didn't know any better how to behave," I said. "It wasn't his fault."

"Oh, Max!"

"Couldn't blind old Have Pity that way just for being a dog."

"Being a softy-heart like that will get you killed some day," she said.

"Maybe today."

She looked around at the tight- locked doors off the hallway.

"How come nobody came out to help you?' she asked. "That monster made a real racket."

"Everyone's either doped up or listening to their music in this building. Nobody would even hear Angel Gabriel blow his trumpet in the car port. Even if they could, they ain't getting involved. Now, let's get you back with Yan."

"Oh, nooo! You still wanna try that silly hustle? After that pit bull nearly put you down for good? You should be in a hospital, Max."

"Physical or mental?"

"Oh, Max. Come on."

She led me to the laundry room.

"You smell disgusting. Let's clean that crud off you."

She switched on the faucet on the deep sink.

"Could be fear-sweat," I said. "I'm still scared. Pit bulls kill six out of ten bite victims. That's just one breed. Ex-cons who can't carry guns sometimes feed pit bulls gunpowder mixed with food. They're convinced that gunpowder eats the pit bull's brain and makes him attack for no reason. It's a jive myth, but they still use a pit bull as their own secret weapon. They can kill an enemy in seconds."

"Hush up and wash."

"Cold water only, huh? I need a new shirt anyway."

"That curling up when the Pity was attacking you, that really works?"

"If you got no weapons or big garbage cans, it's the best way to survive a dog attack. Covers up all your arteries."

"I could never stay that still, when a dog is attacking me. Takes discipline, Max. You have it. I don't. Not that much."

"No, I don't," I said. "I was afraid to move."

"Funny man."

"Zygolt, you can play this scene with Yan. It's just like any other play. Worry about your lines and fret in rehearsals but once you're on stage, your training will take over and you do it, no thinking. You'll turn in an Academy-Award-winning performance."

"Aw, Max. goddamn you. You're gonna get me killed this way."

"If I get you killed, I promise to water your plants back in Basta."

"Oh, okay," she sighed. "After you risk your old tail out here, I guess I gotta try one more time."

"Thanks, Zygolt. You can pull off the act. Now, my favorite actress forever, get in there and break a leg."

Zygolt heaved a huge breath, and we went back into the vestibule.

She tiptoed back up the stairs, then waited at the landing.

℣

Zygolt knocked.

My hands clenched into hitting tools when I heard that. But that was foolish. If Yan saw me, her paranoia would explode, and she'd kill both of us,

Damn fool jackass, I thought. Should have brought that garbage can up with me. Or picked up a baseball bat myself. Something.

Zygolt's knuckles tapped the door again.

"Get away!" Yan shouted.

"I can just give this money away to somebody else," Zygolt said, "But that's silly. It's yours for the taking. You deserve it."

Yan ripped open the door, Bowie knife flashing.

CHAPTER 50.

Breakthrough
or
It's About Time

"Put that away," Zygolt told Yan.

Her voice started to quake. I winced.

Actress that she was, Zygolt covered her nervousness with a cough.

"I've got your interview fee," Zygolt managed to say.

She was sticking to the script. My lips cracked a smile.

"Here," Zygolt said. "One thousand dollars, for a short interview about Ms. McKissick and you."

Yan was weighing her chances. All her life, strangers had drifted near her and taken her by surprise. They had tried to sell her everything from vacuum cleaners to their bodies or their friendship.

Usually, their promises came up short. Those experiences shaped her into the angry person that she became, hanging in her own lumpy doorway, deadly sticker in her mitt. With the drugs and anger mixed inside her, she could kill.

"Got nothing to say," Yan said.

Zygolt hung back.

My back teeth crunched together. The tropical mix garbage reek wafted up from below.

I used to think that Los Angeles was an antiseptic town. MGM had brainwashed me, but now I could smell the garbage and corruption.

"How well did you know McKissick?" Zygolt asked.

"She's just a last name to you, is that it?" Yan asked.

Yan sounded like she was veering between peaceful and furious. Knowing her routine, I figured that the drugs were tossing her around some more. Who I was hearing was not the same whispery lover from before.

Zygolt said nothing.

"You don't care much about her, huh?" Yan said. "Just another homeless Black bag-lady. Not White or hoity-toity like you."

Zygolt still said not a word.

It sounded like she was losing ground.

The street outside stayed quiet. No more whirlybirds choppered our eardrums. Hopefully, Los Angeles might be hushing down.

My neck muscles ached from straining to hear Zygolt and Yan. The thought of crawling into a bed, made my mouth quirk with pain. It was not going to happen soon.

"I can't force you to talk to me," Zygolt said.

"C'mon, Zygolt," I muttered. "Use those yard sale bargaining wits. Pretend to walk away. Push her into a corner. Don't fold on me now."

Part of me felt like the director urging the unknown starlet to get out on stage and carve her name into the eyes of the theatergoing audience.

Somehow, we connected.

"Goodbye," Zygolt said.

True to the police interview training I had given her long ago, she dropped Ms or Mrs., any courtesy title at all. The trick was to degrade your interview subject. It was a technique of stating that you stopped caring about them. They were not important to you anymore.

Rolling those dice, I snaked my head around the corner and watched them.

Heads turned away from me, Zygolt and Yan only paid attention to each other, not seeing me.

A car drove by outside. Its earsplitting rap song added more hammer blows to those already pounding my head. Maybe the music showed that life was slip-sliding back to normal here in Hollywood.

Yan stepped into the hall, still holding the Bowie knife.

"What about that money?" Yan asked.

Zygolt stopped again.

So did my breath.

"What about that interview?" Zygolt asked.

"Oh, snap," Yan said. 'Why should I fricking sell out what I got for just a thousand? Think I'm a dumb kid or something, you stuck-up slut?"

"I'm afraid that you don't understand today's media, my dear. 'cause your story could be worthless tomorrow. Officer Patty Alwer could resign or kill herself. More witnesses could come forward to condemn Officer Alwer or exonerate her."

"Okay," Yan said. "I knew McKissick."

"It seems that everyone is claiming that now," Zygolt said. "How well did you know her, may we say? "

"Had a tattoo on her hip."

"That is difficult to ascertain now. Which hip was that?"

"Let's see."

Yan crinkled her eyes and stared at an imaginary McKissick.

"Facing me, her left."

"A tattoo of what, may you tell me?"

"A red rose."

"How did you happen to see that tattoo?" Zygolt asked.

Her tone sharpened. Now Zygolt was switching characters too fast for Yan to notice. Zygolt was trying to ape a harsh law-yer zeroing in a court-room cross-examination. She spoke faster and faster. That forced Yan to speak faster, to keep up. It did not give Yan time to think. Lying required thinking. At speed, Yan could not lie so well.

A dog barked below us. Then he barked again, scaring me. It sounded just like my old pal, Have Pity.

"I don't know," Yan said. "Where's that money?"

"Money? My goodness gracious, I have it right here."

"Give it up."

"Let us first establish some ground rules," Zygolt said, shifting characters. Now she was playing this scene as a grande dame lady editor like Dorothy Kilgallen, a revered society reporter back in the golden years of print journalism. Zygolt was talking down to Yan, reminding her who was calling the shots.

"Our financial arrangement must stay confidential. The mainstream media does not seem to grasp that working people such as yourself need to be compensated for their time. They say that paying for interviews damages integrity. I call that poppycock and puffery."

Zygolt was saying all the lines that I had given her. She put them out like they were hers. My smile stretched.

Yan gaped.

"You betcha," Yan said. "Me, too."

"And we shall have the autopsy report quite soon. If the cadaver has no such tattoo, then you will not have any future with us for a true-crime book or film rights to your story."

"What film stuff can you get me? How much money?"

"What do you have to prove that you and she were friends?"

"Close friends," Yan corrected.

That meant that Yan could smell cash and wanted to deal.

"Letters, photos, things like that," Zygolt said. "Hard evidence, as it were."

"I have that stuff right in here," Yan said.

My senses screamed.

Now Yan was planning a rip-off. Her voice showed it. A bad feel corkscrewed up from my gut.

"Come inside here," Yan said. She turned back. She still held the Bowie knife. "Forget about the knife. I'm putting it away. Promise."

"Are you sure?"

Yan stepped away. When she came back, her hands were empty. Now she had no knife. She must have stashed it somewhere. I hoped that she was calm now.

"D'you want this stuff or not?" Yan asked. "Use it or lose it. Right now."

"Okay," Zygolt said. "If you say so."

Zygolt was back playing her role as a reporter. She was leaving reality behind.

I vaulted down the hall.

Downstairs, the pit bull barked again. He was getting closer.

But Zygolt was already going inside her apartment. Yan stepped back and reached under her own shirt. The knife blade flashed.

CHAPTER 51.

**Less Talk, More Laceration
or
Cutting**

Knife hanging in her right hand, Yan snickered and yanked Zygolt deeper into the doorway with her left.

Then both of them were inside.

The door was closing.

I bounded down the hall.

"Hold it!" I hollered.

My foot flew up and stopped the door. It hurt.

"Max!" Yan spat out.

The knife's fat blade pointed at me.

The door opened more. I threw myself into the opening and was inside the apartment again.

"Get out of here!" Yan shouted.

Up close, her eyes darted everywhere. She was on drugs again. She could not think now. That would help.

"Zygolt, GO!" I hollered.

I put my body between Zygolt and the knife.

Yan charged.

The knife-point caught my belt. It glanced off the big antique brass buckle and snagged my dog-bit shirt.

Yan twisted the knife. The blade went by my ribs and cut flesh.

It felt like my flesh, too.

"Oh, no," I said. "This won't do."

Being thick, I talked silly when scared.

Yan stabbed out again.

"Won't do at all," I said.

Zygolt foundered near me.

"Max, go!" Zygolt said. "I can talk her down."

My plan needed me alone with Yan and the bookcase.

Before, I had fixed that bookcase just right.

Yan stepped back, staring at us. She seemed slow now. But that could change.

My foot kicked out and caught her shin. She slipped backwards and went to the floor. She slithered back up again, lunged at me and missed. Maybe the drugs were slowing her down. But she still terrified me.

"Zygolt, you go!" I shouted. "And no cops."

"I can't leave you!"

"Leave," I said. "Can't protect me and you at the same time."

"Max —"

"Go!" I shouted. "Leave the door open."

My plan had to run this way.

Zygolt bolted out the door and down the hall and kept going, banging her elbow on the wall. Zygolt was safe now. Yan lunged at me and missed. My body sponged sweat. Yan could gut me while I ran for the door. Now I could not escape the knife.

"Yan, you didn't know McKissick!" I spat out.

The trick was to sound as nasty as possible. Yan should hate me now. Being a rat might save me.

"Yes, I did!"

"You didn't!" I snapped. "You're just using her to score cash."

"I knew her! We were like sisters!"

"McKissick was a letter-writer," I said. "Everyone says so. She was compulsive. Even when she was homeless. When she died, I saw a wad of letters in her pocket. You say you knew her. But that's a lie. You're just trying to build yourself up. Where are the letters, if you knew her?"

With her free hand, Yan yanked a brown Manila envelope from the bookcase. She waved it and flailed at me with the knife.

Outside in the hall, something fell over with a crash. Clicks followed.

"I read them all the time!" Yan shouted.

"She wrote that she wanted to kill herself, right?"

"Everyone gets depressed."

"How come you didn't help her?" I asked. "Get her into treatment."

Yan fell into my trap.

"I tried!" she shouted.

That cinched it. McKissick HAD been suicidal.

Up until now, I had been guessing and bluffing.

Outside, the clicks got closer. I knew what they were. I had to time this just right.

"And she had already tried suicide-by- cop?" I asked, bluffing again. "Don't try lying to me. I KNOW.""

"That wasn't my fault!" she said.

"That means 'Yes'," I said. "She had tried it. And you were the only one who knew it. She trusted you, told you."

Now, I had to get those letters.

"You picked me up," I said. "You don't think I don't know when someone's tailing me? I'm a pro, Yan. Something felt all wrong to me back there. I think that you saw me on TV on the first day. Then you saw me leave the Hollywood cop station in the TV van, tailed me and saw me sit down in that restaurant. And I'm a type that's easy to talk to. Great with strange lovely women."

"Real easy!" she spat out.

"And then I fell a little bit in love with you," I said.

It felt like the truth.

My eyes drilled hers, trying to shame her. She stayed still.

The clicks sounded at the door. I knew what they were and jumped onto a chair next to the bookcase. The jump jolted my cell-phone out of my pocket. The phone fell and spun across the floor, out of sight.

Have Pity charged from the hall into the room towards Yan. Those clicks were his nails on the floor outside.

"Agggh!" Yan shouted.

Garbage stuck to his coat.

She stabbed at him.

He bounded at her.

She slashed Have Pity with the knife across his snout. Blood spurted. He sprang away.

I lunged for the manila envelope and got my hand on it.

Yan jumped next to me.

"Gimme that!" she hissed.

She cut my forearm. Pain exploded.

My blood hit the envelope. She slashed again and got my ribs. Have Pity barked and went for her leg.

She grabbed my belt and pulled the knife back. I was still on the chair, trapped.

"I got you dead!" she screeched.

Her knife flew to my chest and cut my shirt some more.

"NOW!" I shouted. "Time to move."

CHAPTER 52.

Leaving Law Behind
or
Joy

My knee kicked the hand holding my belt.

I leaned back and grabbed the tilted bookcase with both hands.

I pulled the bookcase.

Stacked books rained down.

Shelves crashed. The bookcase caught her square. Books exploded, wood crunched as it tumbled down over her and the dog.

"AWWWGH," Yan cried and Have Pity yelped as the book case pinned them to the floor.

Have Pity's paws clicked again. He tried to scramble free. But the bookcase covered them both. Neither could move.

My arm stung. Blood slathered from my ribs and left thigh.

Yan must have cut my thigh when I dodged her. That meant cuts on the ribs, arm and this thigh. I could bleed out and die.

All this time, I was clutching the manila envelope.

That was today's treasure.

Time to visualize victory, I thought. Just like my coach Mr. Marcelino used to say at Saint Blaise's School for Young Men.

Have Pity whined. That stopped me.

Gotta get those letters to Brookings and his whiz-bang Grand Jury, I told myself.

My blood kept pumping out.

"Blood's dark," I said, continuing my own pep talk. "That's good. Ain't an artery. So I might make it."

Exhaustion washed my body. Lying down to rest felt like a good idea to me.

Except I might die.

Have Pity pawed his way out from under the bookcase and collapsed. A bone in his right leg had broken and punctured the skin. He could not walk.

"Aoooh, aoooh!" he mewed like a kitten.

"Sorry, old Have Pity," I said. "But I'll have the vets fix you up. You been a big help just now. Perfect distraction."

Putting my back against it, I moved the bookcase off Yan. Her chest still rose and fell. The Bowie knife lay alongside her.

"I'll even pay for you, Have Pity," I went on. "Real money. No plastic."

My fingers checked Yan. She had a clear airway. Moving her now might cripple her. So I let her lay. Nature could fix her better than I could.

As a coda, I pinned the Bowie knife through her blue jean cuff and to the wooden floor. If she wanted to flee from her own apartment, she would have to strip off her jeans and run away naked. In her condition, she might be unable to reach the knife and yank it free.

"A Royster-type handcuff," I panted. "Or jean-cuff."

Passing out felt like a seductive idea as I stumbled down the stairs.

❧

Somehow, I made it onto the street.

It lay empty. Nothing but parked cars, steering wheel locks firmly in place. No signs of a riot, but nobody was prancing on the boulevards, either.

My hand patted my pocket.

No cellphone.

It lay somewhere back in that mess. If I went back to retrieve it, I would never come out.

"Hey!" I shouted, "Call 911! I'm bleeding to death here!"

Nothing happened. No windows went up.

"911!" I hollered. "Get me an ambulance."

Snake eyes.

It felt like I was whispering to myself.

Inspired, I used whatever strength I had left to grab up a rock from a tree box and smash a Honda's side window with it. The safety glass broke.

Dead silence.

The next window felt harder. It took longer.

Two cars later, a Mazda gave off a tinny alarm when I broke the window.

That's how to get the LAPD rolling on you, I thought. Just damage some taxpayer's car.

The alarm kept keening.

Even in a riot-type deal, the taxpayers will scream if somebody steals their ride, I mused. A call will go out.

Yan had scared me so much that I forgot my own safety. Tunnel vision did that. The Bowie knife had scared me into panic.

Tearing off part of my shirt sleeve, I wadded it up and tried to stop the blood flow from my thigh. But it kept oozing out. Starting to shake, I slowed my breathing.

A black-and-white screamed up with lights and sirens going.

It screeched to a stop, and two LAPD cops got out. A chunky, dyed Latina blonde, and a Black man, whose skin gleamed against the blue uniform and shiny gun leather. A scar threaded along his right jaw, past quirky eyes.

The woman held a pump shotgun at port arms. The man pointed his Glock at the ground.

The pair looked like high-school kids in over their heads. They were tense and nerved up,

This week, maybe we all were.

"New York police," I said.

"What's that?" the younger one asked. "What the hell happened to you, man? All bloody and stuff."

"NYPD," I said. "This envelope contains evidence in a murder case. If you lose it, that's a felony. Big problem with your

PSB. Contact Lt. Ling or your Watch Commander. Then, you call Brookings in the DA's office. He's got the murder case, and he needs this envelope. Or else, an innocent person goes down."

"What kind of innocent person?" he asked. "You a New York liberal?"

"Maybe. ACLU," his Latina woman partner said, "American Communist Lawyers Union."

"If you only knew," I sighed. "But I'm holding this envelope until I see Brookings."

"ACLU sucks brown wind," the man said.

"My legs are numb. I can't walk. Maybe I'm going into shock."

This scared them.

They moved faster now.

More black-and-whites pulled up on the scene.

My cops traded me off to another car that came up. They argued about who would write the damaged vehicle reports.

The second car had old-timers with graying hair and hash marks on their sleeves inside. One wore reading glasses.

Their badges read "Detective." It looked like everyone was pressed into uniformed anti-riot patrol today.

Cops from the second car groused but called for an ambulance.

❧

A red-and-white ambulance rolled to me.

A third LAPD car squealed to a stop and a Latino cop, a crew-cut youngster wearing sunglasses and chewing sunflower seeds, hopped out. He helped the paramedics lift me onto a folding gurney . smelling of rubbing alcohol and strapped me onto it. The Latino cop climbed in and settled in the jump seat.

"Guy's losing some blood here," an Asian paramedic man said. "Hooked him up with stuff already."

The Latino cop kept taking calls on his cellphone. Through all this ride, I did not pass out. Maybe they were hoping that I would.

"Where you taking me?" I asked.

"Cedars-Sinai," replied the Asian paramedic.

"Cedars-Sinai," I muttered. "Where the Beautiful People go to expire. Mama Royster, I have finally arrived. Didn't Elizabeth Taylor die here?"

"Who's she?" the cop asked.

❧

The ER wheeled me to a private room on the ground floor. Putting the envelope under my good leg, I slept on the gurney.

Brookings shook me awake, along with two grizzled detectives in pricey dark suits. One, bald and chunky, had an unlit cigarette in his mouth and kept staring at me. His partner, Black and bearded, with gold-rimmed glasses, kept scribbling notes on a pad.

Brookings read the letters while nurses kept sticking me with needles.

"Wow," he said. "McKissick wanted to try suicide-by-cop. She writes all about it. After her career and life tanked, she made up her mind but good. With these letters, Alwer is clear."

"So there won't be any indictment," I said. "That's good."

"But I still need you."

"That's bad."

"Just a couple of days."

"Why?"

"There was never a riot here over this," he said. "Just some civil unrest. Hollywood Division reports some vandalism and Riotous Assembly arrests but that's all."

"You can't sell the public that," I said.

"We already have," Brookings said. "Nobody wants another LA riot. That just hurts everybody,"

"Speaking of hurt," I said. "My body may be worse off than you think. 'cause my legs are numb. I can't walk."

"That's not possible," a thin-faced Asian nurse with gold rimmed glasses said. "You should be able to walk."

"The NYPD fired Mr. Royster," Brookings said. "For having delusions."

"Yeah," I said. "Like justice for all. There's a delusion for you."

"Nobody really knows what's in his head," Brookings said.

"I understand," the nurse said.

"If you do, tell me," I said. "Because I sure don't."

She and another nurse left the room.

"A unit hit Yan's apartment right away," the detective with the unlit cigarette in his mouth said. "And we got one officer bit."

"Have Pity?"

"Thanks, but he's gonna be okay."

"Have Pity is the pit bull," I explained. "He's got a busted leg. How could he bite anyone?"

"Wasn't the dog," the detective replied. "It was the female suspect. The injured one. She bit the officer. We need you to tag her for ADW with her knife."

"Sure thing," I lied. "I'm a good citizen."

"Let me get some papers out of my car," Brookings said.

His words chilled me. He would be getting the Material Witness order and serving me with it.

"Keep Housekeeping out of here until I get back," he told the detectives. "Nobody talks to Royster. You got that?"

"We know our job," the Black detective said.

"And we gotta call our captain," the Cigarette Detective said. "He's gotta call the commander. Chain of command. Gave us a direct order. Doesn't make sense to me. Be right back."

"Sure thing," I said again. "I'll be right here."

Then I was alone in the room.

"Come, Our Hero," I said aloud. "Let us away."

My clothes and wallet lay on the table. Blood still caked the shirt.

I ripped armholes in the pillow case with my teeth.

The pillowcase would make a weird-looking shirt, I figured. But that's Hollywood outside this door. I'll fit right in.

The orderly had cut my pants to dress the knife gash. My teeth went to work on the remaining pants leg. Now they were shorts. The dark color hid the bloodstains.

Scared and jerky, I stepped out into the hallway, looking maybe okay. My shoes oozed some blood. Nobody had noticed this before.

"Hey!" someone shouted. "Where you going?"

It was the Latino young cop, still chewing his sunflower seeds. His muscles bulged under the uniform. He was almost touching me. I was trapped.

"That lawyer," I said. "Wants me down into the lounge to meet his boss. That's nuts. But you know how lawyers are."

He looked me over,

"You betcha," he said.

He leaned against the wall near my door.

Limping, I made it to the corner in the hall. Then I turned the corner.

I ached through a door to the stairway and hobbled down the steps.

At the ground floor, I stepped out into a huge parking lot and kept going.

❧

A green cab cruised on the street near the lot. He saw my hand fly up and stopped his cab.

Moving with hysteria, I closed the gap between me and the cab.

Maybe they would be watching flights to Miami. They might think that I was important enough for that.

But the Mexican border was too big for them to check every U.S. citizen crossing it. I would hit Mexico first and then throw them off my trail. Just like the movies.

"Hey, you!" someone shouted behind me. "Hold it! Police!"

My feet moved. I hopped like fury.

Over my shoulder, Brookings and the detectives and the Latino uniform were dashing across the parking lot. But my cab driver was looking the other way. I reached his cab, fell inside and panted. He shot through a yellow light, putting thirty yards between us and the law.

"Where to, sir?" he asked in a Middle-Eastern accent from inside a short black beard.

"Greyhound station," I panted. "For a bus to Mexico. Now, I'm the one getting away."

Special thanks once again to...

To Detective-Investigators Mark Baldessare and Gerry McQueen and all the other cops and federal agents who taught me so much about hunting our real-life serial killers.

To the *Spy, the Movie* team – Jim MacPherson, Alex Klymko, Charles Messina and all the rest of the gang for a grand adventure in screenwriting.

To Kieron Edwards, the newest member of Team Pigtown, for his vivid cover illustration.

To Nad Wolinska for her always inventive cover illustrations.

To Richard Amari for his equally inventive cover design.

To my screenwriting partner, Lynwood Shiva Sawyer, for his support and encouragement over the years.

To my eagle-eyed proofer, Malcolm Brenner.

And my thanks to that wonderful woman, companion and friend from Guangzhou, China, who shares my adventures and my life.

If you enjoyed reading *Max Wisecracks Hollywood (Foxtrotting for Justice)*, you'll definitely like Frank Hickey's other Max Royster novels:

When the Whistle Blows, Everyone Goes

Federal agents jail me for murder. That's me, Max Royster. Aging. Fat. Broke. And innocent. How do I clear myself from inside my cell? Nobody believes me. A hate group tries to rape and kill me. But Mother Royster always said to keep smiling no matter what. So to chase away the jailhouse blues, I organize a hipster group and swing dances among the inmates.

A Manhattan tycoon frets about his beautiful daughter.

She is cavorting somewhere near Palm Springs, California.

He pays me, Max Royster, to find her.

This simple job turns into a hairball.

She leads me astray.

Someone kills her boyfriend.

The U.S. Park Rangers blame me for it and lock me up in a federal prison.

Me being me, I try to stay cheery by organizing swing dances between male inmates.

An inmate hate group tries to rape and kill me.

Other inmates protect me for kicks.

Some enjoy the dances. Anything beats prison routine.

The warden and the correction officers suspect me of spying on them for the FBI.

Things look grim for our hero.

Can I swing-dance and laugh my way out of lock-down to find the real killer among the Beautiful People in Palm Springs?

Everyone wants to see what happens next.

You will, too.

I, Max Royster, fat, broke, divorced, thrown off the NYPD for mental illness. Now in Flatbush, Brooklyn, I find new love, new murder and new career. Can I keep my love? Crack the case? Can I inspire and change private security? And maybe regain my NYPD shield?

Flatbush, Brooklyn, a neighborhood that used to be the borough's jewel.

Sixty years later, street crime plagues the area.

My love, Cooper, and her friends want to clean up the neighborhood and improve Flatbush's image. That way, they can 'flip' their homes and triple their profits

I join a security agency, thinking I can transform the guards from unhappy minimum wage-earners to passionate, hardworking crime fighters.

If I succeed and make Flatbush safe for Cooper and her friends, we will buy a home there and enjoy a happy marriage.

My new employees and I fight to take back the Flatbush streets. I give them better training, uniforms and weapons. The guards buff their new badges with pride.

My boyhood friends, out-of-work actresses, barflies and story-tellers, join us in our quest.

But some guards refuse to let go of old vices. Others turn vigilante and bully innocents.

Curbing their zeal, I try to teach them to uphold civil rights as I hunt the suspect in the comedian's murder.

Then, under cover of night, good and evil clash at the Lefferts Historic House. Facing disgrace and prison, I must decide what matters most in life to me.

Come walk with me on that razor edge between brutality and staying alive as Cooper and I, my Flippers and my guards give everything to try Softening Flatbush.

Can Showbizzers Crush Crime?

Can I, Max Royster, fired from the NYPD for mental disease, on crutches, train a ragtag group of performers, my Showbizzers, to use their skills and bodies to stop a genius crime lord in the High Desert town of Basta, California?

Freezing, grieving my lost shield, I hobble aboard an Amtrak train. America passes by outside my window.

When we reach the California desert, my spirits rise. Hope for a new life makes me exit in the small sandy town of Basta.

The sun and beauty cheer me. But the town suffers from crime. A thug mugs me, taking my cash and ID.

That turns me sad again.

A group that I dub "My Showbizzers" – out-of-work dancers, actresses, dog trainers and writers – rescue me. They remind me of my live-for-the-moment cronies back in Manhattan, "The Playpen Irregulars." Thrilled by their energy, I fall in love with Koy, a beautiful Asian dog-handler.

Some Basta deputies duck work or bully innocents. Their sloppiness angers and frustrates me, and their laziness helps a local criminal genius, Crostwaite, rob a bank.

My Showbizzers have many skills. Maybe they could use those talents and creativity to fight crime. They might do better than some lazy deputies.

Nobody else believes in my idea. Locals mock me. The sheriff and the FBI block me. But I force myself to push my idea forward, while my Showbizzers must fight their own bias against government and rules.

But when Crostwaite starts killing, I train my Showbizzers. They go undercover. Their beautiful bodies use sex as a weapon. Koy trains dogs to burgle homes and seize evidence.

To avenge his childhood of horrors, Crostwaite vows to destroy Basta.

Frightened but passionate, without guns, power or respect, my Showbizzers and I risk everything to stop Crostwaite.

Our deadly showdown will answer the question once and for all: *Can Showbizzers Crush Crime?*

Brownstone Kidnap Crackup

When Max witnesses a debutante's kidnapping, he becomes the FBI's prime suspect. Or is he actually their salvation?

It's Christmas in Manhattan.

A blizzard whips the city.

The Beautiful People, in the elite Upper East Side, celebrate in their brownstones.

Until a kidnapper seizes a beautiful young debutante.

Max Royster, fired from the NYPD for mental illness, fights the kidnapper but loses.

The kidnapper flees. Stripped of gun, shield and power, Max has only his wits to save the victim.

The FBI treats Max like a suspect and tramples roughshod on his rights.

During this long sleepless night, an unknown FBI agent cracks up. Over the radio, he quotes J. Edgar Hoover and plants false clues.

To solve the case, Max must smash through the facade and mysteries of millionaires in their snug brownstones.

Exotic women tempt him to give up.

The blizzard worsens.

As the winds howl and snowdrifts deepen, Max risks his life and his freedom in a desperate bid to save the victim.

Once again, Max Royster is back on the street in *Brownstone Kidnap Crackup.*

Funny Bunny Hunts the Horn Bug

To catch a sex killer targeting Upper East Side beauties, misfit NYPD cop Max Royster goes undercover...as an NYPD cop!

The Upper East Side of Manhattan is one of the richest neighborhoods in the world.

But Max Royster, a maverick, outspoken and erudite NYPD foot cop, who grew up working-class in this tony area, calls it "the Playpen." Money protects the bluebloods in this area like the bars on an infant's playpen.

Late one night, patrolling wealthy brownstones, he sees a burglar attacking a rich actress. Max chases him. They fight but the burglar escapes.

The burglar is a sexual predator, known in cop-speak as a "Horn Bug".

For losing the suspect, Max's captain deems Max "a Funny Bunny," too unstable for police work. He strips Max of his gun and badge, then orders Max into Bellevue Hospital for observation and maybe for the rest of his life.

Without any tools or support, Max has ten days to stop this Horn Bug.

The Gypsy Twist

Max Royster's hunt for a sadistic serial killer takes a startling turn when he realizes that not all predators are born alike.

One autumn night, someone strangles a teenage boy jogging in Central Park.

In Brooklyn, street cop Max Royster risks his life to disarm a madwoman with a knife without harming her. Nevertheless, her lawyer charges Max with brutality. The Department decides to punish Max.

Max's protector is Sgt. Lipkin, an expert detective working the Central Park murder. Lipkin knows that a killer like this seeks a new sexual thrill, a "Gypsy Twist," with each new murder. The dead boy is the son of one of the wealthy elite of the Upper East Side. Max is the only cop in the city from that world, and on scholarship years before, Max had even graduated from the dead boy's school.

Lipkin summons Max for the assistance that only Max can provide.

Max probes the tony school and neighborhood, ignoring bosses who, out of jealousy, try to block his progress.

A beautiful, free-spirited reporter, Diana, woos Max to try and make him reveal insights about the case. Denying him nothing, she lures Max onward.

The killer seizes another school-boy who was playing soccer in the park and drags him to death with a car.

Wealthy New Yorkers scream that someone is butchering their sons. The city rocks.

One night, muggers attack Sgt. and Max, who freezes on the trigger. The muggers cripple Lipkin.

The Department moves to fire Max.

But the dead boy's tycoon father hires Max to track down the killer. Max and Diana live below the radar in the New Orleans and San Francisco underworlds, hunting the killer until a shocking conclusion reveals the killer's true identity.